Bolan had to protect Paul and Jabari at all costs

Leading the terrorist a yard or so, the Executioner pulled the trigger and drilled a round through his target's chest. The Boko Haram gunner looked shocked, as if he'd just awakened from a strange dream he didn't understand. With his last few ounces of strength, he tried to lift his weapon.

Another round caught him in the nose, and he dropped to the floor.

The echoes of gunfire suddenly stopped. And when they did, Bolan heard distant shots coming from the direction he'd sent Paul and Jabari. The gunfire told him one thing: the battle raged on.

Pivoting on the balls of his feet, Bolan changed directions, Kel-Tac leading the way.

DON PENDLETON'S MACK BOLAN®

INSURRECTION

A GOLD EAGLE BOOK FROM
WORLDWIDE®

TORONTO • NEW YORK • LONDON
AMSTERDAM • PARIS • SYDNEY • HAMBURG
STOCKHOLM • ATHENS • TOKYO • MILAN
MADRID • WARSAW • BUDAPEST • AUCKLAND

Recycling programs
for this product may
not exist in your area.

First edition March 2015

ISBN-13: 978-0-373-61575-9

Special thanks and acknowledgment to
Jerry VanCook for his contribution to this work.

Insurrection

Printed in U.S.A.

We make war that we may live in peace.
                                    —Aristotle

Some people seem to have nothing on their agenda other than murder and mayhem. We call those people terrorists and must track down that evil and eradicate it. No quarter given.
                                    —Mack Bolan

PROLOGUE

A disconcerting premonition of impending doom fell over Bishop Joshua Adewale like a cloak as his name was announced over the loudspeaker. He rose from his seat amid the applause all around him. The sinking feeling that had appeared so suddenly in his chest now dropped to his stomach. The anxiety intensified even further, making his legs feel as if they were filled with wet concrete that was one step away from setting.

Adewale walked down the aisle to the stage and mounted the steps. He stopped behind the pulpit, then turned to face the congregation.

The bishop took a deep breath as he looked out over the sea of faces that made up the Catholic Bishops Conference of Nigeria. Even now, as the gathering applauded, he realized his emotions were in conflict. He was delighted—and somewhat nostalgic—to have been invited back from New York to address the conference at this seminary where he had studied so many years ago. In the country of his birth. But at the same time, he couldn't shake that sense of foreboding.

There had been rumors of an Islamic extremist attack planned against the conference attendees. And in Nigeria, Islamic-based terror almost always meant Boko Haram.

Adewale squeezed his fingers even tighter on the wooden podium as he cleared his throat. He knew in his heart that if he died this very second he would be on the fast train to meet Christ. Yet a small amount of the fear of death remained.

"My brothers," he said into the microphone in front of him, "it is an honor to—"

Adewale never finished the sentence.

The bomb shook the chapel as if hurricanes were assaulting it from all four sides. Bricks flew out of the walls like missiles, several finding human targets at the same time as a section of the roof blew down and fell in a huge chunk on one section of the pews. The screaming men in those pews disappeared in a cloud of plaster and splintered wood.

Amid the shock of noise, Adewale felt helpless as debris continued to fly. The roiling smoke overtook him on the stage. It was only then that he realized he was no longer behind the pulpit. The blast had thrown him to the floor on his side. The pulpit was no longer in sight. It had been uprooted by the blast and sent sailing somewhere out over the congregation.

Through the dust Adewale could make out dozens of other bishops whose black cassocks were now dingy gray. Those who were still mobile were scrambling toward the aisles. Many of the wooden pews had been blown from the bolts fastening them to the floor, and jagged pieces of wood and steel acted as shrapnel, slicing through flesh in the panic.

For a moment Adewale lay frozen in surprise. Then pain seared through his left forearm and he looked down to see that something had cut deeply into him just below his elbow. But the dust was so thick, he couldn't identify the object.

His eyes burning, Adewale clamped his right hand over the wound in his left arm, and the bleeding slowed slightly.

Through openings in the thick dust clouds the bishop could see human remains—a few bodies, others blown to pieces. The few who had been spared serious injury helped others down the aisles.

Still stunned from the blast, as well as the horror before him, Adewale realize what was in his forearm: a small metal hinge—undoubtedly from the pulpit.

The bishop rose to his knees. "No! Don't leave!" he yelled. Under the current conditions they were safest right where they were, inside the ruins of the building.

He knew what awaited any bishops who made it outside.

Adewale tried to shout again, but when he drew in a breath he was choked by the dust. He fell back to his hands and knees, as the panicked clergymen surged forward.

Someone at the front of the stampede of men finally got the door open and the bishops who had survived the explosion began fleeing into the sunlight. Adewale reached the door just in time to see Boko Haram terrorists surround the clergymen, their razor-sharp machetes gleaming in the sunlight.

Then what was left of the chapel roof behind him collapsed, and something struck the back of his head.

As his eyelids fluttered shut, Bishop Joshua Adewale knew he would be spared.

There was something he still had to do.

Six blocks from the main chapel of Saints Peter and Paul Seminary, Fazel Hayat sat cross-legged on top of the tin roof of a mud-and-plaster house. A pair of Steiner 10x50 power binoculars were pressed to his forehead. They had provided a close-up view of the explosion in the chapel, and now did the same for the machete slaughter.

Hayat couldn't help but smile. Dhul Agbede's improvised explosive device had worked perfectly. But then the man's weaponry always did. Hayat's right-hand man, and Boko Haram's top assault expert, knew more about weapons than anyone else in their network.

Hayat glanced to his side, where his second-in-command now sat quietly. For a moment, he wondered just how much Dhul's given names might have influenced his interests and studies as he'd grown up. *Dhul Fiqar* meant "name of the Prophet's sword" in the Yoruba tongue, and the man's last name, Agbede, translated roughly as "blacksmith." Dhul *was* a blacksmith by trade, and in addition to the elaborate gold-inlaid and ivory-handled machetes both he and Hayat wore in the sashes around their waists, he had forged the more rustic, yet equally deadly blades the Boko men in the distance now used to eliminate the Catholic bishops who had survived the bomb inside the chapel.

Hayat kept the binoculars close to his face, but watched Dhul in his peripheral vision.

The man's eyes betrayed no emotion of any kind. The fact was, they were a dull black, and reminded Hayat of a shark. The Boko Haram leader shook his head. He had seen Dhul construct bombs and then put them in place with a completely deadpan expression on his face. He had seen him kill innumerable Christians and Jews with his gold-inlaid, nickel-finished machete. Deadpan again.

Hayat wondered if the fact that the man never showed any outward emotion might be because he *felt* no emotions. If that was the case, it meant he was truly a psychopath.

The Boko Haram leader shrugged and turned his attention back to the slaughter going on at the seminary. It mattered little if Dhul was a sociopath. If so, he was certainly a useful one.

Hayat watched as two of the remaining bishops attempted to get away. A pair of his Bokos went to work, hacking them down. A heavyset clergyman had picked up a loose wooden plank with nails extending from one end. Grasping it with both hands, he swung it at one of his assailants. The Boko parried the spiked weapon of opportunity, then swung his machete in a reverse stroke. The overweight bishop fell to his knees, gripping his slashed neck. Fazel Hayat watched as his head threatened to separate from the rest of his body. But with his left hand clutching his throat and the fingers of his right encircling the large crucifix suspended around his neck, the heavy man hit the ground dead, but still in one piece.

The Boko who had killed him went back to the bishop he had been working on.

The discrepancy brought a shrug to Hayat's shoulders. Men—even trained men such as his Boko Haram army—often reacted strangely in battle.

A second later, the entire building came crashing down behind the pile of dead bodies. The blood-splattered Boko Haram fighters stepped back when stone and scraps of wood flew through the air as if a second explosion had taken place. Dust rose as if a million hookahs were blasting their smoke toward the sky. Then the Bokos made their way through the killing field, clutching their blood-drenched machetes as they searched for any remaining life. Each time one of the men on the ground twitched— either as a last sign of life or in an involuntary muscle spasm after death—one or more machetes slashed downward, putting an end to the movement.

In all but one of them.

Suddenly rising from a pile of bodies, a bishop wearing a cassock more gray with dust than black climbed to his feet and began stumbling away. It was the bishop from America, Joshua Adewale. He walked directly past several of Hayat's men, who appeared not to notice his presence.

A cold chill twisted down Hayat's nape and along his spine to his lower back. What he was seeing was impossible. It was unnatural. It could not have been happening. He had personally witnessed a huge concrete block strike this man in the back of the head. It should not only have rendered him unconscious, it should have killed him.

He turned toward his second-in-command. "Dhul," he said quietly, "did you see that?"

"Did I see what?"

"That bishop. The one who just stood up and walked away."

"I saw it," Agbede said. "He was lucky. But do not worry. We will get him soon, somewhere else."

"Then it was not my imagination?"

"Not unless it was my imagination, too."

"It was the American, Adewale," Hayat said. "The one who was scheduled to speak first." He let his binoculars fall for a moment, resting his eyes. "He was holding his arm. It appeared he was injured."

"He was lucky," Agbede repeated.

Hayat watched the gray-black, ghostlike figure as it stumbled on, growing smaller and smaller, walking away from the chapel. The phrase "It was more than luck" fluttered through his brain, but the thought was disturbing, and he repressed it.

CHAPTER ONE

The Learjet bore no military, police, national or corporate emblems, only the bare minimum of markings required by international law. It had flown directly from the United States to Argentina, where the big man, who was Jack Grimaldi's only passenger, had provided officials with documentation that he was an executive for Gulf Oil.

The trip from the US to South America had been nothing but show. It was a simple ruse on the million-to-one chance that any of the world's antagonists had stumbled across the Learjet's real destination.

After refueling, Grimaldi, the number-one pilot at Stony Man Farm, had charted a new route, from South America across the Atlantic Ocean and then the Gulf of Guinea, allowing them to enter Nigerian airspace from the south without tripping the radar of any other country.

During the flight, the big man had changed from the perfectly tailored suit he had worn in the guise of an oil mogul into faded blue jeans, well-worn and scuffed hiking boots, and a gray T-shirt beneath a khaki photographer's vest. Now he was a freelance photojournalist.

But beneath this outer shell was the man's true identity. He was not a photographer.

Mack Bolan, aka the Executioner, was a warrior.

Hidden beneath his long, multipocketed vest, on the left side, was a Concealex nylon shoulder holster that had been specially designed to carry his Beretta 93-R machine pistol. The weapon was equipped with a custom-made sound suppressor threaded onto the barrel.

On his right side, connected to the other end of the shoulder rig, was a double magazine carrier. Its rigid form held the twin mags securely, without the need for retaining straps or other devices that would slow down a reload. Also on Bolan's right side, secured on the thick leather belt threaded through the loops on his jeans, was a holster that toted his mammoth .44 Magnum Desert Eagle.

At the small of Bolan's back was a Cold Steel Espada knife, which bore a notch in the top of the blade that enabled it to be drawn, hooked on a pocket or belt, and snapped open in one fluid motion.

Last but not least was a tiny North American Arms .22 Magnum PUG mini-revolver. The small but mighty weapon had saved Bolan's life on more than one occasion as a last-ditch, hidden "hold out" weapon.

The landing gear of the Learjet descended and

locked into place. Ahead and below, Bolan saw the runway. He knew that much of the clothing and other gear he had brought along would not be needed. But the cameras and other photographic equipment backed up his cover story. And in regard to his combat accessories, the soldier's philosophy had always been that it was better to have it and not need it than to need it and not have it.

The largest of several screens set into the control panel in front of the two men blinked twice. Then the head, shoulders and chest of a man wearing a gray suit and burgundy necktie appeared. "Good evening, Striker," the man said.

"Evening, Hal?" Bolan queried. "Does that mean it's evening where you are or where Jack and I are getting ready to land?"

Hal Brognola, the man on the screen, pulled a ragged-looking cigar from the breast pocket of his jacket and shoved it into a corner his mouth. "Sounds like you just woke up," he said around the cigar stub.

"I caught a few winks after we left Argentina," Bolan answered.

"It'll be early evening by the time you touch down in Ibadan. You may want to reset your watch. How much sleep did you get?" Brognola looked slightly concerned.

"Enough. I slept all the way from the US to Argentina. Then caught another nap after we took off again. I'm good to go." He studied the man on the screen. Hal Brognola was a high-ranking official at the United States Department of Justice. But he was also the director of Sensitive Operations at Stony Man Farm, the top secret counterterrorist command center with which Bolan often worked.

"So tell me what I'm getting into, Hal," he said.

"I could *tell* you, but I think it'll mean more if I *show* you."

The screen went blank for a few moments. Then a grainy video, probably shot by a cell phone, began to run. In the short clip Bolan saw the ruins of what looked to have once been a church building. Bodies were strewn among the rubble of what might have been a chapel. Partially burned books—Bibles and hymnals, perhaps—were scattered here and there. Chunks of scorched wood that resembled the corners of pews and the top half of a broken crucifix lay among smoldering embers.

But the setting took a backseat to what was happening in front of the decimated church. Men dressed in the odd combination of civilian and military clothing so often found in warring, developing countries, were swinging their machetes at other men wearing the long cassocks of Catholic clergy. The weaponless men in the long garments all looked as if they'd been inside when the explosion had detonated; they were covered head to foot with ash.

The Executioner felt his eyebrows lower and his

jaws tighten as he watched the barbaric mass murder. The clip ended with one of the bishops being slashed across the throat and falling forward to the ground. Bolan concentrated. Something had caught his attention, but he wasn't sure exactly what.

Brognola's face returned to the screen. "Ugly stuff, Striker."

"Some of the worst I've seen. Where'd you get it?"

"A CIA snitch happened to be close to the action and recorded it," Brognola replied. "We hacked into the Company and made a copy."

Bolan paused, letting the righteous anger filling his chest recede slightly. Out-of-control anger would not serve him. If a warrior let rage take over, he ended up like the men bleeding out on the ground in the clip. And no one was helped.

"That was a meeting to kick off the Catholic Bishops Conference of Nigeria," Brognola said. "In Ibadan. Opening day."

"Aside from the fact that no one deserves that type of treatment," Bolan said, "how do we fit into this picture?"

"One of the men in attendance was a Nigerian-born but naturalized US citizen. Bishop Joshua Adewale, from New York."

"I take it the bad guys are Boko Haram?"

"Have to be," Brognola replied. "It's Nigeria, after all. What's a little unusual, though, is that the Bokos have operated primarily in the northern part of the

country up until now. Kano, Maiduguri and the surrounding regions. But I guess the Catholic bishops
conference in the south was more than they could
resist. Made it worth the trip."

Bolan's ears popped and he realized that Grimaldi
was still bringing the Learjet down through the sky.
Glancing at the pilot, he said, "How much longer,
Jack?"

"About five more minutes."

Turning his attention back to the screen, Bolan
said, "The Bokos have ties to al Qaeda, don't they,
Hal?"

"We're 99 percent sure of it. There's a rumor about
some 'super assassin' from al Qaeda who's running
with the Nigerian terrorists." Brognola pulled the
cigar from his mouth for a second. "Informants don't
know who, though."

Bolan squinted slightly at the screen. "I saw something on that clip," he mused. "I'm not sure exactly
what, but it got caught on the radar between my ears.
Can you run that video again?"

"Sure thing, big guy." A moment later the grainy
film was on the screen again and the machete massacre was repeated. The Executioner continued to
frown, concentrating more on the top, bottom and
sides of the screen than the main action on which
the photographer had focused. As the clip neared its
end, he saw what only his subconscious had caught
the first time.

Just before the final bishop's throat was slashed, to his side and almost out of the frame, two men with machetes were attacking other victims. One chopped at an arm. The other went for the neck. But what seemed weirdly out of place was that another bishop walked unsteadily right between them. Both men with machetes turned and saw him, but ignored him.

"Take it back a little, Hal," Bolan said. "Then pause it."

The clip ran in reverse, with machetes leaving the cuts they'd made on the bishops and returning to the raised hands of the attackers. Blood flew back through the air, reentered the bodies of the men in the black cassocks, and the bishops who had fallen stood up.

"Stop it right there," the Executioner said, and the clip froze on the screen. "Did you see what I just saw?" he asked Brognola.

"I didn't until just now," the director of Stony Man Farm admitted. "There's barely enough room between those two Bokos for the man to squeeze through. And they both obviously saw him—they turned their heads and looked directly at him. I'll have our computer team run a facial recognition comparison, to make sure, but I recognize the man who walked out of the picture. That's our American. Bishop Joshua Adewale."

"Any idea where Adewale went?" Bolan asked.

"No. Like I said, I hadn't even noticed him until you pointed him out. But I—"

Bolan heard a phone ring in the background and Brognola said, "Hang on. That's Aaron. He's got a copy of this footage and he may have found something."

Bolan waited. By now he could see the runway below. Aaron "the Bear" Kurtzman was Stony Man Farm's resident computer genius and one of the most knowledgeable computer experts in the world. He viewed what he sometimes called his "magic machines" with an eye for both science and art, and was an invaluable asset to the Farm.

As the plane's tires hit the tarmac, Brognola came back online. The frozen image of Joshua Adewale walking between the two Boko Haram terrorists was still on the screen, but Brognola's voice could be heard behind it. "I'm putting you on speakerphone, Aaron," he said. "Tell our man in Nigeria what you just told me."

A second later Kurtzman's familiar voice said, "Hello, Striker."

"Hello, Bear. What have you got for me?"

"Not much, I'm afraid. I'm staying tapped into the CIA because it was their snitch who shot the clip. I noticed the bishop walking between the two machete-wielders myself."

"Great minds working independently," Brognola said with a trace of humor.

"Yes, whatever," Kurtzman replied. "In any case, the same informant tried to follow Adewale. They walked away from the university chapel and into a low-rent housing area, where the snitch lost him."

"But we know he's alive someplace?" Bolan asked.

"Well," Kurtzman replied. "We know he *was* alive. At least for a while after the bombing and ma-chete attack. But we've got no idea where he might be now."

"Thanks, Bear," Bolan said. He turned his at-tention to Brognola. "Okay, Hal. My guess is you'd like me to find Adewale, as well as track down the terrorists responsible for this and eliminate them?" Before the big Fed could answer, he went on. "I'm assuming the rest of the conference has been can-celed?"

"There aren't enough bishops left to continue it," Brognola replied. "There were two who arrived late and were still at the airport when the explosion oc-curred. The Vatican ordered them to get out of the country immediately. The Nigerian officials recom-mended they do the same. So they're on their way to Rome. The church is going to have to reorganize its entire structure in Nigeria, and that's going to be a monumental job."

"Sounds like my mission's clear," the Executioner said. "Rescue Joshua Adewale. But with no more to go on in locating him, I'll plan on going after Boko

Haram. I've got a feeling the bishop will pop up somewhere along the way."

"How you operate is your call," Brognola agreed. "As always."

"How do I stand on entering the country, Hal?" he asked.

Brognola knew exactly what he meant. "I pulled a few strings through a CIA friend of mine. You'll be met by a customs agent named Sean Azizi. He'll walk you through customs and immigration and stamp your passport himself. No search of your bags or person."

"Sounds a little too good to be true."

"My friend just happened to have an informant in the right place at the right time," Brognola said. "You know how that goes. A guy who knew a guy who knew a guy, the last guy being Azizi. Anyway, unless Azizi or one of the other *guys* can't keep from flapping their gums—and they're all getting paid big bucks to keep it a secret—no one else in Nigeria should be aware that Matt Cooper is anything other than the photojournalist he says he is. And even Azizi won't know who you really are or why you're there."

Bolan cleared his throat. "It won't matter," he said. "Everyone in Nigeria will know about the chapel bomb and the machete attack. If my cover ID gets burned, it won't take a genius to guess why I'm there."

"True," Brognola said. "Their first thought'll be that you're CIA."

"It always is. Okay. I'll play it by ear, Hal. Who's my initial contact?"

"A woman named Layla Galab," Brognola said. "You'll find her at the Isaac Center. Any cabdriver should be able to take you there."

"Affirmative."

"Good luck, big guy."

Bolan paused before answering. He and Brognola both knew that luck rarely entered the picture. For the most part, a warrior made his own luck. So finally, he said, "Thanks," as the Learjet's wheels quit rolling on the tarmac of Ibadan Airport in the state of Oyo, Nigeria.

BISHOP JOSHUA ADEWALE'S unconsciousness couldn't have lasted more than a few seconds, he realized, as he opened his eyes again. He could still hear the screams and shrieks he had heard right before being knocked out by whatever had hit him in the back of the head. And as he rose to a sitting position on top of the bodies of several other bishops who had been cut down by the machetes, he saw the massacre still going on outside the chapel.

The pain in the back of his head was bad but tolerable as he stood. A strange feeling of remoteness seemed to come over him. He could see the angry, cursing men with the wicked blades, cutting and slashing and severing heads and limbs from the bodies of men who were dressed similarly to him. The sight made him sick to his stomach. But he knew, somehow, that *he* was invulnerable to their attack.

Adewale began to walk forward. He had no idea where he was going and only the vaguest memory of where he was and even *who* he was. His body ached from the top of his head to the soles of his feet, as if someone had punched him repeatedly in the face, then the sides of his head, then his chest and every other square inch of his body. Each step he took brought on new pain. It hurt to walk, but when he stopped briefly between two of the blood-crazed attackers, he realized it hurt just as much to stand still. Turning a full 360 degrees in an attempt to get his bearings and remember where and who he was, he saw the remnants of what looked to have once been a chapel.

Only one wall still stood, and the bishop did his best to focus his fuzzy eyes on a stained-glass window that had miraculously been spared. Spared from what? he wondered for a moment. Then he recalled a loud noise. As his vision began to clear, he continued to look at the stained glass. It featured Jesus Christ on the cross, his forehead bleeding from the crown of thorns that had been placed on his brow. The sight brought back another piece of Adewale's past, and he remembered that he was a priest—no, a bishop.

He turned away from the ruins and saw the men on both sides of him. One swung his machete at Adewale's neck. Miraculously, the assault fell short, but the ugly black steel came close enough that he felt the air move against his throat.

The compulsion to walk came over him again, and he moved on, passing between the two attackers and wondering why he had no desire to run. But the same remoteness, a feeling that even though he was in the presence of evil, he was invulnerable to the blades, continued to coax him on.

Still wondering why he felt no fear, the bishop left the screams and cries behind him and walked on. He did his best to take stock of the situation, focusing his brain on what he could remember as he continued to walk down an asphalt street.

He was a bishop; he remembered that now. A bishop in New York City. But he was not in New York at the moment. Was he back in his home country of Nigeria? He thought so.

Adewale pushed himself on, one wobbling step after another. Something had happened in the chapel, where he'd been speaking to a group of fellow bishops. A bomb? Yes. A bomb set by terrorists. Thugs who were now chopping the survivors to pieces with their machetes. He had been spared. Why, he didn't know, but he knew that they might still find him and kill him.

The bishop realized he had entered a low-income housing area. Every block he passed exhibited a little more poverty than the last. Soon the rough asphalt ran out and was replaced with dirt streets.

Finally, the bishop came to a corner and halted abruptly. Why he'd stopped was as big a mystery as why he'd felt compelled to walk. He found himself next to a wood-frame house, and his eyes were drawn to the backyard, where a clothesline had been stretched from the building to a rough wooden pole in the ground. Most of the clothes hanging on the line looked like women's, but right in the center, waving gently in the breeze, were a pair of khaki pants and a matching work shirt.

The bishop glanced down at his cassock. It had been black, but was now covered in so much dust it was gray. It would still identify him as a Christian bishop if the terrorists who had bombed the chapel came looking for him.

Adewale knew he needed to change clothes. He would take the pants and a shirt from the line. He started that way, then halted again.

Thou shalt not steal ran through the bishop's mind. Taking these pants and the shirt would be wrong. He didn't want to steal. He particularly didn't want to steal from anyone so poor they had to live in this crumbling shack.

But what if he took the pants and shirt and left the cassock? That would be a trade rather than a theft. Wouldn't that be all right with God?

The bishop's mind was finally losing the fuzziness he'd been experiencing since the explosion. He looked back at the line, then reached into a pocket of his cassock and felt his money clip. Then he looked at the house, and now that the haze that had hampered his thinking was gone, he realized that the people who lived here would probably be eager to sell him the shirt and pants. Particularly since he would pay them far more than the clothes were worth.

That was the answer, the bishop thought. He would *buy* the clothes from them.

Bishop Joshua Adewale's legs still felt a little unsteady as he left the road and walked across the ragged grass toward the front door. The three steps leading up to the porch were made of wood that had rotted long ago. As he mounted the second one, he heard a loud crack, and his left foot broke through the plank to the ground.

That confused him again, and for several seconds he simply stood where he was and looked down at his trapped leg. Finally, he reached down with both hands and, pulling with all his strength, managed to get his foot free of the shattered stair.

The effort left him exhausted.

The bishop realized that while some of his thinking had returned to normal, other aspects of his mind were still numb with shock. Such as the leg he had just skinned. He knew there was pain along his shin, but it was almost as if someone else was hurting.

He moved onto the porch without further incident and stopped in front of the door. The wood in the lower half was as rotten as the steps. The top half featured a large cracked pane of glass, behind which hung a blanket.

As he had done when he'd broken through the step, Adewale stood still, just staring for a moment, wondering what to do next.

Knock. It was almost as if he heard an actual voice in his head, and he realized he was not entirely over the shock he had experienced. His rational brain faded in, then out, then in again and…

The man in the dust-covered cassock slapped himself across the face. Suddenly, the world came back into focus. At least for the moment. He reached out and rapped three times on the flimsy wooden door. He waited, frowning, again trying to remember why he was here.

To change clothes, said the voice in his head. He could hear it more clearly now. You are going to offer to buy clothes from these poor people, and you are going to pay them much more than the clothing is worth because they need it.

But why did he need different clothes? Oh yes. The terrorists. Boko Haram.

Finally, the blanket behind the glass moved slightly at the lower left-hand corner.

Through the tiny opening, Adewale saw a dark brown eye.

Then the door opened slightly and he looked down to see a little girl holding the doorknob. She stared out through the crack, gazing up into the bishop's face. She wore a tiny red T-shirt and blue shorts that looked as if they had originated in America or Europe. Her hair was a mass of braided pigtails that shot out from her head and had rags securing them at the ends.

"Who is it?" called a voice from somewhere behind the child.

The tiny brown figure on the other side of the door didn't speak. She just kept staring up at Adewale.

Footsteps tapped on the wood floor. A moment later, a woman with caramel-colored skin opened the door wider and looked out at him. Her brown eyes opened wide and her mouth opened in a silent *"Oh."*

The bishop and woman looked at each other for a good ten seconds before she finally found her voice. "We heard an explosion," she said in a half whisper, as if she was afraid the neighbors might hear her. "We did not know where it came from. Was it the Boko Haram monsters?"

Adewale shrugged. "That would be my guess," he said. "But I do not know for sure."

"It was Boko Haram," she stated, nodding vigorously. "They started out in the north, but now they have come south. And no one will ever be safe again."

"May I come in?" the bishop asked. A low buzzing sound had been in his ears ever since he'd awakened after the explosion, while the pain throughout his body had been so severe that he had barely acknowledged it. Now, as he continued to regain his senses, the sound seemed to grow louder.

"Most certainly," the woman replied, and opened the door the rest of the way. As soon as he was inside, she stuck her head out, looked nervously both ways, then hurriedly closed the door again.

Turning to the bishop, she said, "How did you escape?"

"I don't know. I just walked away."

"God was with you," the woman declared. "But the Bokos will still be looking for you,"

"I know. I would like to buy some clothing from you…" As he reached into his pocket for his money clip, the hum in his ears grew to a roar and he collapsed to the floor.

CHAPTER TWO

Mack Bolan couldn't resist a slight jab at his old friend Jack Grimaldi as the plane taxied off the runway and onto the asphalt access road. "May I assume you brought a good book to keep you occupied while you await my return, Jack?" he asked.

"Of course." Grimaldi smiled. He tapped the front of his worn leather bomber jacket. "The best book I own." Reaching inside, he pulled out a weathered address book. "Fact is," he went on, "there are a *couple* of ladies in Ibadan who would like to have a good time with an American pilot."

The Executioner laughed softly. There were few airports in the world that weren't within quick access of some attractive female acquainted with Jack Grimaldi. Not that the pilot ever let a woman interfere with his work. As Bolan reached over the seat for his bags, he thought of all the times he and Grimaldi had taken off one step ahead of pursuing criminals, terrorists, enemy military or police. Too numerous to count.

A Nigerian customs official carrying a clipboard walked toward Bolan as he lugged his bags away from the private plane. As the man drew closer, Bolan noted the broad smile on his face. The two of them stopped, facing each other, and Bolan saw that the nameplate on his chest read Sean Azizi.

Bolan set a bag down and extended his right hand in greeting.

"Matt Cooper," the customs agent said, before he could utter a word. "You are a photojournalist. If you please, Mr. Matt Cooper, just call me Sean. I was advised that you were coming." His speech had the sharply clipped accent that came from an African heritage combined with a British higher education.

Yes, Bolan thought as he shook the man's hand. You were advised, all right. And smile or no smile, you were paid off royally as well, no doubt.

For a second the men stared into each other's eyes, both sizing the other up. The soldier reminded himself that most officials who were willing to break their own laws for money played both sides of the fence for all they were worth. Most were also willing to go back on their original agreements if an offer of additional bribery presented itself.

The Executioner made a mental note not to forget about Sean Azizi and the potential threat he represented. The customs agent might not know exactly who "Matt Cooper" was or what he was doing in Nigeria, but he knew he was American, and that he was there under false pretenses and using false identification. So somewhere down the line the man might just find another market where he could sell such information. And if he did, Bolan definitely got the feeling that the man would take advantage of it.

But for now, everything went as smoothly as Brognola had promised it would.

The customs agent guided Bolan through both customs and immigration and updated his passport. Their last stop was at a currency exchange.

Fifteen minutes after the Learjet had touched down, Bolan said goodbye to Azizi, loaded his luggage into the trunk of a battered taxicab and settled into the backseat.

"The Isaac Center," he told the driver, who nodded, threw the transmission of his twenty-year-old Chevy into Drive and pulled away from the airport.

The man tried several times to start up a conversation, mentioning the unseasonably cool weather, suggesting a few tourist spots that Bolan should see and finally offering to get him the most beautiful prostitute in Nigeria at a fair price.

"Beware," the cabbie went on, as he moved the steering wheel back and forth. "Other taxi drivers and men will tell you they will get you the best women *cheap*. I do not promise cheap—that means ugly and diseased. You get what you pay for." Bolan saw him look up into the rearview mirror, waiting for a response.

When he didn't get one, the driver finally shrugged, gave up and fell into silence. Bolan stared through the open windows as the taxi passed block after block of mud-and-plaster dwellings with shiny tin roofs. Ibadan, he knew, was the home of close to a million Nigerians, and the capital of the Western Region. One of the largest cities in Africa between Johannesburg and Cairo, it boasted a top-notch hospital and medical school, as well as the country's premier university.

They drove through three market areas crowded with pedestrians buying fresh vegetables, yams and spices, as well as clucking chickens. They passed huge piles of cotton cloth, much of it the blue color favored by Yoruba tribesmen. Twice the cabdriver was forced to stop as wedding processions of dancing and singing men and women streamed by.

Bolan took in the sights, sounds and smells around the cab as they passed more pedestrians on the crowded streets and sidewalks. It was a colorful and vibrant city.

The taxi began climbing a steep upgrade, and at the top Bolan saw the destination he had given the driver. The center had been named after Isaac, the son of Abraham, whose faith and devotion to God had been demonstrated by his willingness to sacrifice his only son. Not only was the story of Abraham and Isaac a prelude to the sacrifice of God's own son, it symbolized the orphans who lived at the center. Isaac had been spared at the last second by the hand of an angel. But Boko Haram had shown no such mercy. In their own twisted version of the Old Testament story, the terrorists had sacrificed the parents instead of the children in their ongoing war against Christians in Nigeria.

The Isaac Center now provided a home to over three hundred Nigerian orphans. The main entrance to the relatively modern building was centered on a circular drive. Behind what appeared to be a one-story reception and office area stood a three-story section that could hold dorm rooms. To the right, new construction was going on, with framers raising skeletal two-by-four walls on top of a concrete slab. From the general layout, it looked to Bolan as if more dorms were in progress, which could mean only one thing.

The Isaac Center was expecting even more orphans.

The sharp hiss of electrical-powered nail guns sounded as the cabbie pulled up to the front door and killed the engine. Bolan got out of the backseat. Together, they lugged his bags through the front doors and into the lobby.

"This is far enough," Bolan said. He reached into his pocket, pulled out several naira bills, pushed them into the hand of the driver, then turned back toward the building's interior.

Under the watchful eye of an elderly black woman, roughly a dozen little boys and girls were playing on wooden rocking horses and other handmade toys to the right side of the lobby. Their laughter made it obvious that they had been too young to know how much they had lost. At least they had been spared the bloody memories that would haunt the Isaac Center's older residents for life. The Executioner vowed that the terrorists responsible would pay.

The big American stepped up to the front counter as the cabbie exited the building. English had been the official language of Nigeria since British colonial days, so he had no trouble when he said, "My name is Matt Cooper and I'm looking for Layla Galab."

"One moment, please," the receptionist answered pleasantly.

Bolan studied the woman as she reached for the telephone. Around thirty years old, she had well-defined but still feminine arm muscles revealed by her sleeveless blouse. She worked out at a gym—a fairly unusual luxury in such a country as Nigeria. And while Bolan was hardly a fashion expert, what he could see of her skirt looked to be more expensive than the clothing on most of the other women he'd seen since landing. Two gold rings, one featuring a large diamond, the other an opal, flashed on her hand as she lifted the receiver to her ear.

As was the case in many developing countries, the rich got richer as the poor became poorer, and Bolan guessed this woman had come from a wealthy family. Perhaps her conscience had gotten to her and she had taken this job to help those less fortunate than herself. In any case, he doubted the rings or clothing had been purchased with money from her Isaac Center salary.

A moment later, the woman placed a call and

spoke into the receiver. "Miss Layla, there's a Mr. Cooper here to see you." A short pause ensued and then she said, "Okay," and hung up. Rising, she took the time to bend and smooth her short skirt over her thighs. "If you will follow me, please, Mr. Cooper." She strode around the end of the counter, then stopped and looked down at his baggage. "Your luggage should be perfectly safe right where it is," she said.

Bolan thought of what the bags contained, then glanced in the direction of the children. "I think I'd better take it with me, just to be careful," he replied.

The receptionist frowned. "Perhaps you are right," she said. "You must have many thousands of dollars' worth of photographic equipment inside, and even the most well-behaved children become curious. I would hate for them to break any of it."

The soldier reached down and grabbed the handles and straps of the bags. He wasn't worried about the "equipment" inside the bags getting broken. He was worried that some of it might harm any curious children who got their hands on it. All the firearms inside were loaded, cocked and locked. It wouldn't take much for a kid to accidentally blow one or more of his friends away. And Bolan didn't intend to take the chance of that happening.

The receptionist started down the hall, her hips swaying in what the Executioner suspected was a slight exaggeration for his benefit. He followed, his rubber lug-soled hiking boots making soft thuds in time with the woman's clattering high heels as they crossed the tile.

A moment later, she stopped at a door on the right side of the hall, twisted the knob and pushed it open. Then she stepped back from the opening.

"If you would, Mr. Cooper," she said, smiling up at him.

Bolan had to turn sideways to get the equipment bags strapped over his shoulders through the doorway. But as soon as he had, the door closed behind him, and he found himself alone in a small office with a strikingly beautiful woman.

She had risen from behind her desk, but held a cell phone to her ear as Bolan entered. "Yes, Mother," she said, looking up and smiling. "No, Mother. Leave the laundry for me. I will do it as soon as my duties permit. Yes, Mother. I love you, too. Goodbye." She lowered the phone from her ear and clicked it off.

Layla Galab smiled as she extended her hand across the desk. "Mr. Cooper," she said. "You will excuse me, please. My mother's mind is failing and I must check on her several times a day."

Bolan nodded in understanding as he set his bags on the floor. Her smile appeared genuine, but he noted that her lips stayed pressed together as they curled up at the corners.

The Executioner took her small hand in his, noticing that while it was delicate, her fingers and palm were covered by calluses. This woman was not just a sit-behind-the-desk paper pusher. She got out and *worked* for the welfare of the children who lived at the Isaac Center, perhaps even helping with the on-going construction next door.

"Miss Galab."

"You will excuse me, also, I hope," she said, turning her hands palm up and glancing down at them. "But as you no doubt saw when you arrived, we are constructing new housing, and I often go out to help. I am afraid it has taken away the femininity from my hands."

"No," he said. "It just emphasizes your other feminine qualities." The Executioner stared down into the woman's chocolate-brown eyes. She was indeed beautiful, and he could feel the electricity passing back and forth between them.

Breaking eye contact, Galab pointed to a chair in front of her desk and said, "Won't you sit down, Mr. Cooper?"

"Thanks." He sat, then looked back across the desktop and said, "But call me Matt."

"Thank you. Please call me Layla."

She resumed her seat and said, "Now, Mr. Photojournalist Matt Cooper, can you tell me the real reason you are here? I do not think it is to take pictures for *National Geographic*."

Bolan crossed one leg over the other. "I understand you've helped Americans before," he said.

Galab gave the room a 180-degree glance, as if it might be bugged, before nodding. Then, in a low voice, she said, "And I will help you in any way I can." A second round-the-room glance seemed to take some of the stress from her face. "I will do anything to keep the terrorists from murdering more mothers and fathers and creating more orphans." She leaned down and pulled open a drawer in her desk. A moment later, a bottle of antacid appeared in her hand. "You will excuse me if I—" she began.

Bolan interrupted her. "Of course."

"I'm afraid I have developed an ulcer from all of this," the woman said, as she twisted off the cap.

A faint odor of chalk floated across the room as she took a long drink. Bolan chuckled to himself. The woman was self-conscious about the calluses on her hands, but didn't seem to mind looking like a wino who'd just found a bottle of Mogen David 20/20 when it came to her ulcer.

Enough pain, Bolan knew, had a way of chasing self-consciousness right out of the soul. Besides, he thought. Like her calluses, chugging the medicine straight from the bottle somehow emphasized her femininity rather than detracted from it. It made her seem more human.

When she had finished, Galab screwed the cap back on and returned the bottle to her desk drawer. She pulled a tissue from the same drawer and dabbed daintily at her lips before turning her attention back to Bolan. "Let us get to the topic at hand," she said. "Are you able to tell me what you have planned?"

"Up to a point," Bolan replied. "I'm primarily here to find Bishop Joshua Adewale and get him safely back to the US. But I also plan to do all I can to rid your country of men like those who killed the parents of the orphans you have here. I just haven't decided exactly how I'm going to accomplish that."

The statement was meant to be blunt, and Galab took it that way, shrinking back slightly at Bolan's words. "Let us make sure I understand you correctly," she said in a small voice. "Do you intend to arrest or simply kill these men?"

Bolan paused a moment, looking deeply into the woman's eyes. "I have no power of arrest in Nigeria," he said. "But Boko Haram has gone way past that point. Even if I could arrest them, with all due respect, the Nigerian government has become so corrupt they'd probably be set free again." He stopped speaking for a moment to let his words sink in. "So I intend to do what I have to do."

The woman got the message. But instead of recoiling further, as Bolan would have expected, she seemed to relax. "I would like to help you, Matt, but I am neither trained as a fighter nor do I have the temperament to be one." She paused and took in a deep breath. "I can, however, take you to men who can and will help you."

"Can these men be trusted?" Bolan asked. "Both to be on our side and keep their mouths shut?"

"I believe so," Galab said. "They are good men, I think. But they do not have a good leader." She paused a moment, then added, "At least they haven't had a good leader so far."

Bolan uncrossed his legs and leaned forward slightly. While Galab seemed to be a caring person, he didn't particularly trust her judgment on who could be counted on and who couldn't. Many "good" people tended to think others thought, and behaved, as they did. And that was often not the case.

The soldier's only option was to meet these men and decide for himself.

"Okay," he said. "I'll need a base of operations, too. Someplace I can store my gear and hide out when it becomes necessary."

"Do you think it *will* become necessary?"

"At one point or another," Bolan replied, "it always does."

"Do you want to meet these men now?"

"There's no time like the present," he told her, standing. "Do you have a car?"

"I do." Galab rose in turn. "Since I suspect I know what some of the things in your luggage are, I think we should take it with us."

Bolan nodded. They left the building through a back door and found themselves in an alley. Two minutes later, they had loaded Bolan's bags into the back of Galab's Nissan Maxima.

The Isaac Center director was backing the vehicle out of her parking space behind the building when the first explosion of gunfire erupted.

A volley of rounds shattered the car window next to Bolan, missing both his and Galab's heads by centimeters. Then more gunfire broke the side window next to the woman behind the wheel.

She screamed.

Another burst of bullets, this one coming from the front, turned the windshield into tiny fragments of glass. In his peripheral vision, Bolan saw a man wearing green fatigue pants appear to the side of the Maxima, pull the pin on a fragmentation grenade and roll the bomb under the vehicle.

"Hit it!" Bolan yelled. His left foot shot across the front seat and stomped down on Galab's right, flooring the accelerator. She shrieked again, her voice blending in with the screech of the Maxima's tires. They tore away from the grenade in reverse, peeling rubber like some teenage show-off leaving the local youth hangout.

Two seconds later, the grenade detonated, but they had cleared the kill zone and nothing but a few pieces of shrapnel hit the Maxima and skidded off.

Bolan had drawn the sound-suppressed Beretta, but not for the usual reason. He didn't need to try to keep the 9 mm explosions from being heard by whoever was attacking them—in fact, the sound of return fire would actually have helped, telling their attackers that he didn't plan to go down without a fight. But that aspect of the impromptu battle was overshadowed by the fact that Bolan didn't want to burst his and Galab's eardrums inside the Maxima. And if he counterfired with the massive Desert Eagle, there was every chance of that happening.

Even with the windshield and side windows blown out, the .44 Magnum explosions inside the car would be deafening.

The Executioner dropped the front sight of the Beretta on the man who had thrown the grenade as the Maxima fishtailed farther away. Thumbing the selector switch to 3-round burst, he squeezed the trigger and sent two 9 mm rounds into the attacker's chest. The third hollowpoint round rode high, grazing the top of the white turban on the man's head.

Their attacker jerked with each shot, but kept running. And as he did, he pulled the pin on a second grenade. His final burst of energy ended abruptly. The grenade slipped from his fingers as he fell, dead before he hit the ground.

But the grenade was far from dead.

Galab had twisted the steering wheel, skidding the car in a half-circle. But then her mind seemed to stall and she froze in place. Bolan started to reach down and throw the transmission from Reverse into Drive, but before he could, the director seemed to come out of her trance and did it herself.

Bolan twisted in his seat, now seeing through the back window the man who had just fallen. His lifeless body lay on the concrete in the parking space they had just vacated. Next to him, the second fragmentation grenade still rolled and wobbled.

Then it came to a halt and prepared to explode.

Another man—by now the Executioner had seen enough to convince him that they were indeed Boko

Haram terrorists—appeared dangerously close to the grenade. Bolan aimed the Beretta his way and sent another trio of rounds through the back window of the car to pound into his throat and head. This time the turban stayed on but turned red.

Bolan switched his attention back to the grenade in the parking space. It still lay where it had come to rest, and he was surprised that it had failed to explode. There had been more than ample time for it to detonate, since the pin had been pulled.

A dud. It happened. Particularly when weapons and munitions were purchased on the black market, the way terrorists usually obtained them.

But the Executioner had no more time or need to contemplate the stroke of luck. The workmen had all hit the concrete or found other cover. Bolan glanced toward the front of the Isaac Center and the dorms just beyond.

None of the bullets flying through the air, or the grenades, were heading that way.

"Get us out of here," he ordered.

"But the children—" the center's director started to say.

"Aren't the target," Bolan stated. "*We are.* Now move it!"

She floored the accelerator, moving forward this time. The Maxima began to fishtail again, but the woman behind the wheel kept control and straightened it. They sped to the end of the alley, turned right and emerged onto a street. Suddenly they were cruising away from the attack, and the only danger left was the possibility of severing an artery on all the broken glass inside the Nissan.

"Praise God, Christ and the Holy Spirit," Galab said around choking gasps for oxygen. Then, as the Maxima blended in with the other traffic, she drove on, skillfully weaving in and out of the flow until they reached the edge of the last market area the cabbie had driven through when he'd brought Bolan to the Isaac Center. The soldier thought back on their escape from the alley. At first the woman next to him had panicked, but then, suddenly, she'd settled down and reacted almost like a professional stock car driver. It was as if she'd become a different person.

"I thought you told me you weren't a fighter," Bolan said.

Galab glanced his way, her expression curious. "I did. I am not."

"Well," Bolan said, "once you got over your initial fear, you operated that steering wheel and foot feed like a lifelong hillbilly moonshiner trying to lose the Feds."

The metaphor was obviously out of Galab's frame of reference. "I do not understand," she said, frowning.

"It just meant that you've got the skills of a well-practiced race car driver," Bolan said.

"Ah, yes," Galab said as she patted the steering wheel with both hands. "I have driven in rescue missions many times to get the children. I suppose I have picked up some skills along the way." She paused, took in a deep breath, then let it out slowly. "But driving is not fighting. I do not think I could ever pull the trigger of a gun and take a human life."

"You wouldn't have to," Bolan said, chuckling softly. "You could always just run them over in the street."

The woman's only answer was a smile. A moment later she turned into a parking lot, then settled the Maxima in an empty space. "It is better if we go from here on foot," she said.

The soldier glanced around at the shattered windshield, shards of broken glass and bullet holes now decorating the vehicle. "Yeah," he said. "I suppose we might draw a little unwanted attention in this thing."

"And we should take your bags," Galab stated. "Where we are going will be as good a place as you will find to store them until they are needed."

Bolan nodded, got out and pulled the straps of several bags over his head to hang from his shoulders. "Aren't I going to draw a lot of attention with all this?" he asked.

"Certainly," the woman said. "But the path down which I will lead you will be away from interested eyes. At least for the most part."

A second later they left the parking lot and started down a deserted alley behind the busy market.

CHAPTER THREE

He had designed the room himself, all the while keeping his tongue pressed firmly into his cheek. It was a joke in many ways, a humorous glimpse into the life of an old-style caliph. A cross between modern reality and a cartoon view of what it was like to be a wealthy oil sheikh. But to Fazel Hayat it was fun and certainly exciting. Maybe not quite as exciting as blowing up a chapel full of Christian bishops, or watching on his laptop screen as his men shot at this mysterious American agent.

Hayat thought back to the bombing of the seminary chapel. They had killed many of the bishops. But the primary target—Bishop Joshua Adewale—had escaped, and that made the Boko leader angry. He had wanted to kill the man because he was a Christian bishop, but also because he was an American. In addition to disrupting the bishops' conference and destroying the seminary, Hayat had been planning to humiliate the United States and show the world how the Satanic democracy had lost power, will and influence.

That part of the plan had failed, but he would correct the error.

The soft purr and splash of the artificial waterfall built into the wall and leading down into the indoor swimming pool had a relaxing effect on Hayat, and he stretched out on his side atop the large stuffed pillows. In front of him now was a beautiful shapely blonde wearing nothing but sheer capri pants. Behind him, he felt the large-breasted brunette he had just been kissing reach up with both hands to massage his neck.

The waterfall and pool were the room's central features, but the scantily clad young women swimming and playing in the water also commanded the leader's attention. Other members of what Hayat jokingly called his Boko Haram Harem lounged on huge silk pillows around the room.

The walls of the Haram Harem were of tile, and each one featured a saying from the Koran. At least that was what Hayat had been told. He had never bothered to actually read any of them. For that matter, he had read very little of the Koran.

When he wasn't engaged in some sort of sexual act with the women, Hayat kept busy eating and drinking or planning the next attack on Nigerians who paid homage to the ways of the West. It mattered not if they were Christians or Muslims.

On the other side of the room, across the pool, were two violinists, a string bass player and a harpist. All four were beautiful females. Eerie sounds of music in a minor key came from their strings and guided the steps of three dancers in front of them. These women wore completely transparent pantaloons and blouses, and veils that covered their faces except for their alluring eyes.

Hayat listened to the music and stared at the dancers and musicians. But even in this atmosphere, which had been designed totally for pleasure and pleasure alone, his mind kept wandering. He was now aware that an American agent of some kind— a true specialist, a man whose skills went far beyond those of the usual commando or intelligence officer—had come to Nigeria. He had learned about the man from his contact at the airport, who had been paid by the Americans to guide the man through customs. Hayat did not yet know exactly what this American agent's mission was, but until he received that information, and the man was eliminated, he could not completely rest.

He felt himself frowning. Some of his tracking agents had followed the man as he left the airport in a taxicab. They had tailed him to the Isaac Center, where they had attacked, but been unsuccessful in eliminating him. That was Hayat's own fault, he had decided. He had not taken the threat as seriously as he should have, and had allowed his second team to attempt the assassination. He would not make that mistake again. As soon as they located the American again, he would put Dhul Agbede on the job. And Hayat had not forgotten the Nigerian-born American bishop, either. Joshua Adewale had somehow escaped both the explosion and the machetes of the Bokos sent to the chapel.

He was another enemy who needed to be located. And killed. But Dhul had enough on his plate. Hayat would send Sam to find and kill the bishop from New York.

The second problem on the mind of the Boko Haram leader was almost as troubling as the first. One of his own men—Enitan—had gone over to the enemy. He'd had a dream of meeting Jesus or some such nonsense, and was now calling himself "Paul" after some ancient Christian missionary.

This man, Hayat knew, could be just as dangerous as the American. He, too, needed to be found and killed before he infected other Muslims with his fairy tales and insanity.

That made three men who had to be found and killed: the mysterious American agent, the Nigerian-born New York bishop and Enitan, aka Paul.

In his peripheral vision, Hayat saw a beautiful redheaded woman. She was Canadian by birth, if Hayat remembered correctly. He turned to her as she squeezed in on the pillow between him and the blonde. Her lips were bright red and wet-looking with lipstick, and she smiled seductively into his eyes. She looked as if she wanted to speak, so Hayat said, "Yes, my dear?"

"I am special, am I not?" she purred.

He smiled back at her. "You are all special," he said, as his eyes swept the room. "And what was your name?"

The red lips took on a pouty appearance. "You do not even remember my name?" she cried, in what Hayat knew to be exaggerated offense. "Why, just this morning you and I and Kamilah—"

"I remember what the three of us did," Hayat said. "And it was most enjoyable. But I do not remember your name." He leaned over and kissed the woman on the forehead.

"My name is Patsy."

"From Toronto," Hayat interjected.

Again, she looked slightly put out. "Montreal," she corrected.

"I was close. There are nearly fifty women here," he went on, sweeping a hand around the room. "And new ones arrive every day. I cannot be expected to remember all of your names."

"I suppose not."

"But," Hayat said, "I never forget your *specialties*."

The redhead smiled at him, but to Hayat, the expression looked a little false.

Before he could speak again a sultry brunette approached timidly. He *did* remember her name. Kamilah. The woman who had joined him and Patsy that very morning. Now, she looked nervous, and Hayat could not help wondering why.

He soon learned the answer, as Kamilah stopped

in front of him and Patsy and whispered, "You have a visitor."

Hayat paused. While he allowed other men to watch what went on in his harem through the windows, only two were ever allowed to enter. The most frequent visitor was Agbede. Less frequent, and never showing as much interest in the women as Dhul, was Boko Haram's liaison to al Qaeda, a man who went simply by the name of Sam. So Hayat knew it had to be one of those two when he said, "Who is this visitor?"

"That...*man,*" she replied. "Dhul Agbede. The ugly, perverse one who makes my skin crawl. Please do not make me go with him. The last time—"

Hayat held a hand up and the woman knew to quit speaking. "We will see what he has to say and what he has done," he said. "Go let him in."

She was still shivering as she turned and walked away. Hayat lay back in a half sitting, half prone position on the pillow as he waited. A moment later, Kamilah returned, with Agbede a step ahead of her. Finally, the wretched man reached the pillow where Hayat reclined. Dhul stopped, and Kamilah paused behind him. Then she circled the man and dropped to her side on another pillow, as close to Hayat as she could get.

The terrorist leader chuckled softly to himself. Kamilah was obviously attempting to psychologically distance herself from Agbede and make it appear that she was Hayat's exclusive property. Or else she was just doing her best to get him to forget about her for the time being.

Hayat leaned across the woman, reached over and playfully tapped Kamilah's cheek. He wanted her to know that he had *not* forgotten her. Kamilah, like all the other women in his harem, came and went according to his pleasure. Most had come to him through the human trafficking division of Boko Haram. He doubted that most of them were overjoyed to be where they were. But they knew things could always get worse. Once one of his women was led out of the room with the swimming pool and big pillows, she was either executed or sold again.

"So," Hayat said, looking up at his number-two man. "What do you have to report?"

Agbede dropped onto a pillow directly across from him and reached for a tray holding oysters. After sucking down a half-dozen with a loud, smacking sound, he looked up again. "The man our informant warned us was coming has arrived," he said.

"I am already aware of that. I sent men to eliminate him. They failed. What can you add to this knowledge?"

"I should have been sent to do the job myself," Agbede said.

Hayat stared back at the dirty, greasy man, now splattered with oyster juice. No one else in the organization would have dared speak to him that way. But

Dhul's talents brought him special privileges. On the other hand, the women were listening, and he refused to lose face or look weak in front of them. They had very little to distract them when they weren't pleasuring him, and they gossiped like old hags.

"Yes," Hayat said. "I am aware that I should have assigned that strike to you, as well. But for your own sake, my old and dear friend, be wise in how you speak to me. I am still in charge, and you would do well to keep that in mind."

The veiled threat appeared to have little if any effect on the man. Hayat wasn't sure if it was because he was too dense to pick up on the true meaning of the words, or the fact that due to the outrageous combination of personality disorders that made up Agbede's thinking, he simply had no capacity for fear.

Hayat waved an arm, indicating the laptop that had slid between two pillows. "In any case," he said, "the job now falls to you."

"The man was lucky," Agbede said as he raised another oyster shell to his lips and sucked the contents into his mouth and down his throat. "But I will get him."

"Have we confirmed that he is, indeed, American?" Hayat asked.

Agbede grabbed a handful of red caviar and stuffed it into his mouth. Dozens of the tiny eggs smeared his cheeks instead of his tongue, but he seemed not to notice or care. "I spoke with Azizi, who walked him through customs. He was traveling under the guise of an American journalist."

"Is he from the CIA?" Hayat asked.

"That I do not know. I will try to find out before I kill him if you like."

"If you can, fine. But killing him must be the number-one priority." Hayat shifted his weight on the pillow. "And what of the American bishop? Adewale?"

Agbede grunted, then burped loudly, the sound reverberating around the room. "We have received word that he disappeared somewhere in the slums a half mile or so from the explosion site," he said. "I have men searching for him."

Hayat peered deeply into Dhul's sharklike eyes. Having satisfied his desire for food and drink, the man had begun to stare at the women surrounding him. They had noticed his interest, and all but Patsy had averted their eyes from his, looking at the floor or in some other direction, as if doing their best to make themselves invisible.

Patsy just smiled and snuggled closer to Hayat.

He was growing tired of Dhul's presence. As good as the man might be at his job, there was a limit as to how much filth and grotesqueness Hayat could tolerate. "Go and clean yourself up," he ordered.

Then, turning to Patsy, he said, "Go with him." He felt a leering smile creep over his face. "He will need help. And you will do whatever he asks of you."

Patsy's smile turned to an instant mask of horror. "But…no…please…" she whispered in a trembling, throaty voice.

"You wanted to be special," he said. "Don't you remember? Well, I am making you special. And I am sure that Dhul will think of some very special things for you to do."

Tears began to roll down Patsy's cheeks as Agbede jumped to his feet and grabbed her elbow. Hayat's grin broadened even further. He liked playing these little psychological games with his women.

As Agbede pulled her toward him, the redhead looked over her shoulder and pleaded one last time. *"Please…"* she whimpered in a tiny voice.

"Go!" Hayat shouted, looking her directly in the eye. "And please him. Or you will be sold to the first trader who passes by, and live the rest of your short life in far more unpleasant surroundings than this."

Laughing loudly, Agbede slapped her buttocks, then turned and started out of the room.

"You will be going out in public," Hayat called after him. "Allow her some clothing for appearances sake, at least."

A tall, long-legged blonde had anticipated the Boko Haram leader's words and now appeared in front of Agbede holding two garments. The man set Patsy back down on her feet and waited impatiently while she twisted a wrapper around her body and then shrugged into a traditional Yoruba top known as a *buba*.

"Do not take *too* long with her, my friend," Hayat called after him. "You have an American and a Boko Haram traitor to kill. And other attacks for which we need to plan."

Hayat had settled back on his pillow as Agbede retreated, and was eyeing the women around him again, when Kamilah appeared once more. Stopping directly in front of him, she looked down and smiled. "The other man is here," she said. "Sam."

"Bring him to me then."

She pivoted and walked off, her hips wiggling provocatively. Hayat knew the reason for her sudden change in attitude. He would offer Sam one or more of the women before the man left. But experience had taught him that Sam would not only not hurt them as Agbede did, the liaison to al Qaeda would politely refuse.

A few moments later, Kamilah returned, followed by a short, slightly built man. He was an Arab, originally from Yemen, but his skin was only a slight shade darker than the average Caucasian. His face, which was clean shaved, denoted no particular heritage. And in his work for both al Qaeda and Boko Haram, he made full use of the DNA, which allowed him to portray practically any race he chose to imitate simply by changing his clothes, language and attitude.

The bottom line was that Sam always looked like anything but what he actually was—a radical Islamic terrorist.

Hayat noted that this day, like most days when he was not undercover and gathering information within a specific ethnic group, Sam wore a gray pinstriped, three-piece business suit and a conservative burgundy-colored tie. His jacket was unbuttoned as usual, and Hayat saw the gold watch chain drooping across his abdomen from one pocket in his vest to the other.

Invisible at the small of his back, Sam would undoubtedly have his kris. The wavy, snakelike blade was encased in worn leather and secured by a steel clip to his belt.

Sam had used a wide variety of weapons during the time he had been liaison between al Qaeda and Boko Haram. But Hayat knew a .32 derringer and the kris were his favorites. They were simple, like Sam himself was simple, and they were always with him.

Although, as a member of al Qaeda rather than Boko Haram, Sam didn't answer directly to Fazel Hayat, he had always treated the Nigerian with the utmost respect. So now, as he stopped in front of Hayat's pillow and stood there looking more like some Latin American lawyer than the terrorist he was, he said, "You summoned me, sir?"

Hayat liked the man and liked his manners. They

were in such contrast to Agbede's. "Let us say I *requested* your presence," he said now. "It sounds so much friendlier." He indicated the empty pillow next to him where Patsy had been a few minutes earlier. "Would you like a seat?"

"No, thank you. I would prefer to stand."

"As you wish, then," Hayat said. "I have something I would like for you to do if you would."

Sam nodded. "That is why I was sent here," he said. "To assist Boko Haram in our mutual war against the West, Christianity and Judaism. To unite our two groups."

"The bishop from New York City," Hayat said. "The one who was born here and attended the local Christian seminary, then immigrated to the United States. He returned to be a speaker at their conference."

"So I have been told," Sam replied.

"And somehow," Fazel went on, "he escaped both the bomb inside the chapel and our men outside."

"So I also heard."

"His name is Bishop Joshua Adewale, and how this happened, I do not know. Dhul and I were watching through binoculars from a few blocks away. And I had one man videotaping the machete executions as the bomb survivors tried to run out of the rubble. Dhul and I saw, and our man with the video camera recorded, Adewale clearly walking right between two of my other men and out of the picture."

"I have watched the video," Sam said. "I did not think you would mind."

Hayat shook his head. "Of course not. I am happy that you are already familiar with the problem."

"With all due respect, sir," Sam said. "It appears that the two men he walked between were simply preoccupied with the killing of other bishops. And by the time they were finished, Adewale had left the scene."

"Yes, that is the only answer I can come up with myself," Hayat agreed. "But there is still something mysterious and unsettling about it all. Both men clearly looked at Adewale, but then seemed to immediately forget him and go back to what they were doing." He cleared his throat. "Dhul and I saw Adewale leave the scene and head into a nearby neighborhood, walking unsteadily, as if in some kind of trance."

Sam shuffled his feet slightly as if beginning to grow impatient. "And you would like me to find him and kill him?"

"Yes," Hayat replied. "Dhul has gone after the American agent and the traitor who now calls himself Paul. He will be busy with them, I suspect."

"Again, with all due respect," Sam said, "I should have been sent after all of these men as soon as we recognized the threats they represented. In fact—and I do not wish to overstep my bounds—but I should also have been in charge of the strike against the university chapel itself."

"You are correct," Hayat said. "But I had Dhul manufacture the bomb, plant it and then position the men outside the chapel before he joined me on the rooftop. I thought that would be sufficient."

Sam let a small smile of indulgence curl at the corners of his lips. "Would you allow me to speak freely, sir?" he asked.

"Of course. I value your input. And you possess the ability to disagree without being rude and offensive. Please continue."

"Thank you, sir." After clearing his throat, he said, "Dhul Agbede is an animal, sir," he said. "A mindless mongrel dog more suited to the days of Genghis Khan, Attila the Hun or Shaka Zulu with his scorched earth policy. Granted, there is some use to be culled from the random and apparently conscienceless violence of which he is capable. And he does construct good explosives and forges fine-edged weaponry. Like this." The wavy-bladed kris suddenly appeared in Sam's hand, drawn from the small of his back so quickly Hayat saw only a flurry of movement as the man's suit coat flared out and then fell back to his side. Sam rotated the kris into a reverse "ice pick" grip, then returned it to the sheath behind his back almost as quickly as he had produced it.

Hayat couldn't help being awed. No one could

forge steel into machetes and other edged weapons like Dhul Agbede, but he had never seen anyone who could use those blades with the skill that Sam possessed. The smartly dressed man from al Qaeda was famous for using his wavy blade. Many who knew him compared Sam to a mighty king cobra, who struck so fast with the kris that no man's eyes could follow the movement.

Before Hayat could comment on his skill with the serpentine blade, Sam said, "If there is nothing else, sir, I shall begin my search. May I assume the last known sighting of this Nigerian-American bishop was when he was videotaped stumbling away from the scene?"

"It was," Hayat replied.

"Is there anything else you can tell me that might help me get started?" Sam asked.

Hayat squinted, thinking hard. He knew something else had been unusual, but he couldn't remember exactly what. "No—" He stopped as a memory suddenly returned. "Wait. Yes… It may be of no consequence, but he appeared to have injured his arm."

"And what makes you say that, sir?" Sam asked.

"He was holding his left arm, right above the wrist, as he walked away," Hayat replied. "I remember that clearly now. But it must have been a minor injury. It did not keep him from disappearing down the street."

"Could you tell what type of injury it was? A broken bone, perhaps? Or a puncture…an abrasion?"

"I could not tell," Hayat stated. "Even through the binoculars or on the laptop screen."

Sam nodded and turned, starting to go.

Hayat stopped him, saying, "Would you like a woman or two before you leave?"

San shook his head. "No, thank you, sir. I appreciate the offer, but I am anxious to get to my task."

"Do you think you will be able to find him?" Hayat asked.

Sam turned back briefly with a smile. "Of course," he said. "It is what I do."

Hayat shook his head, which caught Sam's attention. "Is there something else, sir?"

"No. It was just the way you phrased your last comment. It made me think of Dhul. It is also what he does, but the two of you do it in such different ways."

"I certainly hope so," Sam replied. "I believe I would cut my own throat if I thought there were any similarities between the two of us."

And with those final words, he turned quickly and was gone.

GALAB LED THE Executioner along what was primarily a series of alleys. But there were enough streets that had to be crossed, and enough curious eyes falling on them when they did, that the Executioner knew that they and his lime-green luggage would be re-membered.

The bags had been an advantage at the airport, where they hid his weapons and other gear in what looked like typical tourist luggage. But here on the streets of Ibadan they had become a liability, drawing attention to him. Galab herself fitted into the landscape like a stalk of wheat in a wheat field, but with Bolan and his bags along, anyone could see that something out of the ordinary was taking place.

He took in a deep breath and let it out slowly through clenched teeth. Every mission he undertook had its ups and downs. Little things that worked for good as he progressed through the obstacles between him and his goal could easily turn around and hinder him a moment later. He was tempted to abandon the gaudy "sightseer" bags and carry on without them, but knew he might need much of the equipment the bags contained. And by now the damage had already been done. The only thing that would draw more attention than the lime-green monstrosities would be openly carrying the weapons and other equipment they contained.

The Executioner's mind continued to work as they walked swiftly on, hurrying down alleys and crossing streets as quickly as they could. The bottom line was that he needed to find a different, lower-profile means of transporting his gear as soon as possible. But he needed to remember that *some* damage had already been done. The men and women who saw him and Galab would remember them, and that meant that soon the Boko Haram terrorists were going to learn that they had been in the area with their neon luggage.

Galab had to be thinking along similar lines. "We are almost there," she said as they rushed on. "Soon we will be out of sight again and you can store those abominable bags in a safe place."

Bolan just nodded. In all missions, he had found over the years, there were calculated risks that had to be taken. And at this point, the only alternative to allowing themselves to be seen was to turn and go back, forgoing this place where he planned to base his operations. And even then, he had already drawn too many curious looks. If the Bokos didn't already know Bolan and the Isaac Center director were in the area, they soon would. So the best plan of action at this juncture was to make sure they didn't learn *exactly* which building they'd be in.

The soldier clenched his teeth again and moved on. Finally, he and Galab hurried into another deserted alley and the woman from the Isaac Center led him to a back door. The asphalt on which they stood was crowded with stacks of building materials: wallboard, boxes of nails, plywood sheets and other items.

The door led into a building constructed long ago of clay, but that appeared to be undergoing a major remodeling. It was at the end of a half-dozen other clay buildings that shared common walls and looked like some ancient shopping center. A walkway led away from them to the right, and Bolan looked down it and saw that it would take them to the busy street in front of the buildings. As if to confirm his assumption that the building was getting a makeover, he could hear the sounds of various power tools on the roof overhead. Whoever was operating them was too far back from the edge to be visible from below.

Galab caught his line of sight and answered his question before he could ask it. "This structure is old and beginning to fall apart," she said in a voice just loud enough to be heard over the racket. "The roof is currently being repaired. The men are back too far for us to see them."

Bolan nodded. "Just get us out of sight, too," he said, glancing up and down the alley to check if anyone was watching.

"In addition to the bakery out front, the repair work also adds to the cover," the woman added as she raised a fist to knock on the door. "It gives us an excuse for people to be going and coming, in case any of the Boko Haram spies take note."

Without another word she knocked three times on the door, waited a few seconds, then knocked four more times. A moment later, a soft single knock came from the other side. Galab replied with one last thump of her fist, and the door swung open.

A man wearing black slacks and a blue tunic unbuttoned at the neck ushered Galab quickly inside. Bolan took a final look both ways down the alley, satisfying himself that there were no prying eyes taking in this final leg of their trip, then followed.

The man in the tunic closed the door behind them.

Bolan found himself in a dimly lit hallway. Copper pipes and white PVC plumbing, heat and air-conditioning lines were exposed overhead. A steady hum came from the ceiling, punctuated occasionally by a strange buzzing sound. Bolan wondered briefly at its source, then turned his attention to the man who had opened the door.

Galab and he embraced quickly, then stepped back from each other. "Paul," the woman said, "this is Matt Cooper, the American I told you would be coming."

Paul extended his hand and Bolan shook it. "We can use all the help we can get." He had evidently seen the Executioner's glance toward the ceiling. "Many of our converts are skilled artisans," he said. "They are in the process of making the currently unused areas of this building more livable for those who must hide here."

Bolan nodded. Faintly, from the roof, he could hear the same hiss and snap of a nail gun that he'd heard at the construction site back at the Isaac Center. Men on the roof would indeed add to the secrecy of this Christian hideout. It made it even less conspicuous than if the building was left unoccupied. The construction was a perfect example of the old ruse of "hiding in plain sight."

The soldier glanced at Paul, somehow knowing that having workers on the roof had been this man's idea. It was strange, sometimes, how warriors could recognize each other—even in the most peaceful settings. As they'd traveled the alleys, Galab had told Bolan a little about Paul. The man's main mission in life since his conversion to Christianity might be leading other souls to Christ, but his background as a member of Boko Haram—in short, his experience as a working terrorist—made him an excellent strategist.

As Bolan finished that line of thought, he heard the sound of the air-conditioning kick on from the pipes overhead. The sporadic buzz continued, but seemed now to be coming from some more distant source.

He looked upward again just as Paul said, "We have many elderly people here. They dehydrate and collapse easily. So we must keep things at least moderately comfortable for them."

Bolan nodded. Men and women lost resistance to both heat and cold as they grew older, and heatstroke or exhaustion, even hypothermia, could kill them in temperatures that younger, more able-bodied individuals barely noticed.

Paul raised the sleeve of his tunic to his mouth and coughed. Then, lowering his eyes from the ceiling to Galab's, he said, "Did anyone see you?"

"*Everyone* saw us," she replied, pointing at the gaudy green bags. "At least on the streets. But I do not believe anyone noticed our entry here." She looked back over her shoulder at the door, then turned her eyes to Bolan for a second opinion.

He shook his head. "I don't think so. I didn't see anyone when we came in, but that doesn't mean someone didn't see us. There are plenty of places up and down that alley to hide." He turned to Paul. "Bottom line, it's impossible to be sure."

For the first time since Bolan and Galab had entered the building, Paul smiled. "That is the state in which we Christians constantly find ourselves. Not just here but all over Nigeria. We are *never* sure whether we are safe. Not since Boko Haram started its campaign of death and destruction."

He raised his forearm to his mouth, turned his head and began coughing into his sleeve once again. But this time, instead of a single cough, a long series of choking sounds came out. When the fit finally ended, he turned back to Bolan and said, "At the very least, our Boko Haram enemies will soon know something unusual is happening in this area of town. But if we are lucky, they will not know exactly what or where."

Fixing his attention on the Executioner, he spoke

to the woman. "Tell me more about this man, Layla," he said, changing the topic.

"As I said, his name is Matt Cooper." She smiled up at the soldier. "At least that is the name I have been given. I do not know any more about him except that he is from the United States, he is supposed to be the best agent America has to offer and he has been sent here to help us."

The man in the blue tunic nodded. "And you trust him?"

"Implicitly," Galab said. "He has already proved himself in combat against the Bokos. They attacked us as we were leaving the center." She gazed up at Bolan again, her brown eyes filled with feeling. "Without him I would be dead right now."

Paul stared intensely at the Executioner. "Then I will trust him, too," he said. "I will call him Matt Cooper, whether that is his real name or not."

Bolan smiled. "And I'll call you Paul. Although something tells me that wasn't the name you were born with, either."

Paul's head moved back and forth as he returned the smile, but his expression was that of a weary man, one with too much on his mind to waste time or energy on formalities. "No," he said. "I was born with the name Enitan. It means 'person of the story' in the Yoruba tongue. Paul is the name I took after Christ visited me in a dream." He raised a fist to his mouth, coughed yet again, then said, "The dream was much like the experience the Apostle Paul had on the Damascus Road. Are you familiar with it?"

Bolan nodded, remembering the Catholic sermons of his youth. "His name was Saul up until then," he said. "Jesus appeared to him in a waking vision rather than a dream, however. In a sudden light so bright it temporarily blinded him. Jesus asked why he was persecuting His followers."

Paul nodded in turn, and for the first time since they had met let a real smile curl the corners of his mouth. "Exactly," he said. "Up until my dream I had been active in Boko Haram. I had persecuted Nigerian Christians and even brother Muslims, just as the original Paul had persecuted the early Christians for the Sanhedrin."

He stopped speaking and clenched his teeth for a moment. Pain spread across his face at the memory. "There is more to this story," he said. "Background. But I will have to tell you the rest when we have time." The hurt on his face seemed to disappear as quickly as it had come. "The bottom line is that Christ forgave my sins and changed my heart in that dream. And since then I have fought against the persecution meted out by Boko Haram and other Islamic terrorist groups."

Bolan stared down at the shorter man. "That must have delighted your Boko buddies," he said.

Paul let out a sudden laugh that sounded like gravel banging the insides of a washing machine.

"At first they did not know. So I continued to pretend to be a part of them, but leaked information to the Christians." He jerked his chin to one side, indicating that Nigerian Christians were hiding in the building, somewhere behind him. "But then my duplicity was discovered and a price was put on my head. Since that time, I have hidden here. I go out only at night, and even then I must wear a disguise." He lifted his left arm and tapped the sleeve of his tunic. "But I will help you in any way I can. And like the original Paul, I will give my life for Christ if it comes to that."

"It very well might," Bolan told him.

Paul nodded again. "Then let me take you to meet some of the other Christians hiding out here," he said. "A few are warriors and ready to assist us in our struggle. But most—as in any group of people—do not have the temperament for violence, even when it is warranted."

"Not everyone does," Bolan said.

Paul squinted slightly, looking as if he was taking the soldier's measure. "But you do," he said. "You have the capacity for violence. Wouldn't you say you were a violent man?"

"No," the Executioner replied. "I wouldn't. I'm just good at it when it's necessary."

"I understand." Paul looked down at the lime-green luggage Bolan and Galab had set on the floor. "Perhaps we can find some less eye-catching bags for you."

The Executioner let out a small chuckle. "I was going to ask you to do that," he said. "These bags have been an albatross around my neck ever since I left the airport."

Paul turned to lead them down the hall. Overhead was more exposed wiring, plastic pipe, and long strips of insulation stapled to the ceiling. The unexplained buzzing had increased in volume threefold.

Now, the soldier recognized the sound as some sort of electric saw. It was just more of whatever construction was happening on the roof. In addition to the saw, he could still hear the sounds of electric guns spitting out nails, and other hand tools such as hammers, wrenches and pliers twisting metal.

The ancient structure's outside belied its interior, and made a good hiding place for people who had been forced into going underground. The restoration wasn't finished, but the place seemed livable. They passed two rooms that contained stored furniture, canned goods and other "survival" items. An armed man was stationed in each room. In the first, a dark-skinned Nigerian had a Smith & Wesson revolver stuck in his belt. The white-skinned guy in the other storage room held an Uzi in both hands.

Paul and Galab led Bolan through a confusing labyrinth of twists and turns.

"Many of these hallways lead to dead ends," Paul told him. "We have designed it this way in order to confuse any attackers unfamiliar with the layout. Layla and I, and the people hiding here, know the place by heart." He paused a moment and coughed several times. It was a low, grumbling, garbling sound that bespoke some serious upper respiratory problem rather than just a sore throat or allergies. When he had finished, he said, "I doubt that you will be here long enough to need to know the floor plan."

"No, maybe not," Bolan replied. "But it never hurts to know things like that. I've been memorizing these corners and turns as we've walked."

The soldier found more of the same when he followed Paul and Layla around a bend to yet another doorway. The room it led to was larger, and appeared to have been chosen primarily as housing. Men and women sat scattered around the space. Bare mattresses covered much of the floor, and the furnishings consisted of a few mismatched chairs and tables, plus one well-worn sofa. Most people in the room sat on the mattresses or the tile floor. At the rear an open door exposed a white sink and toilet. Although he didn't count them, it looked to Bolan as if there were roughly a dozen individuals present, and the single bathroom appeared to service them all.

Paul stopped just outside the doorway and turned to Bolan. A moment passed during which the Christian convert took in a deep breath prior to speaking.

At the same time, the people in the room suddenly noticed their presence, and all eyes in the room swept to Bolan and Galab as conversation ceased.

In the quiet seconds that followed, the soldier heard faint crunching and swishing sounds somewhere in the distance. He could hardly be certain, but it sounded like someone digging. And it was not all that different from the sounds that issued from Paul's congested chest.

Bolan looked through the door at the uprooted Christians gathered. There were slightly more men than women, and a good number of them suffered from one kind of physical disability or another. Wheelchairs and crutches were prevalent, and one man wore an oxygen nose piece that was attached to a tank by clear plastic tubing.

"I don't see any children," Bolan said.

Paul's chest rumbled when he spoke. "We have shipped the children out of Nigeria to Christian families in neighboring countries," he said. "Much like the British sent children to the United States during World War II. These are people who have been attacked by the Bokos and escaped. Or a few who we know were targeted, but got away in time with their families. Boko Haram has a death list, and most of these people are on it."

Sweat had broken out on his forehead and he used his forearm to wipe it away. "I call this the congregation room. Like the congregation in a church," he went on. "We have several such hiding places around Ibadan, and all are overcrowded like this one." He stopped to draw in another raspy breath. "And we never know from one second to the next when one may have been compromised. We anxiously await attacks that are sure to come sooner or later."

Bolan looked at the faces around the room that had fixed on him. They were dirty and weary and scared. His mind drifted to the happy, playing children he had seen back at the Isaac Center. They had been too young to understand what had happened to their families, but these people were adults, and they understood the danger they were in. Their expressions showed the strain of being forced into a constant survival state of mind. When he looked into their faces, however, Bolan got at least a thin smile from each and every one of them.

They were human, so they were worried. And they were scared. But in spite of all that there was a positive spirit that seemed to emanate from them.

Bolan set his bags on the floor and looked back up again. This time he took note of three men standing against the walls. One leaned back against the far wall of the room, an American-made M16A2 hanging from a sling looped over his shoulder. Two more men—one with a Belgian FAL and the other bearing an AK-47—did the same against the side walls. The man with the M16 was fiddling with the safety. The one holding the FAL was trying to figure out how to adjust the collapsible stock, and the Nigerian who bore the AK-47 was simply staring down at his weapon as if he'd just seen it for the first time.

The soldier remembered the other two men he had seen in the storage rooms they had passed, one carrying a revolver, the other an Uzi. With the eclectic combination of weapons, it was obvious that Paul's Christian resistance, as meager as it might be, was making use of any and all arms they were able to confiscate from Boko Haram, other terrorists or perhaps even the Nigerian army and police.

It was also obvious that most of the men didn't really know what they were doing.

Bolan turned his attention to the noncombatants crowded into the congregation room. Their meager possessions were scattered on the dirty tile around them, stored in everything from worn-out leather suitcases to gunny sacks and old animal feed bags.

Glancing at Paul, the soldier said, "You suppose these folks would like some new luggage?"

He smiled. "That's exactly what I was thinking," he declared. "And I doubt they'll even mind that atrocious color." He fell silent for a moment, scanning Bolan from the top of his head to his hiking boots. "And we need to do something about your clothes. Your profile hasn't exactly been kept as low as we'd have liked it to be since you arrived in country, and this cover as photojournalist has pretty much been blown.

"Layla," Paul said, "if you would be so kind as to wait for a few moments, I will get Mr. Cooper a change of clothes."

"Just call me Matt," Bolan told him. "That's good enough."

Galab had reached into a pocket of her skirt and produced a cell phone. "I am happy to wait," she replied. "As I have said, I am not a warrior. But perhaps I can speak to these people and lift at least a small amount of tension and anxiety from their shoulders. Calm them." She held up the cell phone and punched a button at the top to turn it on. "You are aware of my mother's health, Paul," she said. "I need to check on her. And I also need to find out what happened back at the Isaac Center after we escaped. The police would have arrived, but I want to find out if there was a second attack by the Bokos. That is their usual strategy—to send another group of gunmen, or set another bomb, in order to take out the first responders on the scene."

Paul started to turn down the hallway, but Bolan reached out and grabbed the sleeve of his tunic. "Wait half a minute," the Executioner said. "You told me, and Layla told me earlier as well, that I was here to team up with some Christian resistance fighters." He nodded over his shoulder at the room full of displaced Nigerians. "These all seem like great people," he said. "But except for the man with the wheel gun and the one with the Uzi in the other rooms, and these three here with their rifles, I don't see any weapons. And even the guys with the guns don't look like they're very experienced."

He glanced around the room again and noted several older men. "Do any of the other guys have any combat experience?" he asked.

Paul nodded. "Some of them might surprise you," he said. "A few were former warriors, and although their endurance and speed is not what it used to be, they are still capable of pulling a trigger."

Bolan didn't answer, but he knew the men Paul spoke of weren't going to be much help. Maybe they could "pull triggers," but as he scanned the wrinkled faces in the room, he didn't see any more triggers to pull. Besides that, there were far more aspects to combat than simply firing a gun. Speed, agility and a host of other things. A warrior had to get into position before he actually shot, and he had to have enough strength to hold his weapon steady after he got there.

Paul cleared his throat. "Listen for a moment, Matt," he said, then stopped speaking and held both hands out, palms down, to the people in the room. Again, silence reigned, and the Executioner heard the low, gritty noises of what sounded like shovels digging into a mixture of dirt and pebbles or chips of concrete.

"Do you hear that?" Paul asked.

Bolan nodded. "I heard it earlier, too."

"Then let us go and find some low-key clothing for you," he said. "Then I will take you to the source of this noise and all of your questions will be answered."

CHAPTER FOUR

The first room they'd passed upon entering the building—filled with broken furniture, canned food and other survival gear, also turned out to be the place Paul had chosen to store extra clothing and other supplies.

Bolan followed him to a steel clothes rack on wheels that looked as if it had come from a clothing store. A wide range of shirts, blue tunics, skirts, slacks, jeans and other garments and accessories hung from hangers permanently hooked to the top bar.

Paul pointed to a corner of the room just past the rack. "You can stow those green atrocities there for now," he said. "They'll be perfectly safe."

Bolan walked over and began sliding the carry straps off his shoulders as Paul started looking through the hangers, checking each garment as he came to it, then rejecting it and sweeping the hanger down the bar with a metallic swish. "Finding something appropriate," he said in a low voice, "and big enough to fit you is not an easy task." He glanced up at the Executioner.

Bolan watched him for a few seconds, then let his

eyes move down the rack to a long garment hanging at the very end—a robe like the one worn by the man he had seen earlier with the S&W. He frowned, raising his hand to grasp the front zipper of the photojournalist vest. He had chosen the vest for two reasons. First, it lent authenticity to what he had thought would be his cover. And second, its many pockets could be stuffed with extra ammunition magazines and other equipment he might need. But now that he'd been "burned" as a photojournalist, the vest that screamed that profession to the world had become a liability, just like the suitcases.

Stepping forward, the soldier pulled the robe off the rack. It was big and bulky, and when he shrugged it on it fell almost to his knees. Woven of heavy cotton, it displayed a pattern he suspected was associated with some African tribe or Arabic ethnic group.

Paul watched him try on the robe. "I see what you want to do—cover the vest," he said. "And I understand. I see only a small problem, and one that can be easily overcome."

Bolan turned his attention to the other man and waited for him to finish.

"Robes like that were originally the garments of a small but specific sect of the Yoruba tribe," he said.

Bolan guessed the rest of the problem. "And they're all black men."

"They were at first," Paul said. "But Nigeria is

like all countries, in Africa as well as most of the world." He paused to cough lightly, waited to see if more congestion would erupt in his chest, and when it didn't, went on. "So many people, both men and women, have begun wearing these robes that they have lost their significance."

"Then I'll blend in okay?" Bolan asked as he tied the belt loosely around his waist.

"Yes, I believe so," Paul said. "You are dark for a Caucasian. Probably from so much time in the sun. My guess is you can pass yourself off as a light-skinned Arab or a man of mixed race."

"So the bottom line is I'm still going to draw attention," he stated.

Paul nodded vigorously. "Yes. But not as much as you would in your original disguise. By now, that photojournalist look might as well include a sign that reads Attention All Bokos. Shoot on Sight."

Bolan nodded. "You can't always get everything you want," he said. "Right now, this seems like the best compromise."

Paul continued to stare at the robe for a second. Then the corners of his mouth turned up in a thin smile. "The good news is that I do not think most people, including the Bokos, will give you a second look. These robes are unusual but hardly unseen, and might even cause some temporary confusion on the part of our enemies. You should at least have a second or two during which you are able to open fire on them before they have time to react."

Bolan tied the cloth belt at his waist, making a mental note that the Desert Eagle would be all but impossible to get to without untying it again. But by reaching in at chest level he could access the Beretta in the shoulder holster beneath both the robe and vest. The draw would be slower than usual, but possible. That meant he needed a weapon he could get to quickly.

And he had just the thing.

Reaching inside the robe to the left breast pocket of his vest, the soldier pulled out the North American Arms .22 Magnum PUG mini-revolver. Encased in a small leather pocket holster that also carried five extra rounds, it fit perfectly in the small pocket on the robe's right side.

Paul had watched him and now voiced concern. "I am familiar with the little North American Arms guns," he said. "They are quite reliable. But the .22 Magnums are hardly the best man stoppers."

Bolan looked him in the eye. "Well, then, think of the gun as having two and a half .44 Magnum rounds," he said. "Or consider the very real fact that bullet placement is far more important than caliber when it comes to stopping power." He patted the tiny gun through the robe. "What it all boils down to is that I'd rather rely on a .22 Mag that I can get to quickly than my 9 mm or .44 that's out of reach."

Paul slowly nodded. "It makes sense," he finally said. "At least for a surprise attack. If you have enough warning, you can always draw one of the bigger pistols ahead of time."

"That's the way I see it," Bolan replied. "But what I really need now is a high-capacity long gun. I've got one broken down in one of my bags. But this robe is too short to conceal it."

"Come with me." The other man spun on his heel and walked out of the room. A few seconds later they were down the hall in the second storage room. Bolan had not seen the small armory of weapons when they'd passed the door earlier because they were piled in a corner out of sight from the doorway. But now Paul led him there.

The Executioner's eyes shot immediately to the weapon he needed. Lying on a canvas bag was a Kel-Tec PLR-16 pistol. Essentially an M16 without a stock, it fired the same 5.56 mm rounds and used the same 20-, 30- or 40-round magazines as its more common full-size "cousin."

Bolan picked it up and saw that it had been converted from semiautomatic fire to select-fire only, and could spit out a continuous stream of the popular military cartridges with the flip of the safety switch. The Kel-Tec was far larger than either his Beretta or Desert Eagle, but could still be hung over his shoulder on a sling and tucked under his robe without extending from the bottom.

It would create something of a bulge under his arm, but many of the people in Ibadan carried items in their robes. If he stayed on the move, it wasn't likely to draw much attention.

A dozen or so 5.56 mm magazines were stacked on the floor next to the canvas bag, and all were loaded to the brim. The soldier opened his robe and began stuffing his vest pockets with them. When he'd finished, he ducked into the sling, tucked the Kel-Tec under his right arm, then closed and belted the robe once more. Turning to Paul, he said, "Let's go to war."

"LAYLA," PAUL SAID when they returned to the room of hiding Christians, "it would be best if you stayed here while I show Mr. Cooper—"

"Matt," Bolan said.

"—while I show Matt the rest of our setup here," Paul finished. "You are not a fighter, but few people can match your faith and you can be invaluable reassuring the people that God is watching over them and everything will work out in the end."

Galab nodded. "The Lord has given us all different gifts," she said, smiling, "and I must admit that I don't really know one end of a gun from the other."

The Executioner smiled in turn. "Here's a hint," he said. "If someone points a gun at you and you can see a hole in that end, he's probably not your friend."

Galab chuckled, and once more Bolan was impressed with the positive attitude the persecuted

Christians seemed to be able to keep in the face of deadly danger.

"I will remember that," she said, as Paul and Bolan turned and left the room.

An odor of baking pastry grew stronger as the man in the blue tunic led the soldier toward the front of the building. Bolan had quickly emptied the suitcases he'd used to carry his extra weapons, ammunition and other equipment, and given them to the hiding Christians in exchange for some less conspicuous ones. The Nigerians had been grateful to "trade up" for better luggage, despite the gaudy color. After all, the lime-green bags would be out of sight while they were here behind the bakery. And if they were found and had to flee, it would mean that Boko Haram had identified them, with or without the neon bags.

In the meantime, both Bolan and Paul had cautioned any of them who found it necessary to leave this makeshift hideout, for whatever reason, not to take any of the green bags with them. The outrageous color was undoubtedly known by now, and anyone linked to it would also be immediately linked to the American warrior who had come disguised as a photojournalist to fight the terrorists.

The hallway toward the front of the building was only partly illuminated by the light drifting back from the bakery. Along with the pastry scents, faint sounds of music made it back to them.

Bolan could see several sheets of composite

wallboard leaning against the side of the hall. They looked as if they had been left there to be used in some remodeling project. But as Paul led him that way, Bolan began to see what appeared to be shadowy openings in the wall behind them. When they got there, Paul reached out and pulled the sheets back, just far enough for the Executioner to slip through and enter another hidden hallway.

The "camouflage" covering the opening was low-tech, but effective.

Paul followed him into the darkness, replaced the sheets of wallboard behind him to cover the hole, and switched on a flashlight. The sounds of digging were now louder than ever, and as the two men walked side by side, following the flashlight's beam, the noise level elevated.

Bolan listened as they walked. There was a definite difference in the sound a shovel made when it bit into gravel or other hard particles rather than plain dirt, and those were the sounds he was hearing now.

They turned a corner, then came to another stack of wallboard leaning against the wall. Once more Paul lifted the makeshift hideaway door and both men passed through. The soldier found himself inside another hidden room. But unlike the others, which contained Christian refugees, furniture, clothing and other items, this area's only contents were three old assault rifles leaning against a wall. In the middle of the space, the Executioner finally saw the source of all the digging noises he had been hearing off and on since entering the place.

A pit had been dug in the center of the room, and a trio of men was busy with shovels, deepening and widening it. Bolan looked at the piles of debris on both sides. At the very bottom were scraps of tile and concrete, the first layer that had been excavated. Then came what looked to be plain brown dirt. But on top of that—pulled from slightly deeper down— was earth mixed with a variety of objects like broken pieces of pottery, more ancient tile, scraps of brick and clay building blocks, and even remnants of dried sod with short stalks of straw sticking out of them.

The three men stopped digging for a moment and looked up. Then, seeing Paul, they nodded and went back to work.

"In all of our safe houses," Paul said without having to be asked, "we are digging escape tunnels. Just in case. Here, we have encountered signs of some earlier civilizations."

"Interesting. Any idea who they were?" Bolan asked.

He shook his head. "Nigeria—at least this area that we call Nigeria now—has been inhabited since the Stone Age," he said. "It has been part of several ancient African kingdoms. The Nok empire ruled from roughly 900 BC to 200 AD. Then came the Oyo and the Songhai empires, in the fifteenth and sixteenth centuries. I could go on, but I will give you a history lesson at a later time."

Bolan could see the dust from the digging float-
ing through the air, and it caused him to clear his
throat. But it made Paul suddenly begin to cough un-
controllably again. He held his sleeve to his mouth at
the elbow and spasmed so hard the Executioner was
afraid that his wind pipe might shoot out.

"Excuse me," Paul said when the jerking and near-
choking was over a minute or so later. "I have lung
problems that hamper me in my work for God." He
looked up at the Executioner and smiled. "Like my
namesake, the Apostle Paul, it is a thorn in my side.
No one seems to know for sure what the original
Paul's 'thorn' actually was, but mine is weak lungs."

The soldier nodded. "The rifles against the wall,"
he said. "These men are fighters I can use if necessary?"

"They are," Paul said, and although his coughing seemed to be over for the time being, his voice
sounded almost as gritty as the digging shovels.
"They were Muslims who have converted to Christianity." He pointed toward a large, broad-shouldered
man wearing what looked to be a dirty Nigerian police uniform blouse. Sergeant's stripes on the upper
arms were barely visible through the dust covering
them.

Paul followed the Bolan's gaze and said, "The
man with the stripes—his name is Jabari."

"A cop?" Bolan asked.

Paul turned to him. "Formerly," he said. "The
Boko Haram demons no longer fear the police or

even the military. When they learned about Jabari's and his family's conversion, they staged a home invasion. But Jabari, his wife, their teenage daughter and ten-year-old son had fled their house minutes before. They escaped the unspeakable atrocities that Boko Haram has subjected other women and children to, while making the man of the house watch."

Bolan glanced over at the police sergeant. "Where is his family now?"

"Apparently at another safe house," Paul replied. "It was closer to their home and easier for Jabari to get them there before he joined us in the ongoing battle."

Bolan didn't respond. There was nothing he or anyone else could say about such monstrous behavior.

"Even though Jesus commanded us to do so," Paul continued, "Jabari is having a hard time forgiving the men who did their best to torture and kill his family. He seeks vengeance."

The Executioner knew how that felt firsthand. The deaths of his own family, after all, were what had started him on his lifelong battle against crime, terror and evil in general. "Jesus believed in forgiveness," he told Paul. "But He also believed in justice."

Paul nodded. "I agree. Some Christians, however, get revenge and justice confused."

Bolan didn't respond. The man was right, and there was really nothing more that needed to be said on the subject.

"The other two men digging," Paul said, breaking the short silence that had fallen, "were in the Nigerian army. Both special forces. They converted together and then convinced their wives and children to do the same." He drew in a deep breath that rattled in his chest. "They were on a training exercise when the church they and their family had begun to attend was bombed. Again, all were killed. They, too, will be eager to stop digging and help you. Barkari and Shomari are their names."

The soldier nodded. These three men had good reason to fight the Boko Haram terrorists. But he would need to keep a close watch on them. Sometimes even seasoned warriors could get too close to the fight and let their emotions take over from common sense. One, two or all three might well be inwardly seeking a death that would reunite them with their loved ones in heaven. What complicated things further was the fact that this death wish might not even be conscious.

If that was the case, they would endanger not only themselves but everyone around them.

Paul began coughing again.

"Let's get you out of here," Bolan said, "before you choke to death."

He nodded and the two of them headed toward the hole behind the wallboard. Bolan took one last look at the men digging the tunnel. He knew where they were, and he would call on them when he needed them.

Paul switched his flashlight back on as they started down the dark hallway.

"You promised to tell me the whole story of what got you out of Boko Haram and into all this," Bolan said. "Now's a good time."

Paul chuckled under his breath, but again it sounded like pebbles bouncing off metal. Then his tone turned serious. "I had helped another Boko Haram terrorist—Dhul Agbede, a *terrible* man— wire a local Christian church with plastic explosives. We did it late, on a Saturday night. Dhul had set the timer to go off a few minutes after the Sunday morning worship service began the next day, when the church would be most full. I was asleep, but had set my alarm clock to ensure I would be awake to hear the explosion in the distance.

"Akilah, my wife, and my daughter, Sabah, were not home when I woke up, and I assumed they had gone to the market as they usually did on Sunday mornings. I heard the explosion, and then I waited, drinking tea and laughing to myself about what we had done. But the time when Akilah and Sabah should have returned came and went, and there was no sign of them."

A long silence ensued, during which Bolan could tell that Paul was psyching himself up to tell the rest of the story. Finally, the man spoke again. This time in a smaller, even quieter voice. "The police finally arrived at my door. They escorted me to the church, never suspecting that I had played a part in planting the bomb."

Bolan took a guess at the rest, hoping to spare Paul the painful experience of telling him more. "Your wife and daughter walked past the church on their way home from the market," he ventured. "They were killed by the bomb?"

Paul shook his head almost violently. "That was what it had to be, I thought when I saw what remained of them," he said. "They were in front of the church, on the sidewalk." His face glistened with tears. "Dhul and I had used more than enough Semtex plastic explosive to make sure all of the people in the church would die. And we didn't care if the shrapnel blew out into the area around it." He stopped speaking and began coughing once more.

This fit, the Executioner suspected, was brought on more by anguish than the dust in the air. Emotional and physical health were often tied closer together than most people realized.

When he had regained control, Paul spoke in a low, painful voice. "My wife was struck in the head by a piece of a church pew. Sabah, only ten years old, was nearly beheaded by a huge chunk of flying stained glass. They were still holding hands, on the ground, when I arrived with the police."

Bolan remained silent for a few moments, then said, "That's a sight no father or husband should ever have to see."

Paul turned to face the big American as they

reached the hall door that led back into the main part of the bakery building. "Have you ever lost anyone like that, Mr. Cooper?" he asked.

Bolan thought back again to his father, mother and sister—all victims of the Mafia so long ago. "I lost *everyone* like that, Paul," he said in his own quiet voice.

Paul wiped his face with his other sleeve and pushed the wallboard back so they could exit again. Behind him, the Executioner still heard the steady, rhythmic swishing and chinking sounds of the tunnel-in-progress.

Once back in the main hall, Paul spoke again. "I considered killing myself," he said. "And I cursed Allah and blamed him for the deaths. Why had they chosen that path to come home? It was not the one they usually took and not the most direct route." He shook his head vigorously as if trying to shake the memory out of his brain.

"Then one night, a few days later, I began to picture not my wife and daughter but all the *other* people who had died in the explosion. Christians. But people just like me and my family. All innocent of everything except converting from Islam to Christ. From there I began to think of the other bombings and home invasions and other butchery I had helped orchestrate for Boko Haram, and I thought of the Apostle Paul, who had persecuted the early Christians in much the same way.

"In an attempt to thoroughly know my enemies, I

had read the New Testament, and mocked it to myself and others. But now I was inexplicably drawn to it again, and read it once more. I had not slept for three nights in a row, but fell into a deep slumber with all that on my mind. That next morning I found this letter. It had been left on our living room table, but slipped off onto the floor, and in my grief I did not notice it until then."

He reached into the back pocket of his slacks and pulled out a crumpled sheet of paper. Bolan could see that it had been folded and refolded many times. "There is no need to open this," he said. "I have read it so many times I have the words memorized. But I will summarize them for you." A broad smile suddenly replaced the agony that had been on his face. "My wife and daughter had *not* taken a different route than usual coming home from the market. They had not even gone to the market. They had both accepted Christ as their personal savior the day before, after speaking to a Christian missionary who was not too frightened to speak the truth here in Nigeria. They were not on their way *past* the church, they were on their way *into* it." He stuffed the letter back into his pants and beamed even more brightly at the soldier. "At the end of the letter, Akilah urged me to make the same commitment to Christ."

Bolan had listened to the emotional outpouring without speaking. Now, he took a deep breath as the two men stepped back out into the main hallway. While the sweet smell of pastry had been strong there earlier, it was even stronger now. The main sounds Bolan heard from the bakery area now were of muffled voices and the occasional *ka-ching* of a cash register. But someone had turned on some stereo device and the mysterious, almost eerie notes and chords of traditional African music set in the minor key drifted their way.

Paul led the Executioner to what looked, from a distance, to be a dead end in the hall. Upon closer inspection, Bolan saw a curtain covering a doorway. They entered a kitchen-like room with giant ovens, sinks and counters. A long wooden table in the center held several rolling pins, its surface covered in a light coat of flour. In the corner, a stack of trays reached from the floor almost to the ceiling.

The smell of baking goods was almost overpowering.

A lone man had just opened an oven, and looked up as Paul and Bolan walked into the room. Paul held a finger to his lips. The man saw it, nodded and quietly closed the oven door again.

Another curtain separated the baking room from the counters where the goods were on display to the public. More careful now, Paul stopped just in front of this curtain. Slowly, he reached up, pulled it a quarter of an inch to the side and pressed his face to the tiny opening. and motioned Bolan forward.

Paul continued to hold the curtain open as the soldier peered through the narrow gap. He could see the front counters, complete with workers in white shirts, pants and aprons, and customers wearing a variety of traditional clothing, Western blue jeans and T-shirts, and military surplus. The front of the building was all glass, and through it Bolan could see men and women passing by on the sidewalk, taking no notice of the bakery and completely unaware of what purpose the building really served.

But what caught the Executioner's eye was across the street. Through the glass, he could see a number of men gathering.

Bolan turned away from the curtain. He also understood now why the music was on so loud—it helped cover the sounds of digging that came from deeper in the building.

Paul motioned for the soldier to follow, and the two men crept back through the room with the ovens and down the hallway. The farther they moved from the bakery, the more the building took on an eerie silence. They passed the room housing the Christian converts, where Layla Galab was speaking with several of the women, then walked past the two storage rooms. Bolan's plan—now that he had rid himself of the telltale lime-green luggage and disguised himself in the robe—was to exit into the alley and recon the area outside the building.

He didn't know exactly what it was, but some instinct honed from years of battle, or perhaps some unconscious knowledge that his brain had picked up on, had made him uneasy. He saw no signs that the hideout had been compromised, but uneasiness had crept over him ever since they'd peered through the curtain.

Then, suddenly, the reason behind his caution hit him between the eyes like a brick. It was nothing he had seen inside the building. It was what he had seen across the street.

The men opposite the bakery had been in a huddle formation, not unlike an American football team deciding which play to run next. They were keeping an eye on the bakery. Not staring exactly; in fact, it was more as if they were purposely trying to avoid looking that way. But occasionally, their eyes shot to the glass storefront as if compelled to do so.

The soldier sprinted back down the hall to the curtain and parted it again.

Just in time to see the men across the street tying red sashes around their arms and waists.

SAM WALKED CASUALLY down the street toward the ruins of the chapel on the edge of the university campus. In the distance, he saw the men in yellow coveralls and white hard hats sifting through the wreckage. A dozen ambulances were parked up and down the block, their red and blue lights twirling in circular beams that intersected with each other and made Sam slightly nauseous.

The al Qaeda–Boko Haram liaison man closed his eyes every few steps, fighting off the dizziness swirling through his brain. He forced himself to remember that some men were good in business. Others were gifted writers or sculptors or painters. Yet others possessed the gift of healing as doctors. Or, in their positions as attorneys, the ability to successfully defend even the most rampant and destructive criminals. But even these "best of the best" within their chosen professions had Achilles' heels. Every man had some weakness that he had to overcome in order to successfully call on his talents.

Sam continued to walk on, his eyes closed against the swirling, whirling, twirling colored light. He let his eyelids flutter open every few steps but only enough to ensure he had not veered from his path or was about to stumble over any of the rubble that had been propelled out into the street. The second he felt the nausea in his abdomen or the imbalance in his brain begin to return, he shut his eyes tight once more. Then he moved on.

Sam was not a doctor or lawyer or businessman. If he was forced to squeeze himself into one of the categories he had contemplated earlier, he supposed the closest he could come was that of the artists. His talent, however, was not like that of a Michelangelo, who had chipped away at a block of marble until the statue of David had been "born." Nor did he move his brushes from palette to canvas like Rembrandt or Manet or Monet, creating either classic or impressionistic paintings that could cause patrons to stare contemplatively for hours. He did not write poetry like Omar Khayyam, nor did he spin tales. But Sam had a gift, nonetheless. A gift only a handful of men around the world possessed. He could find a way to locate anyone, anywhere, anytime.

And kill them. With no emotion. And certainly no regret.

Sam's eyelids fluttered open for a moment, then closed again. But during the half second he could see, he noted that in addition to the ambulances, police cars were parked throughout the area, and they, too, were sending flashing emergency lights out to join what looked almost like an American Fourth of July fireworks display. Sam had attended such a show in the District of Columbia when he'd studied at George Washington University years before. He had reclined on the grass with some friends in the National Mall area, watching the bright and bursting and near-earsplitting display that was being launched from the region of the Reflecting Pool. Suddenly, he had become violently ill, falling to his hands and knees and regurgitating until his stomach could produce nothing more than dry heaves.

Sam had already been made aware of his gift for tracking and killing people, but it had not been until then that he had recognized his own limitations. Yes, even the greatest of men, with the most brilliant gifts, had at least one weakness. And Sam's was certain types of lighting. He didn't know exactly how it all worked, nor was it important that he knew. What it all boiled down to was that these lights did something to his brain. They threw it out of balance. They didn't affect his thinking, but they made him want to throw up if he looked at them for more than a few seconds.

So he had learned to close his eyes every so often when he encountered such lights. That didn't completely eliminate the problem, but it did allow him to remain functional.

As he approached the Nigerian cops, emergency technicians and hard-hatted cleanup crew, Sam took a quick final inventory of both his appearance and the mental attitude he needed in order to effectively portray the part he intended to play. He still wore the suit and tie he'd had on when he'd met with Fazel Hayat, but he had added a camera case that hung by a strap around his neck, and he gripped a hand-tooled leather briefcase.

The camera and briefcase added two final touches to the illusion he was creating. First, the briefcase gave him the appearance of a man carrying documents of some kind. This, in the eyes of some people, would vault him high on the importance scale. In reality, the briefcase was stuffed with a gray suit identical to the one he wore.

But the camera and briefcase were also props that helped Sam get into character. They made him *feel* like what he wanted these first responders to believe he was.

Sam closed his eyes as he walked between two police cars, but had to open them briefly as he stepped up onto the curb. Here, just beyond the flashing lights of the vehicles lined up along the street in front of the demolished chapel, the lights were not as bad. Sam thought of the old expression the "eye of the hurricane." It was something like that, now that he was past the vehicles. He could still see the reflection of the rotating lights off pieces of broken glass and other shiny scraps in the rubble that had once been part of the chapel at Saints Peter and Paul. But the illumination seemed to lose its power to sicken him when he wasn't exposed to it directly.

A police officer saw Sam step up over the curb onto the scorched brown grass between the street and the chapel. The smell of smoke was still strong in the air, and to the side of the chapel Sam could see several firemen and an old fire truck. But despite their age, the truck, hose and other equipment seemed up to the job at hand, and as he watched, the firefighters extinguished the last few flames burning the grass.

The police officer—the gold bars on his shoulders revealed he was a lieutenant—reached out and pushed a hand against Sam's chest. "This is a restricted crime scene!" the man barked.

It was a demeaning action and the condescending words and tone of voice made Sam's anger rise instantly. His first instinct was to kill the man right there and then, but Sam had not gotten where he was within the world terrorism by giving in to his emotions. So he forced a smile instead. Then, slowly reaching up into the front breast pocket of his jacket, he pulled out a business card. The smile still on his face, Sam exaggerated his Yemeni accent as he quoted the information on the card. "I am an adjuster from Kasim Insurance. We are based in Yemen but insure businesses and individuals throughout the Middle East and Africa." He paused a moment. "*Surely* you have heard of us?"

The lieutenant's eyes grew harder. Then he said, "Of course I have heard of your company. And I can tell you are an insurance adjuster by the way you are dressed. Do I look like a fool to you?"

That made Sam smile even more widely. Because no one could have possibly heard of the Kasim Insurance Company—it didn't exist. "Of course you are not a fool," he said in his most polite tone of voice. "I can see by your rank that you are anything *but* that. So certainly you can see that I need to—"

The officer cut him off by raising the hand that wasn't still on Sam's chest. "Whatever it is you *think* you must do," he said, "it will wait. As I said, right now this is still a crime scene and my men are not through processing it."

"Do you know when I might be able to gain access?" Sam asked politely. But as patient as he might still appear to be, his rage at this pompous fool with the gold bars on his shoulders continued to rise.

"No, I do not," the officer said smugly. "But if you have not returned to the street within the next five seconds I can assure you that I will help you gain access to a jail cell."

When he remembered it later, Sam suspected it

was at that exact moment that he decided to kill the lieutenant.

"May I ask one more question please?" Sam inquired. He kept the smile on his face, but in his mind he saw his wavy-bladed kris entering the man's chest and snaking its way through his heart.

"Make it brief," the lieutenant replied. "As I'm sure even one such as you can see, I have important work to do here."

Then again, Sam thought later, his decision to kill the man might have come when he'd said the word *important*. "While you and your men investigate the scene, I could spend the time interviewing witnesses. That way I would not be in your way. Are you aware of any witnesses who survived?"

"No," the police officer replied. "Now, if you will—"

One of the cleanup crew happened to be walking by at just that moment, and interrupted the lieutenant. "Someone said they saw one of the bishops walk away from the scene," he said, taking off his hard hat long enough to run his shirtsleeve across his sweating forehead.

Sam turned to face him. "May I ask who told you this?"

"I do not remember," the man stated as he covered his head again. "Someone when we first arrived."

"Did they tell you anything else?" Sam asked.

The man looked up at the sky in thought. "No... wait...yes. He said that the bishop who walked away was covered in gray dust, so had probably been inside during the explosion. And that he was holding one arm with the other, as if he might be injured."

Sam's anger gave way to interest. "Do you know which direction he headed?"

"He went that way." The worker pointed a finger to his right.

"Is there anything else you can tell me?" Sam asked.

As the man shook his head, the lieutenant stepped in again. "There is something else I can tell you," he said. He raised his wrist and looked at his watch. "Your five seconds are up. If you are not gone by—"

Sam stepped in suddenly and whispered into the officer's ear. "I have something of the utmost importance to tell you, but we cannot allow it to be heard by this man or anyone else. It may be the key to this entire attack."

Sam stepped back and studied the lieutenant's expression. He could almost read the words *I want to be chief of police someday* written across his face. The man was debating with himself the likelihood of whatever Sam had to say being a stepping stone toward that goal.

Evidently, he decided it might be "Go ahead," he whispered.

Sam shook his head. "We must have total privacy," he said.

"Follow me." The lieutenant pivoted on the balls

of his feet and started toward the cars parked in the street. Then, looking back over his shoulder as he walked, he added, "But if it turns out that what you have to say is useless, you and your expensive suit will find yourself in jail within the hour."

Approaching the spinning lights again, Sam closed his eyes at every opportunity to keep the disturbing flashes from making him sick. Luckily, the lieutenant's car was one of the closest to the university grounds, so it was less than a minute before the cop was behind the wheel and Sam was taking the shotgun seat. The man from Yemen opened his eyes long enough to see several other cops, hard hats and a few emergency personnel walk by, but paid them no attention.

"Now, tell me what you have and be quick, or—"

The lieutenant never got to finish the sentence.

Sam's kris appeared so fast, the arrogant cop barely had a chance to turn toward him. His hands had been in his lap, but now they started to rise in defense against the twisting blade.

Sam felt the edge of one of the curves in the steel slide between the lieutenant's forearms and leave lines on both wrists. For a brief moment, the marks looked as if they'd simply been drawn on the cop's arms with a black ballpoint pen. Then the blood rushed out, turning his inner arms red.

Sam thrust the kris forward, let the point penetrate lieutenant's chest, then twisted the grip first one way, then another, until all the curves in the blade had glided through the man's flesh and the tip had penetrated his heart. Bright crimson shot from the wound as each twist enlarged it further. Sam felt the blood splash onto his face and chest. He held the knife tightly as the lieutenant jerked back and forth, then side to side.

After several seconds, the cop leaned back against the seat and stopped moving. His eyes gradually dimmed, until they stared off into space but saw nothing.

Sam was covered in the man's blood, from his face to his waist. Some blood had even dripped down his legs to his knees. He watched another man wearing a white hard hat walk by, thankfully ignoring him and the dead cop behind the wheel. But Sam knew he'd immediately draw the attention of anyone who happened to glance his way if he got out of the car.

So, reaching up with his left hand and grabbing the back of the lieutenant's neck, Sam pulled down, slamming his victim's face against the bottom of the steering wheel. He heard the neck snap on the way down.

That was good, Sam thought. More insurance that the man was dead.

And, after all, he thought ironically, he *was* in the insurance business.

Sam held the man's face against the steering wheel until the blood pumping out of his body had slowed to a dribble. Then he wedged the lieutenant's head into the space between the bottom and the center of the wheel, and leaned back in the shotgun seat to inspect his work.

The cop was almost bent in two. He could not be readily seen from the outside. He would be found eventually, and someone would remember the man in the gray suit with the briefcase as being the last one seen with him.

But by then Sam would be long gone.

He took a quick final glance through the windshield and then the side windows to make sure no one was paying attention. Then he dropped his briefcase into the rear seat and crawled after it. In less than a minute he had changed out of his bloody suit, shirt and tie and into the clean clothes in his briefcase. Using one of the pants legs that had escaped being drenched in blood, he cleaned his face and hands.

Crawling back to the front, he pulled down the visor on the shotgun side and found a mirror. By rotating the visor up and down, he was able to see himself from the top of his head to his calves. There was one small red spot left on his face, which he wiped off, again using a clean section of the otherwise soiled suit. Finally satisfied that his appearance in no way betrayed his actions, he reached into the briefcase and pulled out a freshly dry-cleaned tie. Still watching himself in the mirror, he wrapped it around his neck under the collar and tied it in his preferred half-Windsor knot.

This would have to do.

He got out of the police car, lugging his briefcase, which now carried the blood-soaked suit. Again, no one paid him much attention. It seemed that if he stayed in the street instead of getting up on the burned grass he was invisible.

So the man known only as Sam walked down the road, turned the corner and headed in the direction the hard hat had pointed. And he saw, almost immediately, exactly what he had hoped he would find.

The blacker spots on the dark asphalt were not easy to see, and would have probably been overlooked if Sam had not been intentionally seeking them. And they could have been motor oil or any other substance. But they weren't. Sam was fairly sure of that even before he squatted to look at them closer. He started to reach for the black gloves he carried as faithfully as he carried the kris and the derringer, then stopped. Being black like the asphalt, they would not tell him what he needed to know. So he pressed his index and middle fingers into the spots instead.

The spots had dried and his fingers came away clean. Sam glanced around. Again, no one was paying any attention to him. He stood back up for a moment in order to reach into his pants pocket, and when his hand came back out it held a small two-bladed, stag-handled penknife. Squatting again, he slid the nail of his left thumb into one of the slots and opened a short sheepsfoot blade. A moment later he was scraping flecks of the dried substance off the pavement.

Sam held his hand up, staring intently at the tiny specks. Then he nodded to himself. What he had was definitely not motor oil. It was dried blood.

Pulling a white handkerchief from the right-side pocket of his jacket, the al Qaeda–Boko Haram liaison rubbed the fingers and palm of his left hand vigorously with the cloth. He didn't mind having blood on his hands figuratively. But he hated when it was literal. Even when it had dried, as these spots had.

He would remember to wash his hands as soon as possible.

Sam shook his handkerchief out and started to slip it back into his jacket, then stopped. At least a few of the flecks of dried blood had to have stuck to the cloth, even after he'd shaken it. He didn't want them transferring to the inside of his pocket, so he dropped it on the ground as he rose to his feet.

He would have to remember to get another handkerchief at the first opportunity, too.

He looked ahead, in the most likely direction a man would walk from where he now stood. Sam saw no more spots immediately, but when he took a few steps, what he knew now was blood *did* appear again. It confirmed what he'd thought ever since watching the American bishop walk away from the chapel on the videotape. The man had been holding his arm. He *was* injured, but not in a life-threatening way.

Just enough to leave a trail of blood for a skilled tracker to follow.

Sam picked up his pace. He no longer needed to test each spot he came across. He was on the trail—the blood trail. And he didn't think it would take too long to find his prey.

CHAPTER FIVE

The soft yet steady music built around the Yoruba *Bata* drums drifted across the room from the CD player. Dhul Agbede thought that it contrasted nicely with the violence that had ended just a few seconds earlier.

Agbede rose from the bed and looked down at the woman. She was stretched across the mattress almost as tightly as the white sheets themselves, her wrists and ankles tied to the bedposts. Her red hair was damp with sweat and her eyes were shut.

But she was not asleep.

There was no way in the world she could have slept through the things he'd just done.

Agbede chuckled. They had been going after it, one way or another, for nearly three hours, and it had been fun. At least for *him*. He turned his eyes to the sheets again. There was far less blood than he would have guessed, considering what had gone on. Much less, at least, than there usually was when he did similar things to other women that Hayat provided as rewards for services rendered.

Agbede reached quickly to the table by the bed

and slid the gold-inlaid, nickel-plated machete from its leather-covered wooden scabbard. He stared at the intricate pattern he had worked into the weapon, and thought briefly of its identical twin that he had forged for Fazel. The Boko Haram leader had nearly had tears in his eyes when Agbede had presented it to him.

Fazel Hayat was a sentimental fool, but that was fine with Agbede. It just made the man that more easy to manipulate.

He used the machete's razor-edged blade to slice through the ropes that bound the woman to the bed and said, "Open your eyes." As soon as her eyelids flickered, he stood up, returned the glistening machete to its scabbard, then bent and retrieved his OD green fatigue pants from where he'd thrown them on the floor. He stepped into the legs and pulling them up to his waist. A three-quarter–length robe featuring various patterns and designs went around his shoulders, and he donned a dog-shaped cap. He started to tie a belt around the robe, then stopped, remembering the items he still had to hide beneath the traditional garment.

But for now, the Boko Haram killer turned to look at himself in the mirror. He would easily pass for an average man of Yoruba heritage walking down the street. He turned back to the bed.

The redheaded woman's eyes were wide and wild. She had learned the hard way that resisting his orders—or even being too slow to carry them out—

brought on indescribable pain. As he buttoned the fly of the fatigue pants, Agbede stared down into her face. Her bright green eyes contrasted distinctly with her ginger-colored hair. The emerald orbs stared at him, terrified.

"Get dressed and return to Hayat," Agbede said. He started to call the woman by name, then realized he had forgotten it—if he had ever known it in the first place. But as he tied the cloth belt around his waist he let his eyes travel down her nude form, from the red hair atop her head to her painted toenails. He might not remember her name, but he never forgot even one square inch of a woman's body.

Slowly, the redhead rose from the bed. It took her several seconds to straighten to full height and that slowness annoyed Agbede. He had done far more to other women and had them recover far faster. This woman was acting. It was a passive-aggressive attempt to make him feel sorry for her and what he had done, in the hope that he would not do it again.

Agbede found himself growing angry, but smiling at the same time. He grabbed his goatee in his right fist and pulled on it, lifting it up and out into the sweeping curl that had become his trademark. As he shaped the thin, stringy hairs of his mustache, he watched the woman limp slowly toward the clothing he had ripped from her body three hours earlier. When she reached the pile, she looked down. "I do not think I can wear any of this," she said in a small voice. "It is torn beyond use."

The nude redhead turned to face him now. Both her palms were pressed against her lower abdomen as if she might be trying to hold her organs in place beneath the skin. "Even if I can find some clothing," she said, "I do not think I can walk that far." Except for her words she made no sounds. But tears flowed freely down her cheeks. Whether they came from physical pain or the humiliation he had inflicted upon her, Agbede didn't know. He suspected it was a combination of both.

The Boko Haram number-two man walked swiftly to his closet, opened the door and pulled out a short robe. The most basic of Yoruba clothing, this one was a rich red color. Throwing it across the room, he watched it hit the woman in the face. "Wear this," he said simply. "And be gone."

The redhead began slipping into the garment, each movement seeming to cause new agony to shoot through her body. "Can you give me a ride back?" she asked. "I am in such…pain. I still do not think I can walk."

"I think you can," Agbede said. "But if you cannot, you will no longer be of any use to me or Fazel. If that is the case, I will turn you over to my men. There are roughly two dozen here at the moment. They have been without women for some time, and I am sure they can think of many interesting activities in which to include you."

Her green eyes widened in even more horror than before. "I will be able to walk," she stated.

"Somehow, I thought that would be the case. Leave me now."

The woman turned and fled.

Agbede lifted his brown combat boots from the floor and took a seat on the bed, careful to avoid the blood that was beginning to dry into rusty-looking spots. The boots were already laced and tied, and he made use of the zippers on the side, pulling them down to get his feet inside, then zipping them back up with a strangely satisfying snap.

He rose from the bed and walked to a plain wooden chair against the wall. He had looped his gun belt over the backrest and now buckled it around his waist beneath the robe, adjusting the leather flap holster that hid the Russian Makarov pistol and the carrier that held two extra magazines. His machete came next, and he slid it down through the belt until the steel retaining stud, extending from the scabbard, caught on the top of the leather.

Again he thought of the identical machete he had made for Fazel. It, too, was nickel-plated, inlaid with gold and bore grips made of ivory. Both men's names were inlaid in gold on the side, near the hilt. The elegant blades served somewhat as a sign of rank with Boko Haram. Agbede had crafted the machetes carried and used by the other men, as well. But they were of simple carbon steel and covered in a dull black rust-resistant coating.

Either way, Agbede knew, simple or elaborate, his hand-forged machetes had taken the lives of a multitude of Boko Haram's enemies over the years. And of that, he was proud.

Again, he started to tie the belt around his waist, then stopped. Leaving the robe open, he had access to the weapons beneath it. And it hid them adequately from view. The situation with Boko Haram in Nigeria these days was somewhat in flux. They had grown powerful enough that few if any police officers were going to stop a man who *might* be armed and looked as if he *might* be a Boko. But the organization's strength had not yet grown to the point where the open wearing of firearms and other weapons could be tolerated.

In other words, Agbede thought, one such as himself still had to at least give the appearance of trying to hide his guns and blades. As far as the police and military went, it was not wise to rub their noses in the fact that the balance of power was quickly changing in favor of the terrorists.

He snatched his cell phone off the table next to the bed, hit the speed dial with his thumb, then waited for the call to connect. When he heard the voice on the other end answer, he said simply, "I will need men."

"I will have them ready," Hayat replied.

"Make sure they are equipped," Agbede said. "They will need blades as well as bullets."

"They will be prepared."

Without further words, Dhul Agbede walked out of the room and into the night.

AGBEDE HATED LAST-MINUTE changes to his plans. He detested getting psychologically prepared to go do something related to Boko Haram, reveling in the excitement it caused in his lower belly and groin, then having to postpone it all in order to complete some other task that Fazel Hayat suddenly decided was more pressing. It didn't really throw him off his stride, so to speak, or affect the amount of creative carnage of which he was capable. But it was certainly irritating.

Agbede drove the unmarked minivan down the narrow street that led to one of Ibadan's low-rent areas of town. What they had planned was no longer truly a *home* invasion. But it was an invasion just the same, and he was prepared to try to satisfy his thirst for blood by making the family members of the cop who had killed his fellow Bokos scream until they begged for death. He had planned the attack carefully in his mind, visualizing over and over what would happen. He had primed himself to carry out the assault of the police officer's family—particularly the wife and teenage daughter—in vivid color. He had pictured each and every step of what he would do to the man's family before killing the cop himself. If he was there, of course. Boko Haram's well-placed informant had said that the police officer was off helping hide more Christians.

Agbede twisted the steering wheel, curving the minivan around a corner onto a pitted asphalt street.

In his side mirror he saw the other two unmarked vans following.

All three vehicles were packed with Boko Haram warriors, and every last one was armed to the teeth and ready to rape, mutilate and maim before finally killing their victims.

Agbede's mind returned to the police officer's wife and daughter and the special activities he had planned for them. They would suffer complete humiliation in addition to pain. So he was slightly irritated when the cell phone in the BDU pants pocket beneath his robe suddenly buzzed. As the paved street turned to packed dirt, he fished out the instrument.

"Yes?" he said as he held the phone to his ear.

"Where are you now?" Hayat demanded to know.

"Perhaps a half a kilometer from the strike site," Agbede replied, knowing what was about to come. Some change in the plans. If he had actually believed that Allah even existed, he would have prayed that he was wrong. But Dhul Agbede held no religious beliefs of any kind. Life was pretty simple, as he saw it. You were born, you grew up and you took what you wanted from other people who were weaker than you, or who you could deceive. It didn't matter if you hurt them, or even killed them, because once you were dead, you were dead and that was it. Nobody really mattered. So if you took pleasure in the pain of others, that was just fine. It would all be over before long, anyway, and everyone's body would turn into worm food.

He gripped the phone in his hand a little tighter. He had taken the Islamic freedom fighter job as Hayat's second-in-command only because it offered him both money and an outlet for the peculiar sexual acts that he so enjoyed. He didn't waste his time thinking beyond that.

"What is it that you and Allah need, Fazel?" he said, trying to keep both the sarcasm and sudden anger out of his voice.

A moment of silence ensued. Then Hayat said, "You must be careful with what words you speak and the tone of voice in which you speak them. One who did not know you as well as I do might suspect you are being sacrilegious." Without waiting for a response, he went on. "You must save the police officer's family for later. I have just received a tip as to where the traitorous man who now goes by the name of Paul has hidden some of his infidels. And he is there himself at the moment. Possibly with this mysterious American we heard about from our informant."

Agbede rolled his eyes as he continued to drive down the street. Anything that had to do with "Paul" always took immediate precedence in Hayat's mind. The Boko Haram leader had taken the man's defection from Islam to Christianity personally. Agbede knew Hayat would not rest until Paul was dead and screaming in the flames of this ridiculous "Hades" he so believed was a literal place where non-Muslims spent eternity in anguish.

No, a simple bullet to Paul's head while the man was still here on earth was not enough to satisfy Hayat. The leader had grand and torturous plans for the man whose real name was Enitan. Fazel's plans for him were so horrendous that they rivaled anything Agbede could come up with. But he was more practiced in the art of physical and psychological torture, and knew that what Hayat had in mind was so elaborate that it was not likely to ever come true. At least not fully.

Agbede clenched his teeth and blew air between his lips as his foot moved from the accelerator to the brake. Fazel wanted to take Paul alive and crucify him on a hill just outside Ibadan that vaguely resembled Golgotha, the mountain in Israel where Jesus had hung from the cross. It was a ridiculous plan for several reasons, not the least of which being the fact that Fazel Hayat's "blessed Koran" taught that it was not even Jesus who had been crucified on that day two thousand–plus years ago.

The Boko Haram fighter brought the van to a halt at the side of the dirt street and shook his head in wonder. In order to make the most of the opportunity for personal gain he had been offered, he had studied the Islamic Koran, the Jewish Old Testament, the Christian New Testament and the historical writings of Josephus.

They made for interesting reading, but Agbede

took them no more seriously than he would a cheap novel.

He kept his foot on the brake but left the van in Drive. "Give me the new location," he said into the phone. As Hayat answered, Agbede thought about the other reasons that taking Paul alive for crucifixion would be all but impossible. A crucifixion took hours or even days, and although Boko Haram was gaining power almost daily, there was no way they could keep the military and police at bay for such a long-lasting public spectacle.

Boko Haram ruled the northern part of Nigeria, and it was rapidly getting stronger here in the south. But they were not yet powerful enough to pull off a stunt like that. None of which seemed to impact the thinking of a religious dreamer like Fazel. Such men—men who headed up what Israel, America and other Western nations called terrorist organizations—were rarely pragmatists. Which was exactly why they often chose men like Agbede—more criminal than zealot—as their assistants.

Leaders like Fazel Hayat rarely realized it on a conscious level, but it was their criminal-minded number-two men who were actually the powers behind the thrones. It was men like Agbede who made the terrorist cells successful. And while Agbede's and Hayat's goals ran somewhat parallel, they also differed significantly.

Fazel Hayat was in Boko Haram for Allah.

Dhul Agbede was in it for Dhul Agbede.

He continued to listen to his leader as the van's engine idled. But his brain was busy separating the "practical wheat" from the "idealistic chaff." As far as he was concerned, if Paul didn't fall to a bullet in battle, Agbede could still take the traitor to some remote location and illicit screams for days before the man died. Photographs and video footage of the torture, distributed throughout Africa and the Arab world, would produce the same effect on people as seeing Paul hanging from a cross. It would make them realize that resisting Boko Haram meant agony and then death.

When Hayat had finished pontificating, Agbede suppressed a sigh of relief. "Eniton—Paul— whatever you want to call him, I will recognize," he said into the cell phone. "But this big American…" His voice rose slightly as it trailed off, turning the statement into a question.

"The American can be identified by his luggage," Hayat said. "According to my source, he is carrying what we must assume to be weaponry inside bright green suitcases and other matching travel bags."

Agbede frowned. "He will have rid himself of such telltale luggage by now," he said.

There was a pause on the other end of the line. "And how do you know that?" Fazel asked.

"Because it is what I, or any experienced warrior, would do. Such luggage was meant to get him into the country appearing to be a tourist."

"You may be right."

"I *am* right." Agbede took time to draw in a deep breath. "Okay," he finally said, "we will attack the bakery first. If this mysterious American is there, we must take advantage of it."

"And the traitor who now calls himself Paul," Hayat reminded him. "You must do your best to take him alive."

"Yes," he said in the tone of voice an adult might use when responding to a child who kept reminding him he had been promised candy. "I will bring Paul to you while he is still breathing. If it is at all possible."

"Good," Hayat said. "I have men on their way to the mountain even as we speak. They are taking the lumber and other equipment necessary to construct a cross."

Agbede was running out of patience, but he knew that he served at the pleasure of Fazel Hayat, and he wanted to keep that position for his own reasons.

"All right," he said into the cell phone as he looked up into the rearview mirror at the two vans parked behind his. "We will proceed directly to the bakery. If the American has come to war against us, it is doubtful he and Paul will stay there long. And when they leave, we may lose track of them."

"Correct," Hayat said. "Contact me again when it is over. And *hurry*."

"Before we hang up," Agbede said, "have you had any luck locating the bishop who did not die in the bombing at the chapel?"

"I am about to put someone on his trail," Hayat said. Agbede thought of the Nigerian-born American bishop. Hayat wanted him almost as much as he wanted Paul, but for different reasons. The Boko Haram leader wanted Adewale for politics and propaganda. With Paul it was personal.

It didn't matter to Agbede which one they found first. Or if they came across this big American. Torturing men might not be as much fun as women, but it had a certain satisfaction.

Agbede tapped the button to end the call and turned his head. To the man riding shotgun, he said, "Hurry back and tell the other two drivers what you heard. Have them prepare for an assault on the bakery's rear rooms." He waved the man out of the vehicle with a sweep of his hand. "Go. *Now*."

Hayat's second-in-command twisted in his seat and watched through the van's rear window as the man he had just spoken to did as instructed. Killing Paul and the other fools who had converted to Christianity would be fun, and there were bound to be some attractive women hiding in the bakery's rear rooms. But for some reason, he couldn't tear his mind away from the police officer's wife.

She would have to wait. And *he* would have to wait. But she would still be there when he and the other men were finished at the bakery.

When the other man returned, Agbede let up on the brake and made a sharp U-turn. The other two vehicles followed suit, and soon the three minivans were cruising down the narrow streets of Ibadan as they had before, this time in the opposite direction.

Twenty minutes later they had arrived at the edge of the market area. From here they would have to walk. And that would make concealing their AK-47s and other assorted assault rifles more difficult. Some of the men had secreted their long guns in cases designed for musical instruments. A handful had hidden them in cardboard boxes. Still other Boko Haram warriors had no cases or boxes and were counting on their long robes to cover the rifles they had slung over their shoulders.

There were three major problems in regard to transporting their arms the final six blocks to the bakery. First, no matter how the men using their robes for concealment slung their weapons—barrel up or down—either the front sight or the buttstock still hung slightly below the hem. And if they lifted them high enough to avoid this, the other end became visible through the robe's opening at the throat.

The second problem was even more obvious. A group of eighteen men—some carrying instrument cases and others with one arm tucked tightly against their side in an obvious attempt to keep something from falling out from beneath their robes—drew attention.

But the third problem was perhaps the most telling of all: the men's expressions and bearing. They simply didn't look like eighteen members of the Ibadan

Philharmonic Orchestra on their way to a concert. They had the faces of men hardened by battle.

Their faces betrayed exactly what they were.

Killers.

And that drew more attention than anything else.

Dhul Agbede, however, was used to such attention and even took a certain pride in it as he led the way down the sidewalk toward the bakery. Yes, the Boko Haram men looked like trouble. And even though they were not yet powerful enough to hold the public crucifixion Hayat wanted, or even go about the city openly armed, they *were* strong enough, and feared enough, to make the average Nigerian look the other way when he or she saw them marching down the street on a mission of some sort.

As they approached a storefront advertising shoe repair and leather products, Agbede saw two uniformed police officers turn to look at him and the men behind him. Then, just as quickly, the two turned away and hurried into the shoe shop.

Yes, Agbede thought. Boko Haram was gaining power with every day that went by. And the two cops had no intention of trying to stop whatever endeavor they imagined his group was getting ready to carry out. They might notify their superiors from inside the shoe shop that something appeared to be going down, but they weren't about to take on a dozen and a half Boko Haram warriors by themselves. By the time reinforcements arrived, it would be too late. If reinforcements arrived at all.

A block later, Agbede held up a hand and the men stopped. He turned and let the Bokos behind him move up into a tight semicircle. Civilian men, women and children passed by, going both ways on the sidewalk. Agbede watched until he was satisfied that his men had blended in enough that even if someone noted the discrepancy between their looks and demeanor, and their instrument cases and the bulges in their robes, they, too, would hesitate to inform police or military authorities.

Again he reminded himself that if cops or soldiers showed up at all they would be too late. Boko Haram would have more than enough time to carry out the mass murder inside the targeted building.

Sounds of hammering and other construction noises were coming from the roof of the bakery, and Agbede looked up. For the most part, the men on the roof were working back from the edge, out of sight from the sidewalk below. But now and then a man carrying a hammer or some other tool passed in and out of view.

Agbede looked back down at the man who had ridden shotgun with him in the van. "Go inside the bakery and purchase two dozen American doughnuts," he said.

"*American* doughnuts?" the man asked, surprise creeping into his voice. "Would you not rather I bought—"

Agbede slapped him across the face and the smack of the blow could be heard up and down the street. The people passing turned toward the sound, but by that time Agbede's hand was hanging loosely at his side again. "Do not question me," he said in a gruff whisper. "Ask for American doughnuts and do it loudly enough for both employees behind the counter to hear you emphasize the word *American*. Then watch the reaction on each face closely."

Above his gray-streaked brown beard, the facial skin of the man who had been slapped had turned a peculiar shade of reddish gray. He nodded, his head dipping far lower than usual in a sign of both respect and submission. He turned to walk away, but Agbede grabbed him by the sleeve and pulled him back around. "Be sure to note the reaction of the workers and the customers," he said.

The man bowed again, even lower this time.

Agbede and the rest of the warriors waited. The man leading the Bokos watched through the glass front of the pastry shop. Men and women continued to come and go, purchasing a variety of baked goods from two workers in white aprons behind the counter. One of the men was old—Agbede guessed him to be in his seventies—while the other could have hardly been over twenty. Both wore long beards, one a mixture of white and gray, the other as black as the darkest moonless night.

Agbede noted that a doorway was set in the back wall of the bakery. The opening was covered by a black curtain. As he looked that way, the curtain appeared to move slightly. At least he thought it did. The movement was so slight he couldn't be sure.

The man he had sent into the shop had his back to the glass storefront, but Agbede could see the two workers' reaction to his order. The old man showed no emotion whatsoever as he moved slightly to the side, bent over and began filling a white cardboard box with glazed doughnuts. But the young man visibly stiffened—undoubtedly at the word *American*—then glanced quickly over his shoulder at the back wall.

There would be no need to question the Boko with the doughnuts when he came back out of the shop. The young, dark-haired worker's reaction had told the terrorist all he needed to know.

The intelligence information Boko Haram had received from their informant was now confirmed, and since Agbede didn't believe in a deity of any kind, he took a moment to mockingly whisper "Praise luck." Boko Haram's snitch was about as deeply planted in the Christian resistance as you could get without flipping the very leaders at the top.

So now Agbede knew that there were converted Muslims hidden somewhere behind the curtain. And those in hiding included Paul, the Boko Haram defector, and the big, mysterious American.

He was sure of it now. Someone had taken a peek from behind the dark fabric. He knew it, and the younger man in the white apron knew it, which in turn made the young man nervous enough to jump at the word *American*.

The older man might not be aware of the converts' presence. Or else he didn't care. Not that it mattered to Agbede. The men behind the counter were expendable, either way.

The Boko second-in-command waved for his men to move in closer. When he was satisfied that their bodies were blocking all view of his actions from the passersby, he reached inside his robe and pulled out a short red sash. It went around his left biceps and he tied it with a square knot.

Then he looked up and addressed his men. "Red is the color of the day," he said, as the others drew sashes from their pockets and from inside their robes. "It will not only allow you to identify each other once we are all inside, it symbolizes the blood we are about to spill in the name of Allah." Immediately, all heads bowed and a variety of epithets referring to Allah came out of the men's mouths.

Agbede marveled at how easy it was to manipulate them with the mere mention of Allah. He waited silently while the others quickly tied their own armbands. He knew that the building was being remodeled, inside and out, and once they entered, the red arm bands might well be the only way to differentiate friend from foe.

He drew a Ruger .22 Long Rifle target pistol from his waistband. Then, from the front right pocket of the BDU blouse he wore beneath the robe, he produced a custom-made, cylindrical sound suppressor. As he threaded the suppressor onto the Ruger's barrel, he thought of how he could have probably done so in full view of the public moving along the street and sidewalk. But he knew that it never paid to overestimate one's power. And there was never any sense in taking chances when a person didn't have to do so.

His men were close enough now that Agbede could whisper and be heard. "Rashad," he said, looking down at a short muscular man, "take five men and go to the rear entrance."

The man nodded.

Agbede turned to a taller man. "Zaki," he said, "you pick five men and go in the front." He handed him the sound-suppressed Ruger. "Use this on the two men serving and the customers. Then make sure all of the bodies are hidden behind the counter. Use the rest of your men to block the view from the outside while you hide them. I do not want people on the street to look through the glass and see what is happening. Once they are hidden, go through the curtain and immediately begin firing, even before you see anyone. According to our informant, there is a main hallway that winds back to the rear of the building and exits into the alley. I want total confusion and fear on the parts of the traitor and his fellow infidels inside."

Zaki nodded in understanding, took the .22, hid it under his robe and began picking his team.

"You, Lekan," Agbede said to a man whose rifle

barrel peeked out below his long striped robe. "And you, Olufemi. Go with Rashad, and two others that he picks, to the rear of this building. You two are to stay in the alley while the others enter from the rear. Rashad and whoever else he chooses will begin killing everyone they encounter until they meet up with Zaki somewhere along the hallway. Lekan and Olufemi will shoot any of the Christians who may get past Rashad and his men and try to escape through the rear."

Zaki's face creased into wrinkles. He glanced down at the sound-suppressed .22 Ruger, then back across the street to the bakery, where he would lead his men. "Are the pastry workers also Christians?" he asked.

"What does it matter?" Agbede snapped. "If they are Muslim, they will go directly to paradise, will they not? And if they are not, they will awaken in the Hades they so richly deserve." He stared at Zaki, who now looked down at his feet. "That is what you believe, is it not?"

The man nodded.

Agbede kept the scowl on his face, but laughed to himself inside. The man was a fool. In fact, all the men about to kill the Christians inside the bakery were fools. They really did believe all that nonsense.

"Give the rest of us exactly five minutes to get into position," Agbede said, looking from Rashad to Zaki. Then, addressing the remaining men, he said, "You will all come with me."

One of them stared back at him, his eyebrows raised in question. "If *they* go in the front," he said, indicating Zaki with a nod. "And *they* go in the back, where are we—"

He never got the sentence finished.

Agbede reached out and slapped him. "Do not question me!" he ordered. Then he turned to the others. "Do as you are told!"

Without another word, the Boko Haram second-in-command led the remaining men around the side of the building to the narrow walkway, where the workmen had left their ladder leading upward.

CHAPTER SIX

A quick jerk on the short end of the cloth belt holding his robe together allowed Mack Bolan to access the Kel-Tec. As the gunfire coming from the front of the building continued, he glanced to his side.

Paul had lifted his blue Yoruba tunic and pulled out what looked to be a Filipino-made version of the Colt M1911 Government Model .45. Copied from the tried-and-true Colt pattern, the Filipino version was relatively new, but had quickly gained popularity for both price and reliability. It was a no-frills, no bells or whistles .45 automatic pistol, and the only modification Bolan could see was the 10-round magazine that extended past the end of the grip.

Before the blue tunic fell back down, the soldier noted two other things he had not previously been aware of. Paul carried a double magazine caddy on his belt with two more 10-rounders, and the stacked leather grip of what appeared to be a huge Bowie knife of some type rode just behind his right hip in a leather sheath held in place by a stud.

"Let's go," the Executioner said, and both men took off running in the direction of the gunfire.

There was no need to quiet their footsteps now. The explosions from what sounded to Bolan like a mixture of AK-47 and AR-15/M16 fire more than covered the sounds of leather pounding against the tile floor of the hallways.

Bolan hooked his thumb around the Kel-Tec's grip and used it to switch off the safety. He held his index finger forward, pressed against the front of the trigger guard, as he ran. Keeping your finger outside the guard until it was time to shoot was fine on the firing range, where range masters had made the rule in order to more easily see that safety procedures were being observed. But in reality, pulling your finger back inside the guard to the trigger at the last second tended to make a shooter's rounds fly low and to the side.

Bolan had always operated on the theory that the best "safety" was simple. Don't pull the trigger until it was time to do so.

What had begun as a walk to the rear of the building had turned into a full-blown sprint back toward the bakery. Paul had fallen a step behind the Executioner but was keeping up better than most men could, and Bolan took a split second to glance over his shoulder and ascertain that the 10-round—eleven with one already chambered—.45 was aimed away from him, toward the wall.

That was good. Bolan didn't know yet just how skilled Paul was with a gun, but he didn't like the idea of having the back of his head blown off accidentally if the man proved to be a novice gunfighter.

The Executioner and his partner came to the two storage rooms, and Bolan pushed Paul inside the one where the firearms were stored. "Grab a rifle and do it quickly," he ordered. "The .45's good, but you're gonna need more."

Paul was coughing as he stopped at the pile of weapons in the corner, reached down and grabbed an AK-47. He stood back up.

Bolan had stopped in the doorway and was keeping an eye on the hall, but when he saw Paul start toward him again, he shook his head. "Extra mags," he shouted. "And let's move it."

Paul found three more 30-round Kalashnikov magazines and stuffed them in his waistband beneath the blue tunic. A moment later they were running down the hall again. The gunfire grew louder the closer the two men got to it. The tails of Bolan's robe were now trailing behind him. "It looks like you waited a little too long to start the escape tunnel," he called over his shoulder as they raced on.

In his peripheral vision, Bolan saw Paul nod without breaking stride. "We only acquired this hiding place a few days ago," he choked out. "There has not been enough time."

"Well," the soldier replied, "there's been enough time for word of this place to leak back to Boko Haram. You've got a traitor in your midst somewhere. Any idea who it might be?"

He glanced back again in time to see Paul shake his head. Bolan didn't speak further. It was taking all the other man's wind just to keep running. He didn't have it in him to answer questions at the moment. His breathing was already coming in high-pitched wheezes.

The soldier slowed their pace, hoping that would help Paul catch his wind. There were things Bolan needed to know; things he didn't want to run full speed into without any forewarning.

When they were down to a jog, he said, "Can I assume you put some temporary contingency escape plan in place for just this sort of occasion?"

Paul was still having a hard time speaking, but managed to choke out a reply. "Yes. Everyone with a weapon...will be...fighting. The women, children, and men too old for combat...are to get out any way they can."

"That's not much of a plan," Bolan said, twisting to look back over his shoulder again as he ran on. He found he had to speak louder in order for Paul to hear him as they neared the gunfire. "What do these people do after they're out of the building?"

"They are...assigned to deploy to...several other hideouts," Paul said, coughing. "Spread out...across the city. They will make their way there."

Bolan didn't bother to speak again. As he'd already said, it wasn't much of a plan. But if it was all they had, he would just have to find a way to work with it. The trick, as he saw things at the moment, would be getting the Christians out of the building past the invaders.

Because now he could hear gunfire coming from the front of the bakery and the rear alley doors, which meant they were trapped in the middle.

The Executioner found himself frowning as he ran on, wondering just how the terrorists had gotten where it sounded as if they were—not far away, somewhere between him and Paul and the large room where the huddled Christians hid. But Bolan couldn't help wondering how they had gotten so deeply into the building so quickly. He and Paul had passed that room only moments earlier, and there had been no signs or sounds of battle going on then. Even if the terrorists had come in through the front of the bakery, he felt certain they would have shot the Christians before moving on. He also felt sure that the three converts armed with rifles and guarding the others would have returned fire.

But none of that had happened. And why was gunfire also coming from the rear of the building? The two storage rooms were empty of people. There was no reason for the Bokos to fire off rounds in the back unless...

The soldier's mind whirled in thought for a moment, then settled into place. The Boko Haram terrorists firing at the rear of the building were doing so simply for effect. To create confusion. There could be no other logical reason. They *wanted* him, Paul and the others to believe they were trapped, with no means of escape.

Bolan and Paul ran on down the hallways, their weapons ready, but still not yet having fired a single round. They could hear plenty of explosions continuing and growing louder with each step they took.

They came to a corner in the twisting hallway, and the gunfire seemed to reach a crescendo just on the other side.

Years of combat experience had fine-tuned the Executioner's senses to the point where he rarely missed a single clue that was thrown his way. And now, as they neared the corner, he noticed that the dim light was gradually getting brighter. That could mean only one of two things.

The invading Boko Haram terrorists were either utilizing flashlights, or an opening that hadn't been there when Bolan and Paul came down that same hallway only minutes earlier, had been made. And the soldier wasn't betting on flashlights. If that had been the case, the illumination he saw now would be more erratic, glimmering around the corner in short bursts and inconsistent beams as the men holding them shone the lights around.

Five feet from the corner, Bolan hit the dusty tile floor on his side, like a baseball player doing his best to stretch a double into a triple. The difference between Bolan and a nimble-footed batter, however, was drastic. If the baseball player got tagged, he'd be out and would have to walk back to the dugout.

If the Executioner got tagged, he'd be out for good.

Suddenly, he was around the corner and his hiking boots were slamming into the opposite wall, bringing him to an abrupt halt in the center of the hall, with the Kel-Tec aimed forward. Four things happened at once.

Bolan pulled the trigger and sent a full-auto blast of 5.56 mm rounds down the corridor and into a half-dozen men in the process of turning their own weapons toward him.

He heard the familiar sound of an AK-47 going to work just behind him and to the side, as Paul joined in the fight.

The soldier looked up and saw a hole that had been cut in the ceiling, the result of the buzzing sounds an electric saw used by the workmen had made.

A man with a greasy, sparse, curly beard fired wildly toward him, then disappeared around another corner, in the direction of the bakery.

The short battle had begun abruptly, and it ended the same. But now there were dead Boko Haram bodies scattered along the hall, and giant splotches of blood dripped down the walls.

Bolan kept the Kel-Tec trained toward the corner where the bearded man had disappeared. He was fully aware, now that the roar of the gunshots had died down, that anyone hiding nearby might hear their movements. And there was little chance that they'd miss Paul's wheezing and coughing. The man's chest congestion had all but stopped when they'd slowed their pace, but the choking sounds had started up again right after the brief skirmish ended.

There was little the Executioner could do about Paul's lung condition. The noises he made were involuntary and couldn't be stopped. But there wasn't anything wrong with Paul's hearing, so Bolan kept his voice to a low whisper as he said, "Back to the question I asked you earlier. Do you have any idea who the traitor might be?"

Paul had moved forward and now knelt at his side. He shook his head. "No," he whispered back,

"If you have a leak, it's got to come from someone with access to the outside world," the soldier said. "One of the guards maybe. It can't be anyone tucked away in the congregation room." He stopped speaking for a minute, then said, "Unless there's a cell phone hidden on one of them that we don't know about."

"That's…possible," Paul said. "But I believe it's… unlikely. They have little privacy and one or more… of the others would have told me if someone was making calls."

Bolan thought of the tiny bathroom he had seen off the congregation room. It was the only place he could imagine where one of the people might have made calls. But that was unlikely. Every time he had looked into the large room there had been people waiting to use the facilities. Those outside the door would have been able to hear a voice on the other side.

The Executioner could tell that Paul didn't have a clue as to who it might be, if there actually even *was* a Boko Haram mole in their midst.

The soldier took all this information in, but stored it in the back of his mind for future discussion with the convert. If they *had* a future. Right now, it didn't matter how the terrorists had pinpointed this location. All that was important was that they *had*.

The sound of gunfire continued in a steady rhythm from the rear of the building. It was *too* steady. Again, Bolan suspected the rounds were being fired to create confusion rather than because any of the refugees were back there. He turned that way, the consistent *bang*, *bang*, *bang* continuing to sound dully in his ears.

Paul seemed to read his mind. "They are getting closer," he said, tipping his head toward the alley.

Bolan nodded. "I'd expect that," he said, as more rounds exploded from the front of the building. "It's these men we just shot. Here." He indicated the blood-covered corpses in the hallway with red sashes around their arms. "I didn't understand how they got here this fast or how they got past the congregation room without spotting the people huddled inside. Now that I've seen the hole in the roof, I do."

Paul nodded. His breathing was almost back to normal, and there seemed to be little rhyme or reason as to what sent him into coughing and wheezing spells. "Some of them took the electric saw the workmen had on the roof and used it to cut down into the hallway," he said.

"Exactly," Bolan agreed.

"Well," Paul said, "we still face Bokos both front and rear. What should we do?"

"There's only one thing we *can* do," Bolan told him. "I think we've taken care of this contingent of men—these guys who came down through the hole in the roof." His eyes flickered up to the ceiling. "Except for that one guy with the curled up beard, who decided a quick retreat was in order. And who knows where he's gone?" The soldier looked down at the bodies scattered along the floor, then turned to Paul again. "Follow me. But be ready. The men who came in through the bakery are bound to be making their way back toward us by now."

With the Kel-Tec stretched to the end of the sling, Bolan held the assault pistol in front of him as he moved to the next corner in the hallway. Stopping there, he looked back toward the crude hole that had been cut in the roof. Pointing up with the barrel of the pistol, he said, "My guess is there's a whole slew of dead workmen up top. The Bokos would have come up over the side, killed them, then used their saw to cut open the entrance. That explains the buzzing we heard earlier."

Bolan dropped his gaze back to the hallway leading to the front. "I'll head this way," he stated. His mind returned to the men he had seen eyeing the bakery from across the street, when he'd looked through the curtain earlier. "My guess is the strongest attack has come from the front." He was about to tell Paul to go back and spray the Bokos who came through the back door with his AK-47, when the two of them suddenly heard running footsteps to their rear.

Both men turned their weapons that way.

And Jabari, Barkari and Shomari—still covered in dust from their digging—rounded the corner and almost ran into Bolan and Paul, escaping death from friendly fire by only a few light pounds of pressure on the triggers of the Kel-Tec and AK-47.

Seeing Bolan and Paul, they stopped in their tracks.

The soldier motioned them forward so they could hear his whispered instructions. "Take these men with you," he ordered Paul. "Go back toward the rear entrance—carefully—and take out anyone coming in through the alley door."

Paul nodded, turned back toward the other men and led them out of sight around the corner where they'd just appeared. Bolan heard him whisper something, then the sound died.

Gunfire had continued from the front as Bolan had spoken with Paul and the others. But it was sparser now, as if the men involved had taken cover and were peering out only long enough to fire single rounds at their opponents, then ducking back again as fast as they could.

Bolan recalled the location of the congregation room and realized the Bokos he had just encountered had missed it because the hole in the ceiling had been dug farther back in the hallway. The terrorists who had entered through the bakery's door hadn't made it that deeply into the labyrinth yet. If either group of Bokos had come to the congregation room, the people there would have had nowhere to hide but the bathroom, which would be no safe haven even for the few who could fit inside.

Bolan's quick glance into the big room earlier had revealed the three men with rifles, left there by Paul as guards. The gunfight Bolan could still hear wasn't taking place inside the congregation room or the bakery up front. Those two rooms were only the launch sites for the bullets flying up and down the hallway. The Christian riflemen had moved forward and were now using the opening as concealment from which they could lean out, fire, then duck back again to avoid return fire.

The Bokos in the bakery were responsible for that return fire, doing much the same, but shooting between the doorway and the curtain.

Bolan had kept his Kel-Tec aimed forward ever since he'd slid around the corner on the tile. Now, back on his feet, he continued to let the 5.56 mm machine pistol lead the way stealthily down the hall. Although the corridor still twisted and turned, the illumination was becoming brighter as the soldier neared the front. The light from the hole in the roof helped, but now it was augmented by more light coming through the door to the bakery proper, and Bolan had to guess that the curtain had been pulled all the way open or torn down completely.

There was now plenty of light, at least, for the soldier to make out the shocked expressions of two Bokos with whom he came face-to-face as he rounded the last corner before the congregation room.

A 3-round burst of bullets, which all fell within an inch of the center of a bearded man's chest, sent him tumbling to the ground. It was a bullet group that would have made a benchrest competitor proud, and the terrorist was dead before he hit the floor. The M16 in his hands fell from his lifeless fingers and skidded across the tiles to smash into the wall.

Bolan turned the Kel-Tec pistol toward the other man.

Another trio of 5.56 mm NATO rounds drilled through this terrorist's throat, chin and finally an eye. He stood tall for a few seconds, dead on his feet, his face looking like some ghastly Halloween mask hanging on the wall of a costume shop. Then he, too, slumped to the ground and let the AK-47 in his hands fall next to him.

Bolan kept the pistol up and ready as he moved on. Somehow, these two men had been able to move past the congregation room without being shot by the guards. That bit of intel didn't bode well for either the armed *or* unarmed Christians in hiding. The first possibility that occurred to the soldier was that the three guards with the assault rifles might have already been killed. They had not appeared to be familiar with their rifles—or weapons in general, for that matter—and well-trained terrorists could have wiped them out fairly easily.

On the other hand, if all three were dead, the soldier would have expected more than these two terrorists to have advanced deeper into the building. So the more likely scenario was that the guard force had been diminished rather than completely wiped out. If only one or two of the three amateur warriors had fallen to the Boko Haram assault, it might have afforded these two the chance to slip past the doorway while their brethren pinned the surviving man or men down with a barrage of flying lead.

Ahead, beyond the congregation room, Bolan saw another pair of terrorists turn the corner. One wore both the pants and blouse of old, worn Vietnam leaf-camouflage BDUs, and it was anybody's guess as to how Boko Haram had gotten their hands on the ancient relics. The other man wore blue jeans and an OD green T-shirt. They both had rifles, and the holsters threaded onto their belts carried revolvers the soldier couldn't identify at that distance.

The two men weren't strolling casually along as they turned the corner, but they weren't on high alert, either. They seemed to freeze in surprise when they saw him with the Kel-Tec.

Bolan couldn't help but wonder if Paul might have been right. Perhaps the contrast in appearance between his relatively light skin and his tribal-specific robe had caused the momentary confusion.

The brief confusion that caused the two terrorists to hesitate was long enough to ensure their deaths.

The Executioner flipped the Kel-Tec's selector switch to full-auto and pulled the trigger. A steady stream of 5.56 mm hollowpoint rounds sputtered from the short-barreled rifle-caliber pistol and took off the upper half of the head of the man in camo. He fell backward.

Walking the still-firing assault pistol slightly to the side, the Executioner let the next half-dozen rounds catch the other man squarely in the face. He no longer *had* a face as he tumbled, dead on his feet, back and over the body of his friend.

Bolan moved on, passing the door to the congregation room, which was now closed. He took time to try the doorknob and found it locked. The bolt would fail with one good kick, but for the time being the Christians were as safe as they could be inside the building.

Down the hall, in the direction of the bakery, the soldier saw another figure suddenly appear, firing an AK-47. His face was familiar, and Bolan recognized him as one of the men he'd seen across the street when he'd looked through the curtain. Bullets splattered the wallboard to the soldier's side as brass flew out of the ejection port of the man's assault rifle. Above the barrel, the shooter grinned like some demon-possessed maniac.

Bolan raised the Kel-Tec. But at the exact moment he depressed the trigger, the man darted back to cover around the corner. The Kel-Tec's rounds struck the wall where the crazy eyes had been a split second earlier.

The wild-eyed face was replaced by another terrorist. The sides of the Kel-Tec's rear sight curled up like the horns of a ram as Bolan lined up the front post between them and let them come to rest on the center of the enemy's chest.

The man never even got a shot off.

Bolan pulled the trigger back and let another stream of 5.56 mm rounds jet down the hallway.

The missiles tore into the middle of the man's chest. His chin lowered as he looked down at the damage, and his face took on an expression of disbelief before he tumbled away from the wall and onto the floor.

The area just outside the congregation room went silent. But in the distance behind him, Bolan could hear the explosions of a protracted battle going on. That meant that the Bokos attacking from the rear had now engaged Paul, Jabari, Barkari and Shomari. Bolan found himself frowning. He had shot what he suspected were all the men who had entered the building through the impromptu skylight in the ceiling. He had also downed four more who appeared to have come in through the bakery before pushing past the curtain to the labyrinth of hallways in the back. But that surely had not been all the attackers. He had seen far more men eyeing the bakery from across the street when he and Paul had peered through the curtain.

Where were they now? Had they given up the fight and fled? Doubtful. Were they waiting in the bakery proper to ambush a counterattack by Paul and the other converts? Probably. And *him*? The Executioner had no doubt that by now word of the "American fighter" had spread throughout the ranks of Boko Haram.

And while they wouldn't know exactly who he was, they would know that his skills and abilities were far higher than those of the adversaries they were accustomed to facing.

So should he go back and help Paul and the other men at the rear of the building, or continue forward to face the men he knew had to be at the front? And what about the safety of the people in the congregation room? Especially Layla Galab? In his mind's eye, he could see her huddled in a corner, surrounded by other innocents like lambs awaiting slaughter.

The soldier knew such speculation was pointless. It was action—direct action—that he was called upon to take now. The Executioner knew he had to get Galab and the converts out of the building and headed toward the other safe houses Paul had mentioned. Even after he'd rid this building of attacking terrorists, it would have lost its usefulness. The average men or women on the street—no doubt cowering inside stores and shops and praying that no stray rounds found them—would now know that the bakery had been a front for a safe house.

The Executioner was used to making life-or-death decisions in the blink of an eye. And if there was one thing he'd learned over the years it was that you never knew with 100 percent certainty if you were heading in the right direction. You just had to weigh the odds, decide on your course of action, go with your instincts and move on.

He heard the sound of footsteps behind him and whirled, the Kel-Tec aimed at chest level. A moment later, however, Paul appeared, holding his AK-47. Beside him was Jabari, the former police officer, whose uniform was still covered in dust from the digging he'd been engaged in when Bolan and Paul first arrived.

The soldier looked from one to the other. "Barkari and Shomari?" he asked.

Paul looked down at the floor and shook his head. "They are with the Lord," he said.

DHUL AGBEDE CLIMBED the rungs of the ladder against the side of the bakery, leading his men to the rooftop. He knew his AK-47 barrel could be seen sticking out from under his robe, so he did his best to keep that side of his body away from the workmen as he neared the top. And as soon as he got off of the ladder onto the flat, tar-covered surface, he turned sideways to conceal the weapon from the men working on the building.

One by one, the six Boko Haram radicals followed Agbede's lead. He checked his watch. They had roughly two minutes before the others entered through the front and back of the building.

The workmen on the roof had stopped what they were doing and all turned to face the Boko Haram faction. Agbede glanced around. Their weapons were concealed, but when you put all the little things together—the musical instrument cases, the boxes, the gunnysacks, the bulging robes, the fact that they were unknown to the workers and seemed to have no reason to be on top of the roof—they created quite a disturbing sight.

But none of those things compared to the simple fact that their faces seemed to very calmly whisper to all who saw them, "We have seen a million deaths. And we are about to add yours to the list."

Agbede glanced at his watch once more. Less than a minute remained before his men would enter both the front and back of the building. It was time to get done the two things that needed to be done.

With the workmen still staring at the strange newcomers, Agbede walked to the rear of the roof, turned and paced back thirty-two steps. Then, returning to the ladder, he took four paces forward, then pivoted and returned to the spot where he'd started. All measurements were according to his informant.

If each of his steps had been even reasonably close to a meter, he and his men should be able to drop straight down into the room where the Christians were hiding, and mow them all down with automatic fire.

With one final glance at his watch, Agbede saw that only forty-five seconds remained before the attacks from the front and rear began. He knew that once all three factions of the Boko Haram fighters were inside the building, their gunfire would be muffled from the outside world. But up here, on the roof, it would carry for blocks and alert the police or military or both.

So he turned to his men and said softly, "Now. But no guns. We cannot afford the noise just yet."

Broad grins spread across the faces of several of those who Agbede knew preferred blades to bullets. A moment later, the distinctive sounds of his hand-forged black machetes—as well as the gold-inlaid chopping tool he himself carried—came sliding out of KYDEX plastic, leather, ballistic nylon and even wooden sheaths.

The workmen on the roof had all stopped what they were doing and were watching Agbede and his men closely. They knew something was up even before the machetes came out, and they recognized whatever it was as being sinister. These were hard-looking men climbing up the ladder to the roof. And the workers had nowhere to run.

Now, as the machete-wielding Bokos began walking toward them, one of the workmen cried out, "No!" He backed away from the approaching terrorists until the backs of his ankles hit the short retaining wall at the edge of the roof. "Please…"

"We have done nothing!" another man screamed in a high-pitched voice.

"We are simply workers!" cried yet another, holding his arms up, palms outstretched.

A second later, a machete flashed and his left hand dropped to the tar roof. A second after that, his right hand followed and blood began spewing from the stubs at the ends of his forearms like a pair of miniature fire hoses shooting red water.

The rest of the men seemed to fall at the same time, from massive gashes to their heads, necks and chests.

Agbede stepped forward slowly. He wanted to participate in the massacre, but didn't want to miss what the others were doing. Finally, only one of the workmen remained standing. He wore brown overalls and a plain green baseball cap. Agbede's shiny, nickel-plated machete stood out from the black blades in the hands of his men, and the gold inlay glistened under the sun as the weapon whisked horizontally through the air from the assault expert's right to his left. The head of the man in the coveralls toppled to the side, then hit the roof. Miraculously, the green baseball cap stayed on as it landed upright at Agbede's feet and stared up with a deadpan expression at the man who had severed it.

Agbede wasted no time grabbing the electric saw. Pulling the short cord to start it, he let it sputter in his hands, then lowered the buzzing blade to the spot he had paced off. He had followed the directions of Hayat's informant, and the hole should allow them to drop directly into the room where the Christians hid. Now, as the saw sliced back and forth, the combined odors of tar, clay and freshly cut wood filled the air. The Boko Haram second-in-command knew the noise would be heard inside, and he knew that the most peril his men would face would be the second it took to drop down through the hole. They would be much like paratroopers falling from the sky into the middle of a battlefield. Easy targets, and at least partially preoccupied with their landing and unable to operate their weapons at full capacity in their own defense.

Agbede believed the Americans called that being "sitting ducks."

On the other hand, he told himself as the saw buzzed on, the noise was likely to be written off as just another part of the restoration going on up on the roof. That thought made him laugh silently. Christians seemed to have the ability to make themselves believe anything they wanted to. After all, the fools believed a dead man had come back to life.

Agbede continued his assault on the roof. Now he could hear dull thumping sounds below—the muffled explosions of gunfire from the men he had sent in at the front and back, which meant that he was a few seconds behind schedule. But it also meant that the sounds the electric handsaw was now making would drop a long way down the list of the Christians' priorities. They'd be more worried about getting shot by the invading men. And, again according to Fazel's informant, there were only three armed men in what these fools called the "congregation room." And even they were not trained warriors.

Whichever of his Bokos dropped down into the room first could take out the trio of armed men with one steady burst of fire. Maybe Agbede would do it himself, although such simple killing had grown a bit boring over the years. He much preferred inflicting slow and lingering deaths, and leaving these shootings and even the majority of the machete work to his men.

Agbede finished the final side and the ragged rectangle of roof fell to the interior of the building. He tried to peer down through the opening, but his eyes had grown accustomed to the bright sun and the space below was too dark to even make out shapes. If he was looking down into the congregation room as he'd been told he would be, Agbede knew that the falling piece he had just cut out would have caught the attention of the armed men below, even if they had been distracted by the gunshots at the front and back of the building.

He hesitated. His eyes, and the eyes of the men with him on the roof under the bright sunshine, would take a little time to adapt to the darker rooms and hallways below. And that was time he didn't have. So with the jagged, rectangular black hole staring up at him, he dropped the saw and walked to the nearest workman lying dead on the roof. The man was not large, and Agbede had no trouble lifting him by the arms and dragging him to the hole. "Opeyemi!" he called out, and a tall, slender man hurried across the roof to him. "Take one of his arms," Agbede ordered.

Opeyemi let the Uzi in his hands drop to the end of the sling, then threw the Israeli-made weapon around to his back. He grabbed the dead man's forearm and helped his leader lift him over the edge. Together, they began lowering the dead body.

Slowly. Waiting for gunfire to erupt and pound into the target.

And give away the shooter's or shooters' position, which would enable return fire.

But none of that happened, and Agbede and Opeyemi finally let the man fall to the floor.

Agbede bent his head down above the hole. He could hear no sounds—no speech, no rustling of clothes, no reaction of any kind to a hole suddenly being cut in the roof above the Christians, and a dead body falling in on top of them. That could lead the Boko Haram second-in-command to only one conclusion.

He had not cut down into the congregation room. The informant's intel, or his own rough measurements stepping off the distance atop the roof, or something else he couldn't account for, had gone wrong. But whatever the problem was, he and the other men on the roof were *not* going to enter the building where he'd wanted them to.

The firefights at the front and rear of the building were louder now as the sounds of the explosions filtered up through the hole, and both teams of Bokos continued toward the center of the building. Agbede stuck his head into the hole. There was some light, but not much. With his right hand on the grip of his AK-47 and his left stroking his oily beard, he waited for his vision to adjust. The wait was slow and agonizing, even to a man as cold-blooded as Agbede knew himself to be.

He didn't understand it, couldn't figure out exactly where he was in relationship to the congregation room.

Then, as his eyes began to adjust, it became more clear. A yard or so farther to the front he could make out what looked like a wall, and just beneath and behind him was another. Both seemed to be recently installed, and the assault expert guessed immediately that Paul and his fellow Christians below had probably been remodeling the inside of the building to confuse men like him in a possible attack.

He dropped his head farther into the hole, half expecting to have it shot off. But the only gunfire he still heard was that from the front and rear entry teams. Instead, he immediately caught the faint odor of baked goods—bread, cinnamon rolls and African pastries. But as his eyes continued to adjust to the dim light, he saw the real reason his sawing and the dead workman's body had received no response.

He glanced at the saw still in his hands. With the shooting already begun, it was too late to try cutting out another entrance. Better they all drop through this hole and get their bearings once they were inside and on the ground.

The Boko Haram man stood up and stared down at the hole. The building was constructed of hardened clay, but had been reinforced over the years by lumber. And the edge of the hole closest to the side of the building ended just beyond a two-by-four beam. It made a perfect handhold to grasp, swing down into the hallway, and then let go and drop the final meter.

It was so obvious that Agbede didn't even have to tell his men what to do. He simply pointed and said, "Enter, quickly!"

Seconds later, as the explosions still raged at both ends of the building, all but two of his men had disappeared into the hole. Agbede took one last glance around the roof, then let his AK-47 fall to the end of the sling. "You two," he said in a stern voice. "Stay here. It is always possible that some of the converts will try to escape by coming up through the hole."

Both men appeared disappointed. They had obviously looked forward to the opportunity to kill Christians, and now the likelihood of that opportunity presenting itself had just become more remote. Their dejected faces reminded Agbede of just how thoroughly the men of Boko Haram had swallowed the fairy tale about Allah and Mohammed. But they would do as they were told. They knew that to disobey his or Hayat's orders meant their own deaths.

Agbede swung down into the semi-illuminated hallway. As he hung from the two-by-four, he saw that the men he had led up onto the roof were now in a semicircle, facing him and awaiting his next command.

He released his grasp on the beam and landed on his feet, quickly holding his index finger to his lips to indicate silence. The other men nodded. Holding up his thumb and index finger, he nodded at the two men closest to the first corner in the twisting hallway, and waited as they edged around the wallboard.

A sudden blast of gunfire broke out, and the hall echoed with the explosive aftermath.

The two terrorists who had rounded the corner fell dead, barely still in his field of vision. So much for them, Agbede thought. They had served their purpose. They had pinpointed the position of the enemy combatants. At least some of them.

Agbede was an experienced skirmisher and he knew there would be a brief—perhaps half a second—pause before whoever had just killed his two men would fire again. No matter how skilled the shooter might be, he had run out of targets. And since action was always faster than reaction, Agbede quickly swung his weapon around the corner. In the brief microsecond before he fired, he saw three men.

Enitan, the traitor who now called himself Paul, and a big man wearing a long robe and holding what looked like a machine pistol, were creeping down the hallway. Just behind them was the cop whose family the Bokos had killed. Jabari was his name, if Agbede remembered correctly.

Adrenaline shot through his veins when he knew he had an opportunity to kill Enitan. He pulled the trigger back on his AK-47 and sent a full-auto blast toward the men. At least a dozen 7.62 mm rounds sailed down the hallway. But all of them missed the three, and the energetic chemicals pumping through Agbede's body disappeared as quickly as they had arrived. He had *seen* the two men leading the way behind the iron sights on his rifle. First Enitan, when he had initially pulled the trigger. Then he had swung the rifle over to the big American and seen him just as clearly beyond the sights.

It seemed impossible, but none of his rounds had found their mark. Granted, AK-47s had never been known for pinpoint accuracy, but his targets had been less than twenty yards away. How could he have missed? And the big American had reacted faster than any combatant Agbede had ever faced, forcing him to duck back behind the corner before he could fire again.

He fell against the wall and slid down into a sitting position as the bullets from the American's weapon smashed into the wall to his side. He had been missed by less than an inch, he knew, and that was simply too close for comfort. He had anticipated some resistance from inside the building, but nothing like *this*. He knew that Enitan was an accomplished combatant, but the American had the reflexes of a jungle cat.

Agbede sat for a moment as more rounds struck nearby. Then he leaped to his feet. It was a time for action. For *survival*. With his back against the wall and bullets still pounding next to him, he realized he would have to kill the big American. But this was not the time or place. The odds were far too even here and the Boko Haram second-in-command wanted them stacked heavily in his favor when that time came.

But that didn't mean he wanted his own men to know what he was about to do. "Split up," he said. "Half of you go forward. The others, recon the back."

One of the terrorists frowned. "Where are *you* going?" he asked.

"Do not question me!" Agbede shouted, and slapped the man across the face. Then he tapped the handle of his gold-inlaid machete tucked in the sash around his waist. The men's eyes were stupefied with the narcotic of their religion as they nodded in understanding, clearly willing to comply with his orders.

With his authority firmly established now, Agbede let his rifle fall to the end of the sling and jumped up, catching the two-by-four and pulling himself into a chin-up position. "Push me, damn you!" he grumbled to the men below. A second later unseen hands had shoved him up and onto the roof again.

The Boko Haram second-in-command stared at the two men he had left on the roof. He didn't want them to question what he was about to do, either. "I have something important to take care of elsewhere. Stay here and guard the roof in my absence!" he ordered.

Neither man argued. In fact, they both nodded, their faces masks of unquestioning trust. Agbede waited until they had resumed their patrol of the rooftop, then hurried to the ladder. A few seconds later he had descended the rungs to the ground.

The gunfire still raged inside the building as he looked both ways, saw none of the Boko Haram men or anyone else watching, then took off running down a side street behind the bakery.

He was not a coward, he told himself as he distanced himself from the fighting. He was a *pragmatist*. The attack on the bakery wasn't going as easily as he'd expected it to, and his instincts told him it was because of the big American. So discretion had, as always, become the better part of valor.

Agbede still planned to kill the traitor and the big American, but he would do it from a safe distance.

BOLAN WAITED UNTIL Paul had drawn up to his side and Jabari was only a step behind him. In his peripheral vision, the soldier took note that Paul's blue tunic had ridden up over the stacked-leather grip of the huge knife in his belt. Now that the weapon was in full view, the soldier could see it was a Randall Raymond Thorpe Bowie, a huge knife with a thirteen-inch blade.

"Where in the world did you get that?" he whispered.

"From an American mercenary who was here for a short time," Paul said. "He gave it to me with his dying breath."

"It's a fine weapon," Bolan stated.

"It is," Paul agreed. "But we are still engaged in a gunfight. And I am running low on ammunition. So is Jabari."

Bolan turned to see him better. He indicated the man's AK-47 with a nod. "There are dead men all up and down this hallway. Most of them have Kalashnikovs. You can cannibalize their magazines."

An expression of self-disgust fell over Paul's face. "I may have been on the wrong side of things," he said, "but Boko Haram trained me well. I should have thought of that myself."

"It's easy to lose track of odds and ends when you're fighting for your life," Bolan said, as the two began retracing their steps, stooping to pick up 7.62 mm magazines from the dead terrorists as they went. The truth was, the soldier had said what he had because he sensed their need for encouragement and confidence more than criticism at this point.

Bolan's own brain seemed to step up a pace, become faster and more acute, the more dangerous the situation became.

He, Paul and Jabari made their way cautiously down the hallway. "I don't understand this silence in front of us," the soldier said quietly. "There has to be more men on the other side of that curtain." He paused a moment, then added, "And they had to have heard the gunfire on this side."

Bolan looked Jabari straight in the eye before turning his gaze back to Paul. "I think I know what's going on, but I can't be sure."

"I believe I know," Paul stated. "It is a tactic we used when I was still with Boko Haram. If we did not know the exact strength of the enemy we were about to attack, we would send everyone into the battle, but then have most of our force immediately withdraw. The objective was twofold. The sudden show of our entire force created the impression that the target was vastly outnumbered. But the temporary withdrawal ensured that if that was not the case, we did not lose all of our men."

The Executioner nodded. It was right out of any decent military strategy book and exactly what he had suspected. But Paul's inside knowledge of Boko Haram tactics was reassuring.

"Then they're getting ready for a second siege," Bolan said, again in a quiet voice that would not be heard farther down the hall. "That means we'd better get to Layla and the others and set up before they strike."

Paul nodded.

The Executioner turned and headed back toward the congregation room, making sure his hiking boots made as little noise as possible. His robe had come all the way open earlier in the firefight, but it mattered little inside the bakery. In this building, enemies and friends were easy to recognize. The terrorists wore red sashes around their arms and were doing their best to kill anyone who didn't. And considering the wild chances they were taking as they darted blindly around corners and sprinted down the halls, they didn't mind getting a few of their own men killed if it meant taking a Christian or two along with them.

It was little different than the suicide bombers used by al Qaeda and other terrorist organizations who sacrificed themselves in the name of God in order to commit mass murder. And Bolan suspected they all thought such sacrifices put them on the fast track to paradise and however many virgins a suicide was going for on that particular day.

A moment later, the three men reached the congregation room. Bolan stopped at the locked door and turned to Paul. "They'll recognize your voice better than mine," he said. "Tell them to open the door."

Paul stepped forward, and with his lips almost touching the wood, said, "Layla…or anyone…it is us. Unlock the door."

A second later steel scraped against steel near the doorknob and the door cracked open.

Layla Galab peered out.

Bolan took her by the hand, pulled her into the hall, then stuck his head into the room. "We're going to get you all out of here," he said. "But I've got to check on a couple of things first. Stay here until one of us comes back for you."

He closed the door again and led Galab toward the rear of the building, where the hole had been sawed through the roof. Looking up, he wasn't surprised to see what he'd suspected he would find.

If they helped each other, and if he, Paul, or a couple of the other men who had gone from escape-tunnel diggers to shooters assisted them, they'd be able to get some of the converts out that way. But that plan had problems, too.

First of all, the soldier had seen several people in the Congregation room who didn't look as if they could walk, let alone help pull themselves up and out of the building. Two of the converts, one man and one woman, were in wheelchairs. Getting them up, even with the healthier men pushing from below and pulling from above, was going to be time consuming. And every second that went by brought them closer to the moment Boko Haram would attack again.

Bolan felt his eyebrows lower and his forehead tighten as he stared at the opening above his head. And what would happen to these people even if they *could* get them onto the roof? Somehow, they would have to be lowered to the ground. In fact, they might not even get that far. Who was to say that Boko Haram hadn't left some of their men on the roof to blast the converts away as soon as they stuck their heads out?

And more were likely waiting farther back, in the alley.

The Executioner knew there was only one answer to the problem. And even that plan would take more time than he'd have liked. More time during which the terrorists might realize that there were only a few men still fighting them, and decide it was time for a rush.

Jabari looked far stronger than Paul, who was gripped in another series of seemingly endless coughs. "Hold out your hands and give me a lift," the soldier told the ex-cop.

Jabari bent his knees slightly and interlaced his fingers directly under the hole to the roof. Bolan lifted a hiking boot into the impromptu step, steadied himself with his left hand on Jabari's shoulder, then rose with the Kel-Tec in his right.

His eyes had barely risen through the hole when a rifle round whizzed past his head.

Bolan heaved his upper body through the hole, bringing the Kel-Tec with him. He twisted his head to the side. A man wearing a plain white T-shirt and what looked like the pants to a track suit stared back at him, preparing to fire again. Bolan pointed the pistol in his direction and cut loose with a steady stream of 5.56 mm rounds that turned the white T-shirt a reddish black. In his peripheral vision, he saw the dead bodies of men wearing work clothes lying on the roof. Scattered around them were nail guns and a variety of other hands tools. Right next to the hole was an electric saw.

The workmen on the roof had all been cut down—literally. The terrorists had, as they were so fond of doing, hacked the workers to pieces with razor-sharp machetes.

The man Bolan had just shot took two steps backward and then screamed as he fell off the building into the alley. But he wasn't the only terrorist still guarding the roof.

A man in a blue Yoruba tunic, holding an Uzi, stood ten feet to the side of the one who had just plunged from the roof.

Bolan pulled the trigger again as a volley of 9 mm rounds from the blue-shirted man's weapon ripped past his face and neck. His own jacketed hollowpoint slugs were more accurate, with two striking the terrorist's throat and sending a geyser of blood shooting from his throat. The man tried to fire again, but before he could pull the Uzi's trigger, two more 5.56 mm rounds took off the top part of his head.

He fell onto the edge of the roof, one leg dangling over the side.

The Executioner's eyes made a fast 180-degree sweep. Then he twisted his boot—still in Jabari's hands—until he could see behind him. But the only other men on the roof were lying in pools of blood. And instead of tribal or combat clothing or a mixture of both, they wore the overalls, canvas gloves and other garments of workmen.

What had happened was painfully apparent. The Boko Haram terrorists who had climbed to the roof had massacred the innocent workers, then used their saw to cut the opening into the hallway behind the bakery.

Bolan glanced down again. "Jabari," he said. "Lift me up the rest of the way."

The former cop did as he was told, and Bolan let the Kel-Tec fall to the end of the sling around his neck. Quickly, he knelt on hands and knees and looked back down into the hallway. "Paul," he said, and the man appeared next to Jabari below. "You and Layla go get all the people in the congregation room and take them out through the back door."

Paul frowned up at him. "But there are almost certainly more Bokos still out there," he said. "The man we saw earlier with the curled-up beard—I know him. His name is Dhul Agbede, and he is a *monster.*" The former Boko man actually shivered when he said that. "But he is competent. He will not have left the rear exit unattended."

"The alley will be cleared by the time your people arrive," Bolan said. He reached into his vest, pulled out a fresh magazine, then ejected the near-empty box mag by pushing the button on the side of the Kel-Tec.

"But are you sure—" Paul started to say, as the

Executioner rammed the new load into the magazine well and heard it click into place.

"I'm sure." Then he smiled. "I can't work miracles, Paul," he added, "but I'm fairly good at what I do. So have a little faith, Paul. Just have a little faith."

"Faith is all I can rely upon," he answered. "I will—" He stopped speaking suddenly and turned toward the front of the bakery.

Even on the rooftop, Bolan could hear new rounds being fired from the front, inside the building. "It looks like the escape plan is going to have to wait a little while," he said, as he swung back down into the hallway.

Paul just nodded, bent almost double in another coughing fit, then fell in next to Jabari as the soldier led them down the hallway toward the new rounds in this seemingly endless battle.

CHAPTER SEVEN

Like a swarm of angry hornets whose nest had been knocked down, the Executioner's steady stream of fire from the Kel-Tec blew through the men sneaking down the hallway. Some of their bodies jerked back and forth. Others fell to the floor on their faces. A few dropped backward, still clutching their weapons, while more were driven against the walls on both sides of the hall, only to slide down to the tile floor. Wet trails of blood dripped down the recently nailed up wallboards in their wake.

The magazine ran dry and Bolan pressed the release button with his index finger, letting the empty metal box fall to the floor in front of him. With the practiced hand that had reloaded countless similar AR-15–based weapons thousands of times in the past, he ripped another mag from a pocket in his vest and inserted it into the well at the bottom of the gun. A quick palm strike to the end sent the familiar click to his ears as the residual noise from his autofire died down and the magazine hit home.

Behind him—somewhere beyond the confusing twists and turns of the recently man-made maze—

the soldier could hear running footsteps. Men—undoubtedly Bokos—had entered the building from the alley entrance. The terrorists he had just shot had come from the front. And to get to where they were now, they would have had to pass the room that housed the secluded Christians.

Why had there been no gunfire? Why had the Bokos not engaged the armed men in that room? It didn't make sense.

But the rising sound of boots running toward him from the alley door took precedence over trying to figure out that seeming discrepancy, and Bolan waved Paul around the corner to where the Bokos he had just shot lay dead or dying. Before he spoke, the soldier began striding from body to body, kicking rifles and other weapons from the hands of the dead men on the floor. More than once in his career, Bolan had seen "dead men" come back to life long enough for one more pull of the trigger. And he didn't like the idea of Paul, Jabari or himself taking a bullet in the back from a man they thought was dead.

When he came to the last man he'd shot, the soldier saw that there was no need to disarm him. His weapon had fallen, hit the floor and bounced out of reach on its own. The man's chest was still heaving up and down. He had taken a bullet in the side, but he looked as if he still had a chance to survive if he received some immediate first aid.

Turning to Paul, Bolan said, "Use that big knife

of yours to cut some pieces of cloth from one of these guys' robes. Use them as bandages and stop the bleeding."

He turned to Jabari. "Then you keep an eye— and a *gun*—on him while Paul searches the rest of the bodies."

Glancing back at Paul, he said, "Look for anything that might help us figure out where the Boko Haram headquarters are. Or where their next planned assault might be."

Both Paul and Jabari nodded. Paul drew the big Bowie knife from its sheath and knelt next to the nearest body.

Bolan turned around in the maze and faced the rear of the building, crouching at the same corner he had used only a moment before to mow down the terrorists advancing from the front. This time, he would be on the other side and shooting toward men coming from the rear. He pressed his ear against the wallboard, and found the sounds of pair after pair of boots pounding against the tiles growing louder with every second that passed. He shifted the Kel-Tec to his left hand. Going "lefty" would provide him with a better angle of fire when the terrorists reached the final corner. It would also provide him with better cover where he stood.

As the footsteps continued to get louder, the soldier waited.

Waiting for combat that you knew was coming, Bolan had learned early on in his career, was the hardest part of any battle. When violence broke out without warning, well-trained men acted instinctively and didn't have time to think. But when a warrior—even one who had seen action many times in the past—had too much time to think, it tended to make him freeze up from trying to plan the best "counterattack" from many options.

And that was no good. Too many options meant the soldier might still be trying to pick the best one when the action finally began. That could cause too much deliberation. And too much deliberation got a person killed.

Bolan had overcome the temptation to "overthink" combat scenarios as soon as he had experienced it for the first time many years before. The trick was to clear your mind and let your survival instincts take over. A warrior could not afford to get tied up trying to determine the best strategy. What was important was that he do *something*.

After what seemed like hours, but could only have been a few seconds, a terrorist carrying an AK-47 rounded the corner into the Executioner's sight. He spotted Bolan's Kel-Tec, his arms and one eye peering around the next corner almost immediately, and started to bring his Russian assault rifle into target acquisition.

But the Boko Haram terrorist was a half second too slow and 5.56 mm hollowpoint rounds from the Kel-Tec stitched him throat to nose. The supersonic rounds punched through the front of the man's robe and head, then the back, taking body tissue and brain matter with them as they exited his body. The AK-47 dropped to the end of the sling around the man's shoulder and a look of surprise crossed his face as he fell to a sitting position just past the corner. He was still staring toward Bolan, his eyes wide open in shock, as he leaned back against the wall and died.

The second terrorist was less than a second behind the first. He was a short, burly man wearing a ragged beard that fell halfway down his chest. He looked slightly confused as he rounded the corner and caught a glimpse of the first man sitting there.

The burly man stopped in his tracks.

But that didn't save him.

Bolan leaned around the corner again, keeping as much of his body as he could behind the wall. With his left index finger, he squeezed the trigger of the Kel-Tec and sent a 3-round burst to the center of the Boko's big chest. The hollowpoint rounds punched through the beard and splattered blood and heart tissue out their exit holes just as they had the lead attacker. But the burly man didn't sit down to die as his friend had done.

He dropped his own AK-47, fell to his knees, then tipped over onto his back with his feet tucked under him.

It was a strange position in which to die, but the Executioner didn't have any more time to contemplate that than he'd had to wonder why the Bokos had passed the room full of Christian hideaways earlier. The battle was far from over, and until the final round had been fired, staying alive and keeping Paul and the others in the building breathing could be his only priority.

The next Boko to round the corner saw the burly body in his path too late. His boot caught against the man's shoulder and sent him tumbling forward, straight toward Bolan. Another M16 assault rifle—probably taken off some unfortunate American somewhere on the African continent—flew from his hands as he landed on his chest and slid forward. His slide ended less than a foot in front of the Executioner's hiking boot, and Bolan looked down to see him twist to his side, reach under his robe and pull out a Beretta 92.

Another "trophy" taken from the body of an American? Bolan didn't know. But at this point it didn't matter.

He leaned forward slightly, pressed the barrel of the Kel-Tec against the man's temple and pulled the trigger. Already on the ground, the terrorist had no need to fall as his head exploded.

All three men Bolan had just encountered had been killed within five seconds. But that was enough time for the next Bokos who had entered the building from the alley to realize they were meeting resistance. And now, as Bolan dropped to one knee and pulled back as far as he could around the corner, he saw another terrorist doing almost exactly the same thing across the hall.

The only difference was that the man was shooting right-handed, becoming almost a mirror image of the Executioner.

Rounds flew toward Bolan from the barrel of a rifle too well concealed to identify. They blew past his face to the left, striking the wall opposite. Another burst hit the corner in front of most of his body, which proved to be concealment but not cover.

The rounds passed through the wallboard as if it was paper, and the soldier could feel the heat on top of his head as bullets missed him by millimeters.

The big American didn't have time to use the Kel-Tec's sights. But he didn't need them. He had mastered the art of point-shooting with a pistol, then with a rifle, a technique the US Army had originally called the "Quick Kill" method. As he understood it, the term had now been replaced by something more politically correct.

But whatever it was called, it worked.

Bolan stared at the lone eye he could see around the corner in front of him as he flipped the converted Kel-Tec's selector switch to semiautomatic fire. Then he pulled the trigger and watched that eye explode.

The man kneeling behind the corner fell backward, out of sight.

Bolan waited for the next terrorist to show himself, but that didn't happen. A few seconds passed, then the sound of boots running on the tiles met his ears once again. This time they were heading away from him instead of toward him.

The Executioner listened for a moment, frowning. It sounded like a lone man running. Was there only one terrorist left of the contingency that had entered from the alley? Maybe. That would make a total of six. And there had been six men coming toward him and Paul from the other direction. Five of that half dozen were dead and being searched.

But what had happened to the people in the congregation room? Were they still alive or had they all been mowed down like so much wheat at harvest time by the Boko Haram terrorists invading this place?

Bolan didn't know. But before he could go searching for the Christians, he had to neutralize the threats to his own, as well as their, safety. In the heat of battle, priorities had to be kept straight. So he had to face the threat from the alley entrance before turning back to check on Layla Galab and the others.

Bolan rose to his feet and moved out, cautiously turning the corner. He kept the Kel-Tec in front of him, ready to point-shoot again as soon as he saw a target. Carefully, he scanned his surroundings, focusing on what he was stepping over.

But even though the Executioner encountered no more of the enemy, as he moved on he continued to hear the distant sound of running feet. Soon he had passed at least a half-dozen more corners in the labyrinth. But as he approached another turn in his path, something—maybe his battle sense—told him that absence of adversaries was about to change. Taking a deep breath, he peered out from the edge of the wallboard, the assault pistol in his grip.

Ten yards or so away, at the next corner where the hallway twisted out of sight, the Executioner saw a man running in place. He held an AK-47 in his hands as his knees pumped up and down.

Running in place as he was, and obviously trying to make the Executioner and any other enemy combatants think a retreat was taking place, he looked almost like something out of a cartoon. The strategy seemed childish—at first. But for the average soldier, whose ears at this point would have been suffering from all of the gunfire they had endured, it might have worked.

Unfortunately for him, Bolan wasn't the average soldier.

Before the man could react to the sudden sight of him, Bolan saw another man wearing a carefully tended goatee and mustache kneeling on the floor just around the corner. He held a 9 mm Browning Hi-Power pistol in both hands and had it pointed up, directly at the soldier's chest.

The two-man trap was simple, but would have proved effective against an inexperienced warrior. The man running in place was for show, to draw Bolan's attention away from his comrade kneeling around the corner. Training and common sense dictated that the most dangerous threat be taken out first, and the running man was doing his best to appear to be that threat. If he could distract Bolan—

even for a split second—it would give the man with the Browning time to pump 9 mm rounds into the American.

It almost worked.

Bolan's combat-experienced brain took in all of the information presented to him and calculated the likelihood of success of several different responses. There was no way, he knew, that he could fire the Kel-Tec before the Boko with the Browning got off at least one shot.

So, using the momentum he still had from running across the hall, the Executioner kept moving. He twisted to the side, and the double-tap of 9 mm rounds that spit from the Browning's muzzle passed by him. Again, the bullets were so close he felt their heat, this time on his chest rather than his head. And by the time he had twisted back and slammed into the wall to the side of the terrorist, Bolan had turned the Kel-Tec in the direction he wanted it to go.

Still on semiauto, a lone 5.56 mm hollowpoint round slammed into the terrorist's temple, and he flattened out on the floor.

Bolan didn't waste time admiring his work. He turned immediately toward the man who had been running in place. The pistol moved with him and he caught a split-second glimpse of the man. But now he was running for real. Leading him a yard or so, the soldier pulled the trigger again and sent another 5.56 mm round through his arm and then his chest, before it lodged in the opposite arm.

The Boko Haram terrorist turned slowly toward the Executioner. He looked shocked, as if he'd just awakened from some strange dream he didn't quite understand. With the last few ounces of strength left in him, he started to raise his weapon.

Another single 5.56 mm caught him in the center of his nose, and he collapsed onto the tiles of the hallway.

The echoes of the gunfire suddenly stopped. And when they did, the Executioner heard distant shots coming from the direction he'd sent Paul and Jabari. He still wasn't sure how or why the men had passed the room filled with hiding Christians, but the gunfire told him at least one thing.

The battle that he had thought was ending when he'd pulled himself up onto the roof was still ongoing. So, pivoting on the balls of his feet, the Executioner changed directions.

And once again, the Kel-Tec led the way.

PAUL KNEW THAT his birth name, Enitan, meant "person of the story" in the Yoruba tongue. When he had been twelve years old he had asked his parents why they had given him that name. He remembered the glances they had shot at each other, and the slight uneasiness that had filled the room. Then again, Enitan thought, as he walked down the hallway and the big American disappeared around a corner in the opposite direction, *uneasiness* was probably not the correct word. It was more that even at his young age he had sensed that his mother and father were being reminded of some sort of bond they had between them, some inexplicable spiritual tie that could never fully be put into words no matter how hard they tried.

Paul stopped next to the body on the floor. He remembered his parents staring into each other's eyes so long that he had asked the question again. "Father...Mother...why did you give me this name?"

Paul's mother had finally broken the silent stare and turned to him. "Because God told us to do so," she said.

He had been skeptical. "Are you telling me that God appeared to you, here in this house, and said, 'Name the baby Enitan—the person of the story'?"

His father had spoken up this time. "No, my son," he had said. "God rarely appears like that. At least He has never done so to me or anyone I know."

Paul remembered frowning so hard his face hurt. "How, then, did He tell you?" he asked.

"He appeared to me in a dream a few days before your mother gave birth to you," his father said.

Paul still wasn't convinced. "And how did you know it was God telling you to do this?" he asked.

His mother reached out and took his hand in hers. "Because he appeared to me the same night," she said. "In exactly the same way. And told me the same thing. You will name your child Enitan. The person of the story."

Even after all these years, Paul remembered the incident, and it sent a chill down his spine. He knew the importance the Yoruba tribe placed on names. And as he'd continued to grow up he'd done his best to figure out exactly which person of which story he had been named after. His parents claimed not to know. And as he grew to be a man he had successively been convinced that he'd been named after Adam, the first man; then Noah, who had built the ark that saved humankind from extinction; Moses who had led his people to the Promised Land; Jesus, claimed by the Christians to be the son God; and then Mohammed. Since Paul had always believed in a God of some sort—existence itself confirmed that in his mind and soul—he had done his best to serve Him by carrying out His will. But he had never been completely convinced as to which "person of the story" he was.

Until he finally had his own dream.

Paul finished bandaging the wound of the Boko Haram man on the floor, then stopped for a moment to inspect his work. He had done all he could to save this man's life, and if he lived, he might prove to be an invaluable informant. But blood was still seeping out around the edges of the makeshift bandage, and it would be a race against the clock to see if he could lead them to the Boko hideout or the terrorists' next site of murderous mayhem.

Paul turned and looked up at Jabari, nodding to indicate that he was finished with the field dressing. Jabari nodded back and trained his AK-47 on the man on the floor. Paul rose and walked to the body farthest away from them. He dropped to one knee again. As he tore back the blood-soaked robe before him, he remembered Matt Cooper, and the coolness the American had exhibited as he'd downed the six men in this hallway behind the bakery. Cooper looked as if he had been involved in such combat hundreds of times. He had faced their enemies with the ease of a man shooting clay pigeons at a country club, and if Paul had taken Cooper's pulse he doubted if it would have been any higher during and right after the brief battle than it was before the violence erupted.

Now, as he began to search the body, his mind returned to the dream he'd had. It had answered, finally, the question brought about by his parents' nighttime visions. He remembered his own dream as vividly as if it had taken place the night before and in high definition color.

Just as He had done to Saul on the Damascus Road almost two thousand years ago, Jesus had looked Paul straight in the eye and said, "Enitan, Enitan, why do you persecute me?"

It was more than enough to turn his life completely around when he awakened.

Paul began to search the pockets of the BDUs beneath the robe, but his mind remained on that powerful scene. The dream was the event that had finally convinced him exactly which "person of the story" he was, and what his role should be.

He was not *literally* a reincarnation of the Apostle

Paul, but he had been given the name Enitan because his mission in life was patterned after Paul's. It was his calling to spread the Good News about Jesus to the gentiles as well as the Jews, and he had used his position in Boko Haram much like the original Paul had used his Roman citizenship—to assist in that mission.

Paul continued to search through the pockets of the body stretched out below him, but found nothing of interest. As he moved to the next dead terrorist, his mind stayed on the past. With the overnight change of heart and purpose that had followed his dream, he had continued to use the name Enitan as he went about his Boko Haram duties. But secretly, the man who now thought of himself as "Paul" began to leak vital information to the Nigerian Christians. The intel he provided had resulted in dozens of Boko strikes being thwarted, and hundreds of Christian lives being spared. But such duplicity could not go on forever. Finally, his new allegiance had been discovered and he had barely escaped assassination. As it was, a price had been put on his head and he had alternately been running for his life and fighting back against Boko Haram ever since.

The body Paul knelt next to now yielded a pistol and a dagger, but little else of real interest until he came across a small cloth bag in the right front pocket of the man's OD green pants. It contained a few coins and a folded scrap of paper. Paul pocketed the money, which would be used to assist the survival of the Christians. When he unfolded the paper, he felt his face tighten as he stared down at the scrawled address. There was something familiar about it, something in the back of his mind that told him he had seen it before. But he couldn't put his finger on exactly where, or what it was.

He glanced up to make sure that Jabari still had their prisoner covered, then moved to the next body

Paul's brain, however, remained at least partially in the past. As he knelt beside of the next downed Boko, he again riffled through the man's pockets. He had been "Paul" so long now that he knew few Christians remembered his other name. And he had even heard rumors that his former compatriots within Boko Haram referred to him as "Paul." Of course, they did so sarcastically, but he found pleasure in knowing that the terrorists had at least been forced to acknowledge his new belief.

As he patted down the shoulders and ribs of the dead man to see if anything was concealed beneath his BDU blouse, a sudden wave of guilt washed over Paul. Try as he might, he could never forget that before his conversion he had been responsible for more Christian deaths than he could even count, and his chest ached with the memories. It felt as if a heavy ship's anchor had been dropped directly onto his heart. But there was nothing he could do, Paul knew, to change the past. His only course of action was to move forward. He could never do enough good deeds to make up for the evil he had orchestrated. No man could. But he would spent the rest of his life trying.

In the right breast pocket of the dead man's shirt, Paul found two gold-and-diamond rings, a necklace and assorted other items of jewelry. All plunder from some unfortunate victims of one of Boko Haram's trademark home invasions, no doubt. And whoever had lost the jewelry would have lost their lives, as well.

Boko Haram didn't believe in leaving survivors.

Paul pocketed the items. Since there would be no one alive to claim them, he could sell them and use the money to help other Christians who had been uprooted from their homes because of their belief. What was curious, however, was that another scrap of paper was mixed in with the jewelry.

It bore the same address as the one from the previous man's coin bag.

Again Paul tried to tie the address to a specific site or anything else in his past, but the attempt failed. Was it a Boko Haram hideout? A stronghold of some kind? He didn't think so. The terrorists would not need to write down the location of a place so familiar. Perhaps it was one of the dozens of other Christian safe houses scattered throughout Nigeria. There were far too many for him to keep straight in his head. Or it might be the site of the next strike these men planned to carry out. Another church bombing? A home invasion? Paul felt his eyebrows furrow. He wasn't sure what it meant, but the fact that he'd now found the same address on two of the dead Bokos had to mean something.

Pocketing the paper, Paul went back to get the one in the coin bag as well, before moving on to search the next corpse.

He knelt again, patting down another body. But now he was looking specifically for a paper with that address—or anything that might be related to it—that made sense.

This time he found a full sheet rather than a scrap of paper. It had been folded in two, then folded again into quarters and slipped into a back pocket of the corpse in front of him. He unfolded it, to find only a number and two words. And rather than being hand-written, the address had been typed into a computer and then printed out.

But it was the same address he had found on the other two men: 11637 Yejide Street.

Paul slipped the page into a pocket of his tunic with the other two pieces of paper and stood up. His soul soared now; he was elated with the knowledge that he was onto something.

The man who had truly become "the person of the story" turned toward the next body on the floor. His thoughts, as they often did, returned to the original Apostle Paul, and the "thorn in his side." He knew his own thorn was two pronged: weak lungs and the lingering guilt for the Christians he had murdered before his salvation.

He couldn't seem to shake either one, but God

gave him the strength to persevere. Searching through another shirt and pants pockets, Paul found yet another piece of paper. This one looked to be a small lined page torn out of a spiral-bound notebook.

It bore the same address.

He moved to the next body on the floor and bent once more. The man's robe had come untied and he opened it further. As he began the search, he stared into the dead man's face, someone he had never met. In fact, none of the Bokos he had searched, including the one still alive and kept in place by Jabari's rifle, looked familiar.

That didn't surprise him. Boko Haram was recruiting more members on a daily basis, much like the other Islamic terrorist groups.

Paul found another piece of paper scrawled on in pencil. Blood had soaked through the chest pocket where it had been secreted and part of the address was all he could make out. But by now it was more than enough. He stood, and the movement brought on another sudden coughing fit. Paul walked toward the next body. Behind him, he could still hear gunshots and knew they were loud enough to cover his own hacking sounds. But in front of him—toward the bakery—the fire had settled down. So he did his best to quell the telltale coughing, aimed his AK-47 at the next corner in the twisting hallway, and kept one eye in that direction as he crouched and began to search the last man.

This terrorist had died on his back with his eyes

and his mouth open. His bushy black beard and mustache were ruffled, with hairs curling over his lips and into his mouth, wet with saliva that had not yet had time to dry. His black eyes held the dullness of a shark's, and the AK-47 he had clutched across his chest earlier had been kicked to the side. But his dead hands had fallen back in place as if they still held the weapon in a death grip and he was trying to keep someone from wrestling the invisible rifle away from him.

Paul pulled the man's arms off his chest and stared at the face. This man he did recognize, but he could not remember his name or much about him as he began searching the pockets for the piece of paper that by now he knew he'd find.

And he did find it, in the right slash pocket next to a cheap old rusty pocket knife: 11637 Yejide Street.

Paul stuffed the paper into his pocket, but left the penknife on top of the dead man's chest. Finding nothing more of interest, he straightened up and looked again at the AK-47 that had been kicked clear of the terrorist's hands. Paul didn't need another rifle, but he could use the magazine still in the weapon. He lifted it long enough to eject the nearly full box from the receiver and stick it under the belt of his black slacks. Then he retraced his steps, picking up all the AK-47 mags he could find among the corpses.

Three more went under Paul's belt to pinch his

skin, but the pain mattered little, given the situation he and Jabari were in. He passed him three more of the mags and the former policeman nodded in appreciation. Then Paul slung the AK-47 over his shoulder and drew the Filipino .45. It was as good of a man stopper as you could get in a pistol, and much easier to maneuver within the twists and turns of the hallways behind the bakery. He would save the Kalashnikov and the extra 7.62 mm magazines for when he ran out of .45s or needed to make a long shot.

The last dead man wore a brilliantly dyed robe with red and blue stripes running from the shoulder to the hem of the cotton garment. It looked like a rough copy of the "red, white and blue" that symbolized the United States, and Paul wondered if the man he knew as Matt Cooper might not have taken special delight in pulling the trigger on this Boko. But he wondered only for a second. Although he had not known Cooper long, he sensed that the warrior, as great in battle as he was, took no pleasure in killing anyone.

Paul suspected that Cooper simply did what he had to without much emotion of any kind. With him, Paul guessed, killing terrorists would be much like taking the garbage out. It had to be done. And while it might smell bad for a few seconds, it hardly merited worrying about.

In any case, as he bent yet again at the side of the corpse, Paul saw that the red and blue stripes were now marred by giant splotches of dark blood. He pulled open the garment to reveal that the American's rounds had found both the carotid artery in the man's neck and the femoral on the inside of one thigh. Another severe bullet wound had ripped off the man's left jawbone and yet another had drilled through the center of his chest. It was anybody's guess as to which had killed him first—the heart exploding or the quick bleed-out from the arteries.

Not that it mattered, Paul thought as he began to search this man's pockets as he'd done the others. Dead was dead, and every second he spent with Matt Cooper made him a little more in awe of the man's close-quarters combat abilities. Paul wasn't a bad fighter himself, with or without weapons. But he had never seen anyone like Cooper. It was as if God had created him for exactly the role he was playing in life—protecting the weak and innocent from the stronger and evil.

Of course, Paul believed God had created everyone for specific tasks. It was just that Cooper's were so obvious and dramatic.

Paul rose again and looked down at the body. He recognized the striped robe and what was left of the face. Chander was the man's name. Actually, it was an Indian name, and somewhere in the back of his mind Paul remembered that while the man's father had been Nigerian, his mother was from Calcutta.

Paul shook his head as his heart seemed to sink from his chest to his stomach. He remembered a conversation he'd had with Chander not long before his conversion to Christianity had been discovered. Chander was not a bad man. He was just misguided. And he had shared with Paul that he was beginning to question Boko Haram's indiscriminate use of violence against Christians and Muslims alike. He had even considered converting to Christianity himself, but was afraid.

Now, as he looked down at the shell that had once held Chander's soul, Paul wondered if the man had accepted Christ before he died. There was no way to know. But the terrorist-turned-Christian wished he had talked to the man further and shared his own conversion experience with him. And regardless of what state Chander's soul was in when he died, he'd also carried with him a copy of the address on Yejide Street.

Finally finished with the dead men, Paul turned to Jabari and their prisoner again. He started that way, but before he could get to the man, two other terrorists rounded the corner ahead of him and opened up with full-auto fire.

Paul raised his pistol and pointed it at the first man, who looked to be in his later teens and wore a sparse, scraggly beard. A double-tap on the trigger sent a pair of full-metal-jacketed .45-caliber hardball rounds into the man's chest as the young terrorist's own rounds from the AK-47 in his hands passed so close to Paul's head that they singed the hair just above his right ear.

The second man was older and wiser. He tried to duck back around the corner, but he didn't quite make it.

He had turned his side to Paul in his attempt to retreat, but the former Boko fired twice more, with the first round drilling through the man's temple and out the other side of his head. The follow-up shot missed.

But that hardly mattered.

Paul had dropped into a combat crouch during the encounter. Now he straightened and aimed his .45 at the Boko Haram prisoner. "Help me, Jabari," he said. "We need to get this heartless terrorist to Cooper, get the people out of the congregation room and get out of here."

Jabari nodded and the two of them grabbed the arms of their prisoner. His moan turned to a shriek of pain as they hauled him to his feet. Paul scanned him quickly. The blood was leaking out around the bandage faster now, and it appeared as if he was hemorrhaging. Paul could see that if they were to get any use out of him, it would have to be soon.

The man shrieked again, and Paul pressed the barrel of his pistol against the side of the man's head. "Keep quiet and you may live," he said in a low, grumbling voice. "Make noise again and I will kill you where we stand. Do you understand me?"

The prisoner's face was contorted in pain. He nodded.

"Say it," Paul ordered. "And say it softly."

"I must remain quiet or die," the injured man whispered.

"Very good," Paul said.

He looked at Jabari, who clutched the man's other arm with both hands. "Let's go," he said, and they started toward where they suspected Matt Cooper might be.

CHAPTER EIGHT

Combat—particularly close-quarters combat—was an art rather than a science. That was the reason the great ancient Chinese general Sun Tzu had entitled his ageless treatise on strategy *The Art of War* rather than *The Science of War*. Like a great painting, sculpture or piece of literature, every battle was unique. That meant that while general plans of attack could be laid out in advance, the warrior always had to leave room to improvise when unexpected details entered the picture.

And that reality had given rise to a pair of adages that were every bit as true as anything any great general had ever written: "Every plan falls apart as soon as the first shot is fired" and "Always expect the unexpected."

The Executioner knew these things. Knew that, after all the planning and strategizing was over, the true soldier sometimes had to make a decision in a heartbeat.

That was why Jabari and Paul didn't die that day when they rounded the corner behind the soldier, half carrying one of the Bokos. They stopped in their tracks when they saw him. But by the time they had stopped moving, Jabari's face was less than a foot from the business end of the Kel-Tec.

He stared at Bolan's gun for a moment, his eyes crossing in a look that would have been comical had the circumstances not been so dire. Then he stepped back, still holding the arm of the prisoner.

Both he and Paul held weapons in the hands they weren't using to support the man between them. Paul had resurrected his Filipino .45 and Jabari held the grip of a Russian Makarov 9 mm semiauto pistol. Both had slung their AK-47s.

They lowered their guns when they recognized the big American. At the same moment, their injured charge sagged to the floor, dead.

"Take Jabari with you and go back, Paul," Bolan said, indicating the way the two men had just come. "Get the people out of the congregation room and ready to exit the building." He turned to the man in the dirty police uniform. "Jabari, you get hold of those green bags I traded to the converts for their old worn-out luggage. There's a rope that was left in one. I think I saw one of the men shoving it into a gunnysack. We'll need it."

"Aren't you coming with us?" Jabari asked.

Bolan shook his head. "I'm heading back to the roof. There's still likely to be Bokos waiting in the alley. I'll take out all I can see, but some will still be hidden. The idea is to split their attention, so divide the people up. Those who look physically capable of running on their own will be sprinting out the back door and heading in different directions. At the same time we're going to take those who can't run up through the roof and then carry them down the ladder in the walkway. If they can't be carried, they'll be lowered over the side with a rope."

Paul's eyebrows furrowed. "That's going to be a slow process."

Bolan nodded. "Yeah, it is. But the lane between the buildings is fairly secluded. The Bokos will have a hard time setting a man up for a shot without exposing themselves to my fire." He glanced back to the ex-cop, who was leaning away from him, anxious to get on with the plan. "And while you're at it, find a chair or a table or something to serve as a step, and leave it directly under the hole."

By now, Paul had caught on to the Executioner's plan. "The people who can run will sprint out the back and spread out in different directions," he said, to confirm his conclusion.

"Correct," the soldier stated. "It doesn't matter which way they go. Tell them that as soon as they're away from the battle area they should head to the other safe houses you assigned them to go to during just such an emergency."

"How are they to know when to start?" Paul asked.

"We're going to be getting the physically disabled down off the roof at the same time," Bolan said. "We'll start it all when I fire five consecutive auto rounds. I'll wait one second between each shot. That should differentiate the signal from the rounds I'll be firing at any of the Bokos I see *before* we start the evacuation."

Both Paul and Jabari nodded.

"One more thing," Bolan told them. "I'm going to be busy sniping from the roof. I'll be going after Boko Haram who step out from cover to shoot the runners, and hoping I can take them out before they get their own shots off." He reached up and scratched his chin in thought for a second, then said, "But I'll also be looking for any of these killers who figure out that the invalids are being lowered into the pathway to the side. I can do both tasks from the same position on the roof, but I can't be in two places at the same time."

He paused again, frowning. "That means I need at least two men strong enough to lower people over the side with the rope."

A rare smile suddenly crossed Paul's face. "I have just the pair for you," he said. He glanced at Jabari, who was grinning now himself.

"The twins," the former police officer said.

"The twins," Paul repeated. "Babajide and Babatunde. Both of their names mean 'Father has returned' in Yoruba."

From somewhere in the back of his mind, the Executioner remembered learning that the Yoruba had the highest number of twins born in the world, with forty-five to fifty pairs born out of every thousand live births. Scientists believed it was related to a steady diet of yams…

"Usually it is Taye for the firstborn," Paul added. "'The first to taste the world.' The second twin is usually Kenny, short for Kehinde, 'the child that came last gets the rights of the eldest.'" He coughed into his fist. "Those are the usual names for twins. But this pair, who only recently converted to Christianity, are anything but usual."

"All I care about is that they're strong and they can follow orders," Bolan said.

"Babajide won the Mr. Nigeria bodybuilding contest last year," Jabari said. "His identical twin came in second."

"They also win every powerlifting contest they enter," Paul stated. "First one, then the other. And they are not only immensely strong, they are fiercely competitive. They will work themselves to death for you on the roof just for the sake of outdoing each other."

"Why didn't I notice them in the congregation room earlier?" Bolan asked. "They sound like they'd stick out of the crowd."

"If I remember correctly," Paul said, "they were both sitting with robes over the sweatpants they usually wear. Believe me, you will notice them without the robes."

"Okay. Bring them on. I'm going to the roof and I'll pull myself up again. But get the rope and whatever you're going to use as a step to me, as well as these bodybuilding twins, as quickly as you can."

Without another word, the Executioner took off running for the hole in the roof.

BOLAN HAD BEEN pleased with the way the Kel-Tec had performed. But for the sniping job he was about to undertake on the roof, he wanted a long gun with a stock. The shots weren't likely to be far, so he wouldn't necessarily need a bolt action rifle with a scope, which was good, since he hadn't even seen such a weapon in the building. For the most part, AK-47s and a few scattered M16s and M4 carbines had been the rifles of choice for Boko Haram.

The Kalashnikov-designed AK-47s were perhaps the most reliable assault rifles in the world. You could drop one in a mud puddle, let elephants walk over it for a year or two, come back and it would still shoot. That couldn't be said about the American-made AR-15 family of rifles. They were far more "delicate."

But the advantage the AK-47 possessed in reliability had to be weighed against its accuracy—or rather the lack of it. Bolan had shot many of the weapons, which could not even be counted on to hit a silhouette target at a hundred yards. So as he ran back down the confusing hallways, leaping over the bodies of Boko Haram terrorists he'd shot earlier, he ignored the Russian rifles. But when he saw an M16 lying next to a man he remembered shooting earlier, he ground to a halt, reached down and picked it up.

Bolan pulled the bolt back far enough to see a round in the chamber, then pulled it the rest of the way to make sure it ejected that round properly. He didn't want a jam to interfere with his shooting once he was on the roof. So, turning back the way he'd come, he flipped the selector switch to semiautomatic mode, pulled the trigger and sent the next 5.56 mm bullet flying down the hallway into the wall.

The shot was just another test, and it proved that the rifle functioned properly.

Ejecting the magazine from the receiver, he hefted it up and down in his hand. It felt heavy, which meant it had probably just been inserted before the man using the weapon had died. But there was no reason to take chances, even though Bolan still had a multitude of magazines in his vest.

Reaching down again, he found two more loaded box mags on the body of the man who had carried the M16. They would work with both the American assault rifle and the Kel-Tec, so he filled the remaining pockets of the vest under his robe once more. Then he ran on.

Bolan reached the hole in the ceiling, and with the Kel-Tec hanging from his right shoulder, the M16 on a sling from his left, he jumped up and caught the same two-by-four he'd used like a chinning bar earlier. He swung his legs forward as far as he could, then used the momentum built up to swing back and pull himself up onto the roof. As soon as he'd vaulted to his feet, he was sprinting toward the rear edge of the building.

The Executioner slowed as he neared the alley, then knelt and inched toward the short retaining wall. Slowly, he let himself down onto his chest, with the M16 held to one side, the Kel-Tec to the other. Then he raised his head to peer over the edge.

Below, in the laneway where he and Galab had entered the building, were the stacks of plywood, boxes of nails and other scattered building equipment that had been there before. He drew no fire, but Bolan knew that hardly meant the area was clear of Boko Haram terrorists.

The soldier took a deep breath. The next part was going to be tricky. He had not been fired on just now because only his head, from his eyes upward, had been visible to the terrorists. But he was certain enemy gunners had to be hidden below. They had not noticed the relatively small target his forehead presented, or else had decided to wait for a clearer shot before giving their positions away.

Were any of the unseen Bokos in a position to fire down the walkway between the buildings, targeting the invalids who would soon be lowered over the side? At this point it was impossible to know.

The Executioner's quick survey of what he knew was about to become an intense combat area had been the easy part. Now, in order to spot, then shoot the terrorists waiting for the Christian converts to exit the bakery, he would have to expose much more of himself. The M16 had to reach over the retaining wall, and that meant both arms, his shoulders and his upper chest would be in the line of fire.

Not to mention his head.

The Executioner tightened his jaw in resolve. Each shot he fired would help the men below to pinpoint his position, but he saw no other way to handle the situation. He was already dividing the Bokos' attention by sending the ambulatory Christians sprinting off in every direction from the back door. And it wouldn't take long for the enemy to figure out that some were being lowered from the roof. Paul and Jabari would fire their weapons from the back door to add to the confusion Bolan hoped to create, but they'd be on the ground just like their opponents. And he doubted that angle of fire would present them with the opportunity to do any major damage to the enemy.

Would it all work? The Executioner didn't know. It was hardly a foolproof plan, and its success or failure hinged on him being able to take out as many terrorists as possible before the evacuation began. But he had always believed in the old adage that a "good plan now is better than a perfect plan in an hour," and he saw no other choice than to go with it.

Slowly, knowing this first exchange of rounds was likely to be the only one he got before return fire followed his every move, Bolan raised his head again. He spotted the tail of a brightly striped robe sticking out from behind a stack of wallboard. The leather heel of a black combat boot extended slightly to the side, telling Bolan the robe was open and the partly hidden man was on his knees. Trying to delay giving away his whereabouts as long as he could, the Executioner looked down at his side and picked up a large piece of gravel. Then, rising high enough to throw the stone, he tossed it over the wall and watched it strike the asphalt next to the black boot.

The kneeling man leaned back instinctively, and two arms holding an Israeli-made Uzi submachine gun, a pair of shoulders covered by a Yoruba *sokoto*, and a black face and even blacker beard looked out from behind the stack.

The man was less than thirty yards away. Bolan flipped the selector switch from semiauto to 3-round burst and pulled the trigger. The trio of rounds started at the Boko's chin and worked their way up, the second bullet drilling into his left nostril and the third carving out his eye. The terrorist fell to his side on the ground, his body spasming as if he was performing one last dance of death.

The muzzle blasts from the roof didn't go unnoticed.

Different sounds from different calibers, barrel lengths, makes and models of firearms erupted as a hail of lead drilled Bolan's position. He ducked back down behind the retaining wall. Lying on his side, his shoulder against the clay, he felt the vibration each round brought to the ancient structure. The building had been constructed before firearms were prevalent in Nigeria, and while it had been rebuilt and reinforced over the years, it had still been designed to stop arrows and spears rather than bullets.

Looking up, the Executioner saw the top of the retaining wall blow off above his head. A combination of small clay chunks and powder rained down over him, forcing him to close his eyes until the barrage ended.

Bolan could feel the dust inside his nose, stopping up his sinuses. He was forced to breathe through his mouth as he rolled over one complete turn to change position. A seasoned warrior knew better than to ever show his face twice in a row in the same place in a gunfight, and Bolan had moved on beyond "seasoned" years before. So now, as the dust-clouded air billowed around him even after the gunfire stopped, he raised himself to look over the side again.

Return fire forced his head back down, but the rounds striking the top of the building did so in the spot where Bolan had been rather than where he was now. Though his eyes were irritated by the clay dust, he was able to focus in on a frightened-looking man with a beard that had no doubt once been coal-black but now had stripes of gray running from his chin halfway down his chest.

His eyes darted back and forth in his wrinkled face as he jerked the trigger and made his Russian assault rifle spray ammo all over the roof. Bolan was not so much worried that the man would kill him with skill as by accident.

If you threw enough wild shots at a target, eventually one was going to hit. Such an untrained attack had long been termed "spray and pray" by knowledgeable gunfighters.

Bolan switched back to semiauto and squeezed the trigger. A single, relaxed, well-aimed 5.56 mm bullet streaked from the M16 and caught the aging terrorist just to the side of the nose, between the corner of the mouth and the right eye.

The killer of innocents toppled backward, his finger seemingly frozen to the trigger and causing the AK-47 to keep firing in rapid succession toward the sky. It took a few seconds, but the magazine finally emptied and the Russian weapon fell across the dead man's chest.

Sudden movement at the top of his vision drew the Executioner's eye. He looked up and caught a quick glimpse of a man with a rifle. The gunner was nearly a block away and hard to identify, but he looked familiar, and Bolan guessed it was the same man he had narrowly missed in the hall down below. The one with the dirty, stringy mustache and greasy beard that curled up and out, away from his chin.

The Executioner raised his rifle to fire, but before he could pull the trigger, the figure had disappeared again behind a building.

Bolan heard a noise behind him and whirled instinctively. Knee-walking back out of sight from the alley below, he watched a man wearing nothing but red sweat pants and dirty white Nike athletic shoes pull himself up out of the hole. Ducking his head, he turned a somersault on the gravel roof, and in the sunlight Bolan saw the well-cut muscles in his shoulders, biceps, triceps and lats before he rolled to his feet.

The veins and arteries in the man's upper body looked as if they were trying to escape through his skin.

Bolan watched as the man turned back to the hole and grabbed the coils of a rope that had just come up out of the opening as if of their own accord. Then he stepped back and let the thick line straighten as another man appeared, this one in blue sweatpants.

That was good, the Executioner thought, because the color of their pants was the only difference he could see between the two men.

Babajide and Babatunde. The twins. And they not only looked strong enough to lower the disabled over the side of the building to safety, they looked as if they could do the same with a full-grown hippopotamus.

As if by way of introduction, both men suddenly faced the Executioner, then bent over and clenched their fists in front of their waists in what was known as the "most muscular" pose in bodybuilding circles. The mountains and valleys of their upper bodies grew even larger and more defined, and Bolan wouldn't have been all that surprised if their arteries and veins had burst and sent blood shooting out in all directions.

"Okay, guys," he yelled over the gunfire still coming from below. "That's great, but this isn't the Mr. Olympia contest going on here. Get ready to pump *down* some people who need help instead of pumping up, okay?"

Babajide and Babatunde nodded.

Paul or Jabari or both had obviously briefed the two musclemen on what was needed from them, because as Bolan moved back to the edge of the roof, they began fashioning a large loop at one end of the rope. Standing at the hole, near the center of the roof, they were below the angle of fire the Bokos had from the ground. With one of the twins tying a slip knot, the other allowing him to stretch it across his broad back, they soon had a crude but workable lowering cable that might not live up to US government specifications for a static line, but looked as if it would serve the purpose for which it was intended.

Bolan moved back to the rim and caught another Boko—this man firing one of the captured M16s—in the head with another semiauto snipe. From almost directly below him, the Executioner heard new fire from AK-47s. These rounds came from inside the alley entrance of the building, on the ground floor.

He took a risk, rising higher than he had even when firing and leaning out over the retaining wall. Beneath him, he saw the barrels of two rifles.

Good. Paul and Jabari had finally gotten the converts out of the congregation room, divided them into two groups—the able and disabled and were now joining him in battle. Which meant that as soon as the gunfire died down they could start sending people out, and he could direct the muscle twins to begin lowering others over the side.

The Executioner dropped back behind cover. The return fire had lessened significantly, and no rounds had been fired when he'd leaned over the edge to double-check on Paul and Jabari. That could mean one of two things: he had taken out all the Bokos at the rear of the building, or those who were left had figured out that the converts were about to evacuate, and were waiting for easier targets.

The Executioner saw a solitary man belly-crawling behind the stacked boxes of nails, trying to get into a better position to fire down the walkway. Evidently, at least a few of the Bokos had also figured out that some of the converts would be lowered over that side. Bolan wasn't surprised. After all, the workmen's ladder still leaned there, as if signaling the terrorists to keep watch in that direction.

The man crawled on. By the time Bolan had swung the M16 that way, only his legs were visible. So the Executioner switched back to 3-round-burst mode and sent a trio of rounds into his left calf. The gunner screamed and sat up, taking his left hand off the fore end of his Russian rifle and reaching for his injured leg.

His fingers never quite made it there.

Sitting up had exposed his head.

Bolan shot it off.

Then, so quickly it sounded almost artificial, the gunfire died down and an unnerving silence fell over the alley.

The Executioner waited. Whether the Bokos behind the bakery were all dead, or some were ready to pounce on the innocent converts who were getting ready to escape, he didn't know.

But either way, he knew he was about to find out.

Staying low behind what was left of the retaining wall, Bolan flipped the M16's selector switch to semiauto and pulled the trigger. The 5.56 mm round sailed off harmlessly into the sky. He counted in his head, *one thousand and one*, then pulled the trigger again.

The Executioner repeated this three more times. Then his eyes rose over the retaining wall in time to see people from the congregation room emerge from the back exit of the bakery building and take off running in all directions.

BISHOP JOSHUA ADEWALE knew the moment he opened his eyes that he was on a hard wooden floor. But it took a few seconds to remember where that floor was.

Then, as his eyelids fluttered up and down and he tried to sit up, it all came back to him in a rush. The bomb, the machetes, his strangely transfixed staggering away from the malicious carnage at the chapel. The men's shirt and pants on the clothesline, the woman and then...

That was it. His memory stopped there.

The bishop from New York City sat up and discovered that pillows had been placed beneath his head, back and legs. He looked around the room and saw the woman—for a moment he had wondered if he'd dreamed her—with her back to him. She was doing something at the small gas stove in the one-room shack, and the smell of cooking food—familiar food he had eaten as a child here in Nigeria—filled his olfactory glands. Even after all these years he recognized it immediately. *Moin moin.* A form of bean cake. And palm-wine bread that had been baked in the oven.

At the same time that they made his stomach growl they reminded him of his childhood in a tiny house not so different than this one.

"You are making me hungry," Bishop Joshua Adewale said, and his words caused the woman to jump where she stood. A large wooden spoon fell from her hand and clattered to the floor as she whirled to look at him. Then her horrified face suddenly smiled. "I did not know you were awake," she said.

The bishop laughed. "I barely know it myself," he said. "Do you have a name?"

The woman now joined him in soft laughter. "Most people do," she said.

Bishop Adewale continued playing the game with her. It was the first thing that had even come close to adding a little joy to his life since the bombing. "Am I allowed to know it?" he asked.

"My full name is Olayinka," said the woman. "But my friends shorten it to Inka."

Adewale still sat on the floor. He looked up at the woman. Her curly black hair was tied in place with a blue bandanna and she wore a simple dress of cheap cotton. "Well," he said. "You have certainly been a friend to me. May I be a friend to you and call you Inka myself?"

"Of course." She bent over and lifted the wooden spoon off the floor, then wiped it off with a rag and set it on the counter.

Bishop Joshua Adewale was suddenly filled with a rush of sympathy for this woman and all the impoverished souls in Nigeria. He had forgotten so much about his home country, especially what difficult lives so many of its people lived. Certainly, there were wealthy people in Nigeria, but there were even more who lived like this woman.

And, as always, it seemed to be the little things that spoke loudest about people's living conditions. At home in New York, if a wooden spoon had fallen to his kitchen floor, the bishop would have dropped it into his dishwasher without even thinking about it. Here, this woman had to either wipe it as clean as possible or dip it into some vessel of water she'd carried up from the nearest creek or spring. And if she did that, she risked contaminating that water for drinking or other purposes.

The bishop looked down, shaking his head sadly, and noted that the cut on his arm now bore a white bandage of tape and gauze. Beneath the dressing, the wound that had been caused by the bomb still stung slightly, which meant the woman had cleaned it with some type of antiseptic. Along the edge, a tiny amount of a brownish-purple substance roughly the consistency of petroleum jelly had leaked from behind the tape. Joshua Adewale remembered that almost as well as he remembered the smell of cooking *moin moin*. It was a natural antibiotic mixed from a variety of roots, made and used by poor people all over southern Africa.

Adewale looked down past his knee to the pant leg that had been shredded by the rotten wood when his foot had crushed down through the step to the porch. It, too, had been dressed. And now that he noticed it, he also took note of another light stinging, on his calf beneath the bandage.

Inka saw him examining his bandages and said, "The cut on your arm is deep and should be stitched at the first opportunity. But it should hold for now." Her eyes moved to the torn pants covering his lower leg beneath the long cassock. "Your leg wound is nothing," she went on. "Merely a scrape. It should not slow you down."

"I thank you," the bishop said in his warmest voice.

The woman leaned back against the counter next to the stove. "I tried to get you up onto the bed." Her eyes flickered to the corner of the room where a small twin bed stood. "But I could not lift you and did not want to awaken you." She pointed toward the floor next to him. "So I had to settle for rolling you to the side and sliding as many pillows as I could beneath your body."

Bishop Adewale felt as if he'd been beaten all over with a baseball bat. "It was the finest bed I have ever slept in." He stopped, cleared his throat, then said, "You have told me who you are. But you have not asked me who I—"

"I *know* who you are," Inka said. She pointed toward an ancient black-and-white television with rabbit ear antennas sticking up from the top. "Everyone in Nigeria knows who you are." She paused and lowered her voice to a whisper. "And some—like the murderers and assassins from Boko Haram—are trying to find out *where* you are. The bombing and machete slaughter at the seminary chapel has been the primary news story since it happened."

Adewale nodded silently as Inka turned back to the stove, scooped *moin moin* into a plain brown bowl and pulled a metal spoon from a drawer. "Surely, you are hungry," she said, turning back to the bishop and handing him the bowl. She pointed at the small metal table and chairs against the wall.

The bishop from New York took the bowl and said another grateful thank-you. Then, rising from the floor, he took a seat at the table, folded his hands in front of him, and closed his eyes tightly. "Thank you, dear Lord," he prayed out loud. "For this food that I am about to eat, and for this woman who has given it to me, as well as aid and shelter. May your love and protection be with her. Amen."

He opened his eyes and scooped a spoonful of the bean cake into his mouth. He looked up at the woman, who was anxiously awaiting his verdict. "Delicious," Adewale said. "Exactly like my mother used to make."

Inka literally beamed. "There is no better compliment," she said. "Thank you."

The bishop went on eating, but was careful not to speak with his mouth full. This woman deserved the same respect he would give the hosts of the many fashionable New York gatherings to which he was invited. "I seem to remember a little girl," he said, after swallowing a well-chewed bite. "Was I dreaming?"

"It was no dream," Inka said. "My daughter, Dayo, answered the door when you knocked."

The bishop swallowed again. "She has gone?" he asked.

Inka nodded. "When I realized who you were and that you would need time to recuperate, I took her down the street to my sister's house."

Adewale set his spoon down and stared at the woman. "I am putting you in danger, then," he said.

"Life is full of danger," Inka replied. "It is inescapable." The bishop followed her eyes as they moved from him to the wall beside the table. Hooked over a nail to the rough wooden board was a plaster crucifix. Then her eyes returned to his. "Do not worry," she said. "I do not believe any of the neighbors saw you come in. If they had, someone would have already come to my door to find out what was going on." A throaty laugh escaped her. "We are like poor people all over the world," she continued. "We must create our own entertainment because we cannot afford other forms of amusement. So we give the old saying that 'gossip is cheap' a whole new meaning."

The bishop couldn't help laughing with her.

"I would offer to clean your cassock as best I can," Inka said, when they had stopped laughing. "But right before you passed out you said something about changing clothes." She pointed toward the bed. Adewale turned that way and saw that a khaki work shirt and matching pants had been brought in off the clothesline and were now folded neatly on the bed.

"Yes," he said, as he finished the final bite of *moin moin*. "I will buy them from—"

"You will do no such thing," Inka said sternly. "You are a man of God. Consider them a donation from my husband."

"Are you sure he will not mind?" the bishop asked.

"I am sure," Inka said. "He has no need for them

anymore. He is already with the Lord." The smile was gone from her face now, and Adewale could see it had been replaced by some painful memory. It didn't take long to learn what memory that was. "He was murdered by Boko Haram just as they tried to murder you. The only difference was that he was shot. The terrorists invaded a deacon's meeting at our church and mowed down the men of God with machine guns."

"I am sorry," said Bishop Adewale sincerely. But the words came out sounding hollow and inefficient compared to the atrocious mass murder.

Inka shook her head as tears formed in her eyes. "It is the same all over Nigeria," she said. "His crime was loving God. But Jesus said we would be persecuted for our belief and that we must take up our crosses and follow Him anyway."

Bishop Adewale let his eyes fall to the empty bowl on the table in front of him. He nodded, then he looked back up and said, "You will excuse me for asking, because it is none of my business, but if your husband has passed on, why do you wash his clothes?"

A sad smile played at the corners of Inka's lips. "I do not know," she said. "He has been gone over a year now, but I still feel compelled to wash them. I suppose it somehow comforts me, and reminds me I will see him again when the Lord wills it."

Bishop Adewale nodded. "He works in mysterious ways," he said.

"Yes, He does," Inka said. She had leaned back against the counter next to the stove during their conversation, but now suddenly shoved herself away from it with both hands. "The clothes, as you can see, are on the bed. I am sorry we have no other room in which you may change, but I will avert my eyes until you tell me to turn back around."

The bishop stood up and reached the bed in two steps, which reminded him of just how small the house really was. He took a quick glance at Inka, who stood with her back to him only a few yards away on the other side of the room. Then he slid out of the filthy, dust-covered cassock and into the khaki pants. His arms slipped into the shirt, and he buttoned it up his chest before saying, "I am dressed again."

Inka turned and new tears welled to her eyes. "I thought so," she said.

Adewale furrowed his eyebrows. "Thought what?" he asked.

"You are the same size as my husband. The clothes fit you perfectly."

The bishop could see that his presence,especially in her husband's clothing, was bringing new pain to the woman who had taken him in. "I must go," he said simply.

"No. You are safer here than on the streets. As I said, no one saw you come in here. If they had they would have—"

"We cannot be sure of that," the bishop interrupted. "Do you know what Boko Haram will do to you if they learn you have helped me?"

"Yes," Inka replied. "But they cannot do anything to me that God cannot get me through. Even if they kill me, I will be reunited with my husband."

"But what of your daughter?" Adewale asked.

Inka's face changed as if she had not considered that aspect yet. "There is that," she said, nodding as she contemplated the problem. "But still, I cannot turn you away. If I die, my sister will raise Dayo."

Footsteps suddenly sounded outside, approaching the house, then climbing the rickety wooden steps that led to the front porch. Adewale turned that way and stared at the ragged blanket covering the glass in the top half of the door.

Inka held a finger to her lips to indicate that they should stop speaking. "Wait here," she whispered, and tiptoed toward the door. A moment later, she moved the blanket so minutely that Adewale could see no difference in it. But after glancing out for a second, she walked softly back to the bishop and said, "I do not know who it is. He is dressed like an American or a European. In a gray suit." She paused a moment. "What I am trying to say is not only do I not know him, but he looks totally out of place."

Adewale shook his head. "I cannot imagine who that might be," he said. "If America sent anyone to rescue me, they would go out of their way to blend in rather than stand out like that."

Inka drew in a deep breath. "I have heard rumors

on the street of a man," she said softly. "A man who is not really part of Boko Haram but who works between them and al Qaeda. They say he is like a chameleon. He can change his appearance and pass for any race he wishes."

The bishop reached up and put both hands on her shoulders. "I am grateful for your help," he said. "I suspect I would be dead if God had not led me to this house." He stared deeply into her eyes. "But I cannot allow you to risk yourself further. I will leave through your back door."

"I do not have a back door."

Had the tension in the little house not been so great, Adewale would have laughed out loud. As it was, he settled for a smile. "Then I will leave by your back window," he said, and turned around.

"But where will you go?" Inka asked.

The bishop stopped. A second later, he said, "I have no idea. I feel that God spared me for some reason. I believe he led me to your door, and that he has some plan, some deed he wants me to do here in Nigeria. But I do not know what it is."

The woman looked nervously to the door, then back up into the bishop's eyes. "Go to the next block, turn left and keep going. A half-mile or so later you will come upon a small church. Father Adisa is the priest. My pastor. He will hide you."

Adewale threw his arms around the woman and hugged her before he even realized what he was doing. "May God protect you," he said.

"And may He protect you as well," Inka replied.

The grimy glass in the wall next to the stove lifted easily, without the noise Adewale had worried might accompany the window's opening. With every muscle in his body still aching, he climbed up onto the counter. He was inexperienced in clandestine actions of any sort, and was already halfway out the window before it dawned on him that the man at the front might have sent an accomplice around the miniature house to cover the back.

He had seen that done a thousand times by police on American television.

But luck, or probably God, Adewale realized, was with him as he dropped to the ground on his feet. The backyard was empty. Soon he was cutting across the ragged grass into the property on the next block and passing between two more houses that would have been bulldozed down long ago had they been in New York.

Where he was going from here, however, Bishop Joshua Adewale had no idea.

INKA WATCHED the man in her late husband's clothes walk swiftly between the houses of her neighbors, then wiped another tear from her eye. Not only was this bishop on the run from Boko Haram the same size as Lanre, he bore a vague facial resemblance to him. At least Inka thought so. But she had been so lonely since Lan's death she knew the resemblance might only be in her mind. As the bishop disappeared down the next block, she turned back.

Grief caused the mind to play tricks on a person, she knew, and it was likely that—

Another, louder knock came from the front door and pulled her back from thoughts of her husband to the present. Good. The knock meant the man in the gray suit was still there, which in turn meant the bishop had escaped.

But what should she do now?

Inka stared at the blanket covering the window. She knew the man on the other side of the door might well have heard sounds through the thin walls of her tiny house. Had he heard their voices? She couldn't know for sure, but she thought they had stopped speaking as he climbed the steps, and she doubted their words would have carried that far.

On the other hand, Inka knew she was not in the best shape to make judgment calls at the moment. In Lan's clothes, the bishop—whether he actually looked like him or not—had reminded her of her late husband and intensified the grief she already lived with daily. And while she didn't know exactly who it was at her door, she knew it had to be connected to the bishop somehow.

Men wearing suits did not visit this section of Ibadan for fun. And for both him and the bishop to show up one after the other was too much of a coincidence to *be* a coincidence.

So along with the grief, anxiety flowed through Inka's veins and threatened to overcome her.

Quickly, she reached to her side and turned the knob on the television set. A silver-speckled, shadowy, almost ghostly picture appeared on the screen, and both men's and women's voices could be heard. She hurriedly adjusted the antenna, but the picture didn't improve. Still, the voices came through and if the man at the door had heard the bishop and her talking, perhaps he would believe the conversation had come from the TV.

Another knock. Louder still, this time, and, somehow conveying impatience.

Inka considered not answering the door at all. But if the man *had* heard noises inside, that would only heighten his suspicion. It would be best to open the door and find out who he was and what he wanted. If her own suspicion was correct and the man in the gray suit was looking for the bishop to kill him, she could pretend not to know anything about it.

Inka's eyes flickered up to the crucifix on the wall. Her right hand rose and she crossed herself as the priest at her church had taught both her and Lan to do when they prayed. She would probably have to lie to the man on the porch. And she knew that to lie was to sin. But common sense told her that lying to save the life of an honest servant of God would not offend the Lord.

The woman in the miniature, one-room house just wondered how convincing she could be. Since giving her life over to Christ, she had done her best to always tell the truth, and on the rare occasions when she had slipped up and voiced falsehoods, she had done so in such a bumbling way that she had tripped herself up.

It had made Lan laugh, she remembered. But what she faced now was no laughing matter.

Quickly, Inka turned toward the stove and turned the heat up under the pan with the *moin moin*. The gas flame jumped, then simmered down, and she knew the reheating would make the odor of bean cake drifting through the house even stronger than before. Grabbing the wooden spoon she had dropped earlier, she jammed it into the pan in order to get some of the *moin moin* on it, then hurried toward the door.

This time when she reached the blanket she pulled the corner up and made sure both she and the spoon were seen. Inka and the stranger in the gray suit stared at each other for a moment. Then the woman smiled as widely as her face would allow. She dropped the blanket, twisted the doorknob and swung the door wide open to show she had nothing to hide.

"How may I help you?" Inka asked.

The man didn't answer. He was busy looking over her shoulder, past her into the small one-room house. He kept his eyes there while he finally said, "Have you had any unexpected visitors today?"

"Of course not," Inka replied. She forced a small

laugh. "I am a poor widow. Who would want to come visit me?" She looked down at the spoon in her hand. "Are you with the police?" Although she knew he couldn't be, it seemed like a normal question under the circumstances.

The man didn't answer. He just continued to stare past her.

Behind her, Inka could hear the television as whatever program was on continued. She raised the spoon slightly. She didn't like the look on the man's face.

Could he tell she was lying? Why did he keep staring into the house? The bishop from New York was long gone from the tiny structure.

The aroma of *moin moin* filled the house now, and Inka knew the man in the gray suit would be able to smell it, too. Perhaps if she invited him in to eat, it would be taken as a sign that she had nothing to hide. He would almost certainly decline—men who could afford to dress like him often confused poverty with dirtiness. But the invitation itself would show good faith on her part.

The door was already wide open, but now Inka stepped back to clear a path into the house. "Please," she said. "I have just heated some food." Her words sounded completely innocent—at least to her. She forced the smile back onto her face and said, "Won't you join me? It is lonely, eating alone."

She was surprised when the man said, "Thank you, I believe I will," and stepped past her. Her heart seemed to skip a beat. But then she told herself that she had to have been convincing or the man would not have been so polite.

Particularly if this was the mysterious al Qaeda–Boko Haram man about whom she had heard.

Inka closed the door and turned back around. "If you will have a seat I will—"

She stopped in midsentence. The man in the gray suit was standing in the middle of the room, looking down at the bed in the corner against the wall.

And on top of the bed was a filthy bishop's cassock.

CHAPTER NINE

There appeared to be several Boko Haram snipers left as the converts ran out the back door into the alley. One, a man clothed in a white robe, rose with a Heckler & Koch 93 in his hands.

Before he could fire the German rifle, however, Bolan had sent a lone round blasting through his forehead. Only a second or so behind him, the Executioner heard Paul and Jabari open up with their cover fire below.

The converts raced on. Some were fast, others slow. Regardless of their speed, all had rounds fired at them as they ran. But those bullets went wild, missing even the most snail-like men and women.

Within seconds the converts were disappearing around corners of buildings and down the long alley in both directions. They had thinned out and were smaller, isolated, long-range targets. By now another Boko had risen from behind a stack of plywood. In his hands was a pump-action shotgun, which was the wrong weapon for long shots. He fired, then pumped the slide, fired again and pumped again. But his multiple missiles—by the heavy roar Bolan heard he guessed them to be buckshot—fell short of their targets. And by the time the man had realized the problem, dropped the shotgun and pulled an AK-47 up and over the plywood, Bolan had sent a double-tap of 5.56 mm rounds into the gunner's chest. Another 3-round burst from the Executioner's M16 took off three-quarters of the man's head. He slithered out of sight behind the plywood.

Bolan could feel the heat as rounds zipped past him. One of them tore through the shoulder of his robe, searing across his skin like a flat stone skipping across the water. But his visible presence had the desired effect on the Bokos, dividing their attention and giving the running converts the extra seconds they needed.

Another 7.62 mm round whizzed over Bolan's head, and he felt the hot lead twist through his hair. For a second, the skin beneath it burned as if he'd been scalped. Then the pain disappeared from his thoughts as he spied the man who'd fired the round, an older Boko with a gray-and-black beard circling his face. The man wore a shirt made of *adire*, a cloth with various patterns and designs. The Executioner swung his M16 that way and his own shot proved more true. It drilled through the man's face, and he fell to the ground in a pool of blood.

Beneath his feet, Bolan felt the vibration of more full-auto cover fire from Paul and Jabari.

By now, the converts who had not darted around

corners were too far away for any gunmen except the most expert snipers with the best rifles and scopes. And so far Bolan hadn't come across any of either. Three more times, however, he watched Boko Haram terrorists rise from cover and throw reckless and desperate shots down the alley. And three more times he downed the men with the M16.

Suddenly, the war at the back of the bakery building was over.

But the danger to the physically challenged people trying to get down off the roof remained.

Bolan stood up in an effort to draw the fire of any other terrorists who might still be in hiding. When none came, he tore away from the edge of the roof, sprinted back to the hole and looked down.

The muscle twins, Babajide and Babatunde, had placed a rickety table from one of the storage rooms directly below. A teenage girl who couldn't have weighed more than a hundred pounds now stood on it. But even her light weight made the worn-out piece of furniture jiggle as she waited to be hauled on up to the roof.

The Executioner couldn't help but wonder just how long the table would last before the legs broke. Not long, probably. But until the nails were bent beyond hope or the wood snapped, he could think of no better way to get the physically challenged Christians up onto the roof in preparation to lower them to safety.

Bolan took a second to reconsider the situation.

They still had the option of going out the back. He thought he had neutralized the threat out there, but the operative word was *thought*. There was no way to be sure. There could still be unseen gunmen hidden at the rear of the building, and if these poor newly converted Christians went hobbling out on crutches or rolled out in wheelchairs, they'd be easier to take down than a silhouette target at five yards.

No, the Executioner thought, shaking his head. He couldn't take the chance. He needed to stick to the original plan.

Bolan turned his attention back to the twins. Even though they were identical, he knew that if he had time later he'd learn to tell them apart. And he could learn their names, too. But now was hardly the moment to worry about such things. So in his mind he simply thought of them by the color of their sweatpants, "Red" and "Blue."

Blue had rigged a harness out of the rope that could encircle the waist and come up under the arms. Bolan wanted to make sure they got off on the right foot, so he waited until Blue had dropped the harness down and one of the men below had slipped the girl into it. Then the soldier watched both twins haul the girl up as easily as a fisherman who'd hooked a tiny two-ounce perch.

The girl almost flew up onto the roof, which made it obvious to Bolan that he didn't need both bodybuilders hauling the rest of the people up. One of them could be put to better use lowering them to the walkway.

Until she finally reached the roof, the Executioner had wondered why this girl had been placed with the disabled. But now, as she came out of the darkness and into the light, he saw the stump at the end of her right leg. A moment after she had slipped out of the harness, an unseen hand stuck a crutch up through the hole. Red grabbed it, then handed it to the girl.

Bolan grabbed the red twin's arm to get his attention. "Gather them all over there by the ladder," he said, pointing toward the side of the building where the now-dead workmen had ascended. "Most can be lowered, but some we may have to carry down the ladder on our backs. In any case, I want to get them all together first so we can get them down as quickly as possible once we start." He looked the man directly in the eyes. "There's always a chance that one or more Bokos are still hidden out there, waiting."

Red nodded in understanding. The girl had heard, too. She smiled up at the Executioner, then leaned on her crutch and began limping toward the ladder on her own. Red hurried over and took her arm, helping her along.

Bolan dropped to all fours on the roof and stuck his head down into the hole. "Where's Paul?" he asked.

In the background, he could hear running footsteps. A moment later, a hacking and wheezing figure stopped directly underneath. "I'm here," Paul said, as his face emerged out of the semidarkness.

"You got all of the able-bodied people out the rear exit?" Bolan asked.

He nodded. "I think so."

Bolan frowned. "What does *think so* mean?" he asked.

"It means it didn't seem like as many people took off as we'd brought to the back entrance," he said. "But we were busy firing, so I probably just misjudged." He drew in a deep breath, which made his chest visibly expand, then contract as he let it out.

The Executioner felt his face tighten. The mind could play tricks on men when they were in life-or-death situations. Had all the Christians Paul and Jabari had led to the back left the building? Or had some become too frightened to run out, and found places to cower out of sight of their leaders?

"We could hear you firing above us," Paul said. "Could you see how many of them made it away alive?"

"All of them," the Executioner said. "Not even a scratch on one."

"Praise the Lord," Paul said.

"They took off in every possible direction," Bolan said. "I could hear yours and Jabari's cover fire below mine." As he spoke, he watched Blue haul a legless man up and set him on the roof. A second later, two men pushed a folded wheelchair past the Executioner's face and the twin took it.

Bolan turned his attention to Paul, at the bottom of the hole. "Something you said a little while ago bothers me," he told him. "That it didn't seem like all the people you led to the back actually ran out of the building. Send someone back to check all the rooms and hallways where some of your people might have hidden. They could have frozen up at the last second and been too scared to run. If that happened, they'd have found hiding places. But those places will also be found by the Bokos moving through the building. As soon as that happens, they'll be dead."

Paul's face disappeared for a few seconds, and Bolan could hear his muffled voice giving the order to someone unseen below. While he waited, the Executioner's thoughts drifted to Layla Galab, and he realized she had not been among the people escaping through the back exit.

When Paul's face appeared in the hole again, Bolan said, "Where's Layla?"

Paul frowned, silently telling the Executioner that he'd lost track of the woman during all the excitement.

"I don't know. Her mother's been ill and I've overheard her checking in with her several times. But the last time I actually saw her she was counseling the people about to run out the back." He paused and blew air between his clenched teeth. Then he said, "You did not see her leave with them?"

"No," Bolan said. "She's got to still be down there somewhere."

Paul disappeared again and Bolan heard his muffled voice once more as he gave the new order.

When he looked up next, the Executioner said, "Now, you and Jabari. Go out into the walkway and get ready to help when we lower these people. Take them around to the front of the building and off the street into stores or something. I don't think there are many Bokos left, if any, and I don't think they'll go around to the front now that the cops are coming, anyway."

Bolan paused a second and listened to the sirens. They were wailing so loudly now that he had to raise his voice. "Do you have any idea how to handle your former brothers, Jabari?" he shouted.

"Yes," said the former Nigerian sergeant. "Stay away from them. There is no way to know which ones are on the side of Boko Haram."

"And if we *can't* avoid them?" Bolan asked.

Jabari shrugged. "I do not know all of the officers," he said. "Of those I do know, there are a few I feel certain would stand with us. And a few I strongly suspect support the terrorists." He shook his head vigorously. "The problem is I can't be certain."

"Well, that's a problem, all right," the Executioner said. "Okay, this isn't a foolproof plan. But this gunfight has dragged on and on, and by now the cops won't be the only ones on their way here. There may be a whole battalion or more of Bokos coming to start things up again." He paused and helped haul up an elderly lady whose snow-white hair contrasted sharply with her wrinkled brown skin. But she smiled at the soldier as she went past him.

Her wheelchair, folded like the other one, came next.

The Executioner hurried back to the hole. Below, he saw a half-dozen able-bodied Christians gathered. All the men gripped either AK-47s or M16s.

"Come on up here, gentlemen," Bolan said. "A lot of these people are going to need help getting down the walkway once we get them over the side."

The men helped one another up, then started scrambling down the ladder.

The soldier hurried back to where Red and Blue were already lowering the invalids over the side of the building. Looking down, he saw Paul with his hands raised in the air, ready to take the young girl with the amputated leg as soon as she reached him.

Paul grabbed her around the waist, then set her gently on the ground and removed the harness. He let the rope slide out of his hand, and Red pulled it back up and began slipping it around the man with no legs as Blue knelt and lowered the girl's crutch to Jabari, at Paul's side.

Blue turned to the Executioner. "I heard you asking about Layla," he said. "I saw her about a half hour ago. She was calling her office and telling her secretary to contact the police so they could come help us."

Bolan closed his eyes and clamped his jaws shut in a quick moment of frustration. The Nigerian police had already been on their way—the sirens proved that. But Layla's call might have added fuel to their fire. And again, the Executioner was reminded of what a problem it was going to be dealing with them. As Jabari had said, there would be no way of telling which officers were for them and which were against. Layla, being the innocent and kindhearted soul she was, would never have thought of that.

But what it boiled down to was that a person was just as dead if he or she got shot by some smiling individual believed to be a friend as by an enemy who was foaming at the mouth with hatred.

Actually, Bolan thought, there was no sense in blaming Layla or anyone but the Boko Haram terrorists themselves. The situation, as always, was what it was, and complaining or worrying about it was a waste of time. He would have to deal with things as they came.

As he'd been speaking to the man wearing the Yoruba blue tunic, Red had continued lowering the converts who couldn't walk, let alone run. Blue had been making his way up and down the ladder with those capable of clinging to his back riding the rungs with him.

Wheelchairs, crutches and the oxygen tank on rollers had been lowered as well. More than a dozen maimed people bespoke the utter cruelty of Boko Haram. The last to appear was a man in his mid-twenties.

He had lost both arms.

Bolan looked at his shirtsleeves flapping uselessly in the light breeze, and wondered briefly if it had been another Boko bomb that had taken the man's limbs. Not likely. An explosion would not have skipped over the chest and back in between. This man would go through the rest of his life without hands or arms due to Boko Haram machetes.

More Christians were lowered in the harness by Blue. His twin continued to help others down the ladder on his back, then climb back up for the next disabled person. Bolan took up position at the edge of the roof where he could see down into the walkway as well as back behind the building. He, as well as his rifle, were ready in case any more hidden Bokos suddenly showed themselves and tried to find an angle from which they could fire at the helpless people being assisted in their escape.

After two minutes with no more rounds coming from the rear, the Executioner left his post and started toward where the Christians were being helped down to the ground. While he had been concentrating on countersniping since pulling an obese man up onto the roof, he had been mulling over the problem of getting him down over the side. It had been one thing to get him through the hole with six men pushing up and the rest pulling. If they lost their balance, he would fall only a few feet. But if they dropped him now, the fall could kill him.

As he approached the side of the building above the walkway, Bolan took a good look at the man.

He sat in the midst of the disabled Christians, waiting to go down the ladder or be lowered by rope. He was wrapped in two robes, one worn in the regular fashion, the other on backward. The reason was obvious—the man was so morbidly obese that neither robe could be closed. The belts were too short to encircle his girth, and were tied to each other at his sides.

The man looked sad, and the Executioner felt a quick wave of sympathy pass through him. People didn't get that big just by overeating. This man had a glandular problem or some other disease. Yet while most people would treat someone with such physical problems with respect, this man's face reflected a lifetime of ridicule.

Red had left the ladder and got to the group a second ahead of the Executioner. "We might as well get this man down now," he said, "before we have used up too much of our strength."

Bolan ground to a halt. "Exactly," he said.

Without further words, Red grabbed one of the huge man's arms, getting ready to try to lift him over his shoulder in a fireman's carry. Blue stopped him by grabbing his brother's massive biceps and triceps. "I had better take him," he said.

Red shook his head. "No, my brother," he said. "I am the stronger of the two of us."

Blue's voice rose slightly and a tinge of anger crept into it. "Only last night I deadlifted thirty pounds more than you were able to."

"Yes," Red said, "but this man must go down on one of our backs. It will take leg strength beyond what you are capable of. Must I remind you that I squatted close to fifty pounds more than you did?"

"But my bench press was—"

"Pectoral strength will not enter into this," Red interrupted. "The man's weight will fall on the—"

Bolan remembered that he'd been told how competitive these twins were, but this was no time for them to demonstrate it. "That's enough," he said. "Grow up, both of you. I already told you this wasn't Mr. Olympia and it's not the World Powerlifting Championship, either. It isn't important who gets him down or how it gets done. All that matter is that we do it and save the man's life. Now, give me that rope."

As Red began hauling the harness up the side of the building again, Bolan looked around, then turned to Paul. "You find anything of interest on any of the bodies you checked?"

"Yes," he said. He reached into his pocket and pulled out one of the papers he'd taken off the men. "It is an address. They all had it on them. I think it must either be their headquarters or the place they plan to attack next."

"They wouldn't need the address to their headquarters," the Executioner mused. "They'd know it. It has to be their next assault site. Put it back in your pocket. We'll need it later."

Red handed him the rope and the Executioner

began wrapping it around the huge man sitting next to the edge. Below, he could see that all the converts with their various disabilities were being helped—and helping each other—out of the walkway toward the street in front of the building.

Bolan glanced at Paul. "Your people all know how to get to their secondary safe houses, right?"

He nodded.

"Good," Bolan replied. "Now…" He reached down and grabbed the obese man under one arm. "You two," he told the twins. "Help me get him up."

Red and Blue grabbed the man and lifted him to his feet.

"There's no way either of you is going to be able to carry this guy down the ladder on your back," Bolan said. "We're going to have to lower him. And it's probably going to take all of us."

Paul and Jabari joined Bolan and the twins. The two reached down and wrapped their arms around the gigantic man's knees.

The Executioner saw a tear in the overweight man's eye as they lifted him into the air.

"You okay?" Bolan asked.

"I am okay," he answered. "I'm just embarrassed. I am ashamed of myself."

"Don't be," the soldier said. "It doesn't help anything. You've got a weight problem that goes way beyond just eating too much." He looked down at the man's eyes and they truly did appear to be windows to his soul. And this man's soul *hurt*. "We've all got some problem we have to live with. Yours is just more obvious than most."

"Those are kind words," he said, but the tears remained in his eyes.

"Just the truth," Bolan said. "Once you're on the ground, can you walk?"

"Yes. Not fast and not far. But I can get out of this passage below and to the street." He closed his eyes for a moment and his eyelids shone wetly in the sun. "These are tears of frustration because I cannot fight the enemies of the Savior as you and your men are doing."

"You'll find a way to contribute," the Executioner told him. "For now, let's just get you out of here alive." He tightened his grip on the man's arm. "On three," he told the others. "One, two…three." All five men lifted and got the humongous man over the side of the wall. Then, one by one, but quickly, they let go of him and grabbed the rope.

The lowering process was slow and clumsy with so many hands trying to find a place on the rope. Grunts and groans replaced speech, and at one point, they all started to lose their grip, and it looked as if the obese man would fall. But Bolan caught the rope before it could slide completely out of their hands, and held on while the others grabbed the makeshift cradle again. Finally, they got the man down to where the two below could help lower him the rest of the way.

No longer needed in the rescue process, the Executioner hurried back to the hole in the roof. When he looked down, he saw only two men who had been helping the disabled get to the top. He had not paid much attention to them so far, but now saw that both looked physically fit and carried rifles. "You the last two down there?" he asked.

Both men nodded.

"Then come on up here and help us get the rest of the people down to the ground."

The two didn't bother with the rope. One reached up and Blue grabbed his hands, jerking him up through the hole. As he dropped the man on his feet, Bolan did the same with the other one.

The soldier didn't know these men, but one looked to be in his midfifties and had a white beard and hair. Both had been allowed to grow wild, and looked like the fake beard and wig from a Santa Claus costume. The other man was younger and had the three-day growth of black stubble on his face that seemed to be fashionable among young men the world over these days.

Both men gripped the AK-47s that had hung from slings over their backs as they were hauled up to the roof. Bolan looked from one man to the other. "Which one of you is the better shot?" he asked.

Without hesitation the young man said, "He is."

Bolan was about to offer the older one his M16 when the man spoke. "My AK-47 has been worked over. Target barrel. Bench rest trigger." He looked at the Executioner's M16. "It will probably outshoot your American weapon. It is certainly more accurate than my son's."

Only then did Bolan suddenly see the resemblance between the two men. The white beard covered the lower half of the father's face, but his eyes looked like a weathered version of his son's.

"Then you stay on top while these guys carry people down," Bolan said, hooking a thumb over his shoulder at Red and Blue.

Swinging his gaze to the son, he said, "You go down the ladder first. Take care of any threats you can see from ground level. They're likely to be closer, and pinpoint accuracy won't be as vital."

Both men nodded, and then the younger one slung his Kalashnikov over his shoulder and scampered down the ladder. He drew no fire, which might or might not have been a good sign, the Executioner knew. It might mean there were no men hiding at an angle that provided a shot into the walkway between the buildings.

On the other hand, it might mean the area around the building was still packed with terrorists who had figured out what was going on and were waiting for more targets before giving themselves away.

If that was the case, things were going to get tight.

The twins, and the disabled people who would still have to be lowered with the rope or carried down the ladder, would be like ducks in a shooting gallery, exposed and defenseless. Their only protection would be Bolan and the father-son rifle team, who would have to pick off the hidden shooters before they could fire their weapons into the walkway.

He turned to the twins. Their bare chests, backs and arms glistened with sweat now, and looked like topographical maps with veins and arteries appearing to be blue rivers with creeks leading into them. The sharply defined muscles looked like mountains and valleys. "Okay, guys," he said. "Let's put all that time in the gym to good use. Start carrying the rest of these people down the ladder."

And they began to do just that.

DHUL AGBEDE KNEW he was different from most men. He knew he lacked certain emotions, such as sympathy and certainly empathy. And he wasn't at all sure what love was. Lust, yes. He knew lust, and he took particular delight in reveling in that emotion. On the other hand, he knew he had a vast capacity to hate, and sometimes he found himself suddenly angry without having the slightest idea what had brought on that anger.

He had felt fear, but only on a few occasions. And he had not felt fear during the long-running gun battle in the bakery building. A little amazement, yes. He had never seen a man who could fight like this American. The soldier had led the attacks up and down the halls, defending the Christians Agbede and his men had come to kill. Was the man just lucky? Maybe. It didn't seem to him that anyone could have evaded so many bullets and killed so many of his enemies without having luck, or *something*, on his side. So what was that something if it wasn't luck? Agbede didn't know, but he knew *he* didn't have it.

He was a terrific combatant himself. He knew that and had proved it to himself and others over and over throughout his life. But he didn't have whatever it was the American had working for him. And somehow he knew he never would.

What Dhul Agbede *did* have, however, was a good deal of common sense. And as he walked up the sidewalk to Fazel Hayat's front door, he remembered his last sight of this man who had entered Nigeria under the guise of being a photojournalist named Matt Cooper. Cooper—although that was surely not his real name—had still been on the roof of the bakery building when Agbede had fled the scene. After having escaped the American's gunfire inside the building, Agbede had realized that the battle was not going his way and decided that caution was, indeed, the better part of valor, as Westerners said.

He reached out and pressed the doorbell. What had happened back at the rear of the bakery was still fresh in his mind. Moving a block away from the building and taking cover there, he had watched as many of the Christians suddenly darted out of the back entrance and scattered in every direction. And he had continued to watch as his men, stationed around the alley behind cover, were systematically mowed down by the big American, who had switched from his machine pistol to an M16. Agbede had come out from cover himself only once, intending to take his time and kill the man long range. But as if by magic, as soon as he had shown himself he'd seen the American look up and take note of him, as well.

Even a block away, with the gunfire blowing past him having stopped only seconds earlier, the big American had locked eyes with him.

And been ready to kill him. He had already begun raising his M16 as Dhul ducked behind a building.

The door in front of him opened and the woman he knew as Kamilah stepped back to let him in.

Normally, Agbede would have pinched or slapped her behind as he entered Hayat's dwelling. But he was in no mood for such frivolous behavior, and he barely took note of her beauty as he walked past her.

He knew the way to the room with the pool and the women, and he let Kamilah fall in behind him as he made his way down the hall. Her high heels clicked on the tile, a sound he usually found enticing. He barely noticed now. The air grew more humid as he neared the swimming pool, but that fact went largely overlooked, as well. A moment later, he was in the room and surrounded by beautiful women of many races and nationalities.

The man with the curling beard was somewhat surprised that they had no effect on him, either, and he had no desire to make any of them scream in pain.

The oysters, caviar, champagne and other delicacies looked as if they had been recently replenished, but they held no allure for him. The redhead, Patsy, was lying on a pillow next to the one Hayat usually occupied, Agbede noted. She saw him at the same time, and her eyes grew wide with fear. She was on her feet in a second and hurrying out of the room.

He took notice of the fact that she held her lower abdomen and limped as she left. The sight finally brought a small smile to his face.

But the smile didn't last long.

Agbede stopped and let his eyes search the scene for Hayat. When he could not find the man, he turned and addressed Kamilah, who had followed him into the room. "Where is he?" he demanded.

The smile on her face looked forced. Agbede knew that Patsy had to have told her what he had done to her, and now this woman was afraid the same fate might befall her.

"He is in one of the back rooms," Kamilah said. "He wanted privacy for some reason."

The terrorist snorted. He had never understood why anyone cared about privacy during sexual encounters. He didn't *mind* being alone with one or more women, as he'd been with Patsy earlier in the day, particularly if he had thought up some new way of inflicting pain or humiliation. It allowed him to concentrate on what he was doing without distraction. But most of the time, he preferred an audience.

It was fun to see the other women's faces as they watched him make their fellow concubines squirm and scream.

Agbede's eyes moved to the bar in the corner of

the room and he walked toward it. He was not in the mood for champagne, but he could certainly use a drink or two. With Kamilah still on his heels in case he requested anything from her, he pushed through the swing door and grabbed a bottle of single-malt Scotch from a shelf. Uncapping it, he held the bottle to his lips and chugged several swallows. Then, as the taste actually went from his tongue to his brain, where he could take note of it, he spit it out onto the countertop.

He hated Scotch, and he wondered now what unconscious desire had made him choose it. He was just putting the bottle back on the shelf and reaching for some cognac when Hayat appeared through the same doorway where Patsy had just disappeared. He was accompanied by three very tired-looking women, and was smiling as he tied the belt to a silk robe around his waist.

One of the women carried the scabbarded stainless steel and gold-inlaid machete Agbede had forged for Fazel. As soon as the silk strand was tied tight, the Boko Haram leader took it from her and slipped it through the belt.

Hayat spotted him behind the bar and spoke softly into the ear of a woman Agbede knew to be a native Nigerian. She smiled back at him. But her smile looked just as forced as Kamilah's as she bowed her head in deference, then took the other two women by the hand and led them to the pool.

All three wasted no time diving into the water. It

was as if whatever Hayat had done to them, or made them do to each other, had made them feel dirty, and this was their chance to wash it off.

Hayat approached the bar. Kamilah had a white cloth and was mopping up the whiskey Agbede had spit onto the countertop. "I take it you still do not appreciate fine Scotch?" the Boko Haram leader said.

"It tastes like burned leaves," Agbede declared as he took a swig of cognac.

"That is the way it is distilled, Dhul," Hayat said patiently. "It is supposed to have a smoky taste."

Agbede knew that Fazel was patronizing him, and he intended to make the man pay for such comments someday. But not now. Not while the arrangement they had was still working so well and Fazel thought Dhul was as dedicated to Boko Haram as he was. So he said simply, "I prefer the cognac."

Hayat nodded, again in a condescending manner, as he said, "By all means then, consider it your own."

Agbede took another long pull. He watched Fazel's eyes as he drank. He knew that the Boko Haram leader would have one of the women dispose of both the Scotch and cognac bottles as soon as he left. Fazel would never drink anything from a receptacle that had touched Dhul's lips.

Another insult that the Boko Haram leader would answer for someday.

Hayat leaned against the bar. "Your phone call disturbed me," he said. "Am I to understand that even with all of the men you took with you, the mission to kill Enitan and the American was a failure?"

"Unless the men I left there got very lucky," Agbede said. "And that is unlikely."

"You left your men there?" Hayat said, frowning. "You deserted them?"

"No, I left them to continue *trying* to kill Enitan and the American. The men are expendable." He took another drink of cognac. "You only have one of me." He watched Fazel's expression change to one of understanding. The man knew what he said was true. The Boko Haram leader would never find another man with Dhul's talents.

Agbede took another long swig of cognac. He reacted strangely to alcohol. He could drink and drink and drink without ever feeling its effect. But then suddenly, like a bolt of thunder, it would hit him all at once, a sledgehammer between the eyes.

Hayat knew that, and said gently, "Please slow down, my trusted friend. We still have much work ahead of us."

Agbede nodded and set the bottle down. He didn't want the cognac to overtake him any more than Fazel did. He not only *needed* to kill the American and Enitan. He *wanted* with all his heart and soul to kill them. If he'd believed in a soul, that was.

"And what have you heard concerning the bishop from New York?" he said, changing the subject. "Perhaps I should go after him first. He would be easier than…" His voice trailed off when he saw Hayat shaking his head.

"The bishop is no concern of yours," Hayat said. "I have sent Sam after him."

Anger suddenly flowed through Agbede's veins as if he'd mainlined it into an artery. He hated Sam. Hated the prissy little man's attention to his clothing. Hated the stupid little derringer. And he particularly hated the foolish wavy kris he himself had forged for the man at Fazel's request. He had done it to keep the peace until he had planned his exit strategy, which involved leaving Boko Haram with all the organization's money. But most of all, he hated the competition Sam presented to him.

The man was good at what he did. Perhaps as good as Dhul himself, although Dhul's ego would not allow him to believe such a thing. And Sam seemed to have no appreciation for the women around the pool. Or the food or drink or any of the other pleasures in which Dhul reveled.

"I will find the bishop first," Agbede said. In a flash, he drew his machete—the one identical to Hayat's—and held its gleaming blade in the air. "And I will bring you his head."

"Put the machete away," Hayat said. He looked at the cognac bottle. "The alcohol has done what it often does to you. You will take a nap in one of the back rooms to allow it to wear off. Then I have other plans for you."

Agbede realized that Fazel was right. He had

taken one too many swallows from the cognac bottle and now he wanted to kill someone. Anyone. For a second, he considered slicing Fazel's head off at the neck and then leaving. He could be gone before any of the other Boko Haram men even knew about it. But that would mean he would have to leave the country. And while he eventually planned to do just that, he was not yet ready.

But Dhul Agbede was not sleepy, and the alcohol had affected him in another way, as it often did. Suddenly, he was not only aware of the women in the room, he was desperate to have them. "I do not need a nap," he told Hayat. "I need women. That will take the edge off."

"Save the edge," Hayat told him. "I am finally sending you after the wife, son and daughter of the police officer who killed one of our men and has embraced Christianity. It is an invasion you will relish. You may take as many men with you as you like. But it should be a very simple job. All of our men have had the address of the church hideout for some time." He paused, then added, "We will have to save that officer for some later date."

Agbede stuck his machete back in the scabbard. "I am ready now," he said.

"You will be even more ready in a couple of hours," he said. "Now, go sleep."

Dhul nodded. He would do as he was told. For now. But soon, he would have had all of this man he could stand, and even the wealth of perks his position afforded him would not be able to hold him back from killing Fazel Hayat.

"Take Kamilah," Hayat said. "She can give you a massage and put you to sleep."

The woman suddenly stiffened at the bar. Her bottom lip dropped and her eyes widened. Hayat saw her reaction at the same time Agbede did, and laughed. "Do not worry, my dear Kamilah," he said. "Dhul will do exactly as I have instructed, and go to sleep."

He turned toward Agbede. "You understand, do you not?" he said in a stern voice. "A massage *only*. Do not go beyond that."

Agbede looked at the man through eyes blurred from the alcohol. Perhaps Fazel was right. He should sleep. And denying himself sexual release would build up the tension even more for the wife of the man whose home was about to be invaded.

"I understand," he said, and could hear his own voice slur.

He followed Kamilah through the room and down another hallway. He actually was growing drowsy now, and a nap no longer sounded like such a bad idea. If he kept moving, he knew he would be capable of carrying out the strange sexual fantasies that were still dancing in his head. But if he lay down, he suspected he would be out in a few seconds.

Which proved to be the case. Agbede fell forward onto the bed as soon as Kamilah led him into the small room. He was asleep so fast he never felt her hands begin to massage his neck and shoulders.

And he certainly never saw the tears of relief that flowed freely down her cheeks.

WITH THE STOCK of the M16 against his shoulder and ready, Bolan kept one eye on the back of the bakery building as the other watched the men lower a disabled convert to the ground. The sirens blasted into his ears now as the police vehicles grew closer.

Police sirens. Flashing lights. The Executioner had heard them hundreds of times before. Sometimes they were welcome. Other times they weren't. This time, he wished they'd disappear into thin air—at least for a few more minutes. But he knew that wasn't going to happen, and he wasted no more time with such unproductive thoughts.

The new noise sounded strange after the chaotic cacophony of gunfire that had finally stopped ringing in his ears.

Bolan glanced away from the area he was covering long enough to see that only a few of the disabled converts were still atop the roof. An old man who was obviously blind was about to be trussed up with the rope and lowered to the walkway. The soldier turned back and let his eyes skirt the rear of the bakery one final time before leaving his post.

"Come on," he said to the white-bearded father from the team that had joined him only minutes earlier. "It's time for *us* to go."

The words had barely left his mouth when a cavalcade of rounds pounded the wall beneath him. More audible cracks met his ears as bullets flew past them. "Or not," Bolan added, as he turned back and pulled the trigger once more.

Another terrorist had appeared behind the stacked plywood. His entire right side was exposed as he tried to angle shots into the walkway.

The Executioner stitched the enemy from waist to temple, and the man fell out from behind the stacked building material. The white-bearded man was firing his customized AK-47 at Bolan's side, but whoever he was aiming at was out of the big American's field of vision.

What had happened was obvious. There *had* been more Bokos planted behind the building, but they had held their fire, waiting while the disabled were lowered to the ground and helped out to the street in front. The terrorists' objective was clear: they wanted this strange American who'd led the attacks all through the building, and they were more than willing to let the people with disabilities—who weren't now, and never would be, a threat—go free in order to get him after he let his guard down.

Their mistake had been thinking the Executioner was *ever* lulled into letting down his guard.

Bolan continued firing, dropping Bokos, and still looking for the man with the greasy beard he had seen inside the building. Leaders of men could sense it when they encountered other leaders of men, regardless of whether those leaders were good or evil. And the Executioner sensed that the man who had narrowly escaped his gun sights had, indeed, been one of the Boko Haram leaders.

The sirens continued to grow louder and Bolan was reminded that the cops would only confuse the situation further. They would be poorly trained and afraid of Boko Haram. He suspected they'd shoot anything that moved, and when the dust finally cleared, no one would know exactly who had shot the innocent Christians. In addition, he knew that some of the officers' loyalties would be with the Bokos, which meant they'd *intentionally* shoot the innocent Christians, then blame their deaths on the terrorists.

Bolan returned to the back edge of the roof and dropped to one knee. He was exposing more of his body than he'd have liked, but he also knew that by doing so he was serving as yet another distraction for the Boko shooters while the last of the Christians made good their escape. He knew that even though they wouldn't know exactly who he was, word of the presence of a big American skilled with weapons would have spread throughout all of Ibadan by now. It always happened that way. Usually, the common people as well as the enemy assumed he was a CIA agent. And that made the "bad guys" want his head most of all.

Yes, the Bokos would put most of their efforts into killing the big American now exposed atop the building. And that would give this second group of terrified Christians yet another slight advantage.

The Bokos would be quick to fire at him and the

Christians. He would have to be *quicker*. As soon as he saw them, he would have to drop them. Or die.

The Executioner switched the M16's selector switch to semiauto.

But the complications in getting all the converts out of the building weren't over. As he drilled a lone round through the chest of a man who'd stepped out from behind the stack of nail boxes, a second group of people suddenly burst out the back door.

BOLAN HAD BEEN RIGHT. Some of the converts had lost their nerve and stayed in the building. If they'd been walking behind Paul and Jabari, they could have drifted off and found hiding places without being noticed. But whoever Paul had sent back to check on them had found them, and obviously convinced them to finally make a run for it.

The soldier hit the roof on his belly. There were plenty of distractions now without him adding to them. Rising up just high enough to shoot over the retaining wall, he switched the M16 to full-auto and held the trigger back.

A half-dozen rounds penetrated the chest and abdomen of a Boko who suddenly appeared with a machete. The man's arm had already risen and was about to come down on a Christian wearing sweatpants and a mismatched hooded sweatshirt. The convert was looking the other way as he ran and didn't even see the danger.

All Bolan's mass of 5.56 mm fire hit the terrorist in an area the size of a silver dollar. His heart exploded as if he'd swallowed a stick of dynamite.

The man wearing the sweatsuit ran on, never realizing how close he had come to being beheaded.

As the remaining converts sprinted onward, fanning out down the alley as their braver predecessors had earlier, Bolan continued to send steady streams of autofire into the remaining Bokos. Not far away, the old man with the AK-47 was helping him with short bursts of fire. The Executioner tried to count the runners, but it was impossible. His best estimate, however, was that they were roughly a quarter of the number of the original escapees. Like the prior group, they began to disappear around different buildings in the distance.

Bolan continued to fire, lining the barrel up with every Boko who showed himself. The difference between a live Christian and a dead one had boiled down to hundredths of a second. Their saving grace was that in order to shoot, or slice with a machete, the Bokos had to expose at least part of themselves to return fire.

And there was no more accurate or faster return fire in the world than that of the Executioner. In addition to his own deadly rain of lead, the old man with the white hair and beard was proving to be as good as his son had professed him to be.

Bolan switched the M16 to 3-round-burst mode as the converts ran on. When what appeared to be the final Bokos hidden in the alley fell, the gunfire behind the building died down. The Christians had all disappeared from view.

Bolan had run through two 30-round magazines when he at last let up on the trigger. The alley fell quiet, but now the police sirens were screaming. It was impossible to be sure, but it appeared to the Executioner that all the Christian runners had escaped. Maybe a Boko would find one or more of them on their way to their assigned secondary safe houses. Maybe they wouldn't. And there might still be a terrified man or woman cowering inside the bakery below. If so, they'd either be killed by any Bokos still in the building or rescued—or murdered—by the police. In any case, there was nothing more the Executioner could do.

Finally, he made it to the ladder. Most of the men who had helped get the disabled converts down to safety had now gone down the ladder themselves. But Paul and Jabari still stood on the roof, waiting for Bolan and the man with the Santa Claus beard. As the sirens blasted away, Jabari looked out toward the front of the building. "I am very familiar with their somewhat distinctive sounds," said the former Nigerian police officer. "There are four, maybe five police patrol cars. They are almost here."

"*That*, I could tell myself," Paul said.

Jabari closed his eyes tightly and continued to listen. "At least two, probably three or four, of the other sirens are definitely those of ambulances." Then, leaning slightly forward and cupping a hand behind his ear, he added, "I cannot be certain, but another of the sirens I believe comes from a truck carrying men you call SWAT in America. They are actually more military than law enforcement, although they are part of the police organization. And in Nigeria, they are not nearly as well controlled as they are in the United States. Basically, our SWAT teams are trained to just shoot everything they see before them, and try to figure it all out when the dust clears."

It was almost exactly what the Executioner had predicted. All Jabari had left out was that some of the cops who sided with the Bokos would intentionally shoot at them and the disabled Christians they still had to get out of there.

Bolan looked at the sergeant's stripes on Jabari's uniform. "Get out there in front and make sure they see your uniform," he told the former cop. "Use those stripes and do your best to stall them."

Jabari hurried down the ladder and ran up the walkway toward the front of the building.

Bolan looked over the side of the roof. Whether by rope or ladder, the twins and the other men had gotten all but two of the disabled down to the ground. Now, the brothers were both standing on the walkway, looking up. The Executioner motioned for Blue to come back up the ladder, and he climbed the rungs with the ease of a gymnast.

Bolan looked toward the last people who needed help getting down off the roof—the girl with one leg and the man with no arms. "Can you hold on to my back?" he asked the girl.

She smiled and nodded. And her smile was so infectious that even amid all the carnage that had gone on, Bolan found himself smiling, too. He took her crutch and looked down over the side again. "Hey," he called down.

Red looked up.

The Executioner held the crutch over the edge, then let go of it. It dropped straight to Red, whose shoulder and arm muscles seemed to ripple as he caught the well-worn stick.

"You," the Executioner said to Blue, as the twin hopped off the ladder again. "Can you take this guy?" He pointed toward the man who had no arms.

Blue frowned, obviously wondering how the man could hold on to his back.

"When you have been maimed like I have, you learn to improvise," the armless man said, and Bolan could tell by his tone of voice that he hadn't let self-pity creep into his character any more than the young amputee had. "Turn around and squat," the man told Blue.

The bodybuilder did so, but his face still wore a puzzled look.

The armless man stood behind him for a moment, then turned to Bolan. "Now, sir, if you would be so kind as to lift me up," he said. Bolan hoisted him into the air and he wrapped his legs around Blue's waist. Leaning in against the muscleman's back for balance, he said, "Now, take my empty sleeves and tie them around your chest."

It was Blue's face that broke into a smile as he reached behind him with both hands and found the sleeves. It was a tight stretch across his massive chest, but Blue managed to get them secured, then turned and started down the ladder with the man tied to his back.

Paul was coughing again, but he was smiling, too.

Bolan stooped in front of the girl. A moment later, she was on his back and he was going down the ladder behind Blue. Red handed her the crutch as soon as Bolan let her down on the walkway, and she turned, stretched her neck up and kissed the Executioner on the cheek. "Thank you," she said, and started toward the front of the building with the man who had no arms.

The sirens were wailing, and Bolan could see colored lights flashing from the street. He turned the other way. So far, it didn't appear that any of the police had pulled around to cover the back.

"Let's get out of here while we still can," Bolan said. "If we get separated, we'll all meet back at the Isaac Center. And be careful. There still could be Bokos hiding anywhere."

All the men nodded. Then, with weapons ready, they hurried down the walkway to the alley.

CHAPTER TEN

At first, Sam found blood spots every ten feet or so. They were always roughly the same size and ranged in number from three to six or seven. This told the Yemeni al Qaeda operative that yes, Bishop Joshua Adewale was injured, information he'd already obtained from two different sources—the hard hat, as well as Fazel Hayat's videotape of the man walking away, holding his arm. But it told him even more.

The injury was a cut of some sort, possibly a puncture, but more likely a laceration. It was deep, but it had missed all major veins and arteries. And the farther he walked, the farther Sam found the distance between spotting to be. Plus the lighter and smaller the spots.

The bishop wasn't likely to bleed to death before he reached someplace where he could have the wound treated, or treat it himself.

Sam took his time. At each corner he had to stop and stare at all three possible paths—straight ahead, right or left. If no blood spots were visible, he took exactly thirty steps down each asphalt street until he finally picked up the trail again. If thirty steps didn't lead him to more blood, he started over and took sixty steps.

The al Qaeda–Boko Haram liaison man knew he was methodical to the point of being obsessive-compulsive. But he also knew that a light case of obsessive-compulsive disorder could be a tremendous advantage in his line of work.

As he walked on, Sam noted that the houses got smaller and dingier, and the asphalt streets ran out. The dirt roads on which he found himself, and the fact that the bishop's bleeding was slowing, made the trail more difficult to follow. He wondered how the injury had come about. Was it from one of the Boko Haram men's machetes? Not likely. The videotape had not shown anything of the sort when the bishop had walked between the two men and away from the scene, as if protected by some invisible force. Sam shook his head in wonder as he walked on. The Christians, he knew, would turn this whole mess into a legend in which their God had supernaturally protected Adewale during his escape. The fact of the matter was simply that the machetes had been too busy with other bishops to pay him much attention.

So how had the injury come about? Flying debris from the explosion would be Sam's guess. It was the most likely source. Not that it mattered.

The problem at the moment was that the blood trail was getting so light it was difficult to follow. And if he didn't pick up on some other method of tracking the man, or actually find him soon, Sam knew he was going to lose the trail altogether.

He had slowed almost to crawl speed when he finally lost the trail. He stopped in the middle of the dirt road, closed his eyes and pinched the bridge of his nose with his thumb and index finger. The nausea caused by the flashing lights was mostly gone, but he still felt an occasional fit of dizziness. As he stood there, composing himself, he realized that the trail he had followed had not been straight. The bishop had staggered much of the way, and sometimes the spots were on the side of the street, other times in the middle. Once or twice, the man, who was undoubtedly still reeling from the explosion, had actually stumbled all the way to the other side of the road.

Sam opened his eyes, turned and walked quickly back to the last set of spots he had seen in the dirt. They were barely discernible, but when he squatted again and peered studiously at them, he saw that they splattered to the side rather than the front. It was difficult to see with the naked eye, but the spots were a tiny bit larger at the rear of the spatter.

That suggested that the bishop had finally left the road altogether and walked on the grass.

Sam stood up and stared at the house toward which the blood pointed. It was a tiny one-room shack, and there were clothes hanging on the clothesline behind it. All appeared to be women's apparel, but there were several feet of empty line right in the middle, and clothespins stuck up from the cord like wooden exclamation marks, shouting, *"Look here!"*

Sam stepped off the road and onto the scraggly grass. He walked toward the front door of the shack and noted another set of blood spots halfway through the yard. He couldn't help but smile.

As he climbed the rickety wooden stairs to the porch, he had to step over a hole in one of the steps. Someone's foot had broken through the rotten wood. The splintered edges shone a bright white compared to the rest of the weathered steps, so the break was recent. And on the porch just outside the door, Sam saw what he'd suspected he would see.

A tiny trace of fresh spots, where someone had been forced to wait after knocking.

Sam tapped the vest pocket where his derringer was hidden. Then he reached behind his back and felt the kris through his suit coat. All was in place.

He reached out, rapped his knuckles on the door frame and waited. Inside, he thought he heard muffled voices, but he couldn't be sure. What looked like a blanket was hung behind the window in the upper half of the door, and Sam thought he saw it move slightly. But again, he wasn't certain.

He knocked again and continued to wait. Finally, a woman wearing a light cotton dress and carrying a dirty wooden spoon pulled the blanket aside. She wore her black curly hair tied back by a worn and faded blue bandanna, Sam noted, as she smiled through the glass, then opened the door.

"How may I help you?" she asked.

Sam looked over her shoulder. Although the house was breaking down with age, the inside looked incredibly clean. "Have you had any unexpected visitors today?" he asked her.

The woman laughed. "Of course not. I am a poor widow," she said. "Who would want to come visit me? Are you with the police?"

Sam continued to look over her shoulder. He saw a crucifix on the wall. So she was a Christian. Just the kind who would stick her own neck out to help an injured Catholic bishop in need.

The smell of the disgusting peasant food known as *moin moin* filled Sam's sinuses and sickened him, almost as much as the flashing lights had done. But then he saw a dirty-looking garment on the bed in the corner of the room, and the sight took his mind off the smell. It was impossible to tell from the distance whether what he saw was a dress, a coat or some other item of clothing. But whatever it was, it was definitely out of place in this woman's spick-and-span home.

She invited him inside and he accepted.

It took only two steps to reach the side of the bed. And as he looked down at the dust-ridden bishop's cassock, Sam heard the scratchy sounds of the cheap television against the opposite wall. Voices were coming from the white plastic box. *Television* voices. Voices that sounded nothing like the ones he'd heard while he stood on the porch.

Sam's eyes darted immediately to the back of the shack. There was no rear door, but he saw a window large enough for a man to crawl through. As he stared through the glass at two other broken-down shacks, he watched the woman in his peripheral vision.

Her smile had turned to a mask of horror. She knew she was caught, and she suspected she might die.

Sam suspected she might, too,

The Yemeni turned back to the bed, reached down and lifted the filthy cassock. "It does not appear to be your size, my dear," he said. Then, dropping it back on the bed, he turned toward the rear wall. The house was too primitive to have a sink, but there was a bucket of what looked like clean cooking water on the counter next to the stove. A bar of soap rested on a cheap plastic saucer next to it, and a dish towel was carefully folded just behind it. In addition to the dirty cassock he had just handled, Sam remembered the blood that had been on his fingers when he'd picked up the bishop's trail.

"I'm sure you won't mind if I wash my hands," he said, not expecting an answer.

He didn't get one.

Quickly, Sam lathered his hands and rinsed them in the bucket, ruining the clean water for whatever the woman had intended it. That wouldn't matter. She wouldn't need it when he was finished in this little cracker box of a house. He dried his hands on the dish towel, then turned back to her and pulled out the black gloves he had not been able to use to test the blood spots earlier.

They would work just fine for what he needed to do next.

Fifteen minutes later, Sam had learned all about the church and Father Adisa, and Inka lay huddled on her side and crying on the floor.

"Do not be ashamed," Sam said as he carefully took off the black leather gloves and dropped them next to the woman. He did not care to touch the outside of them, and he would remember to get new gloves when he got the new handkerchief. "Here is a souvenir," he told the woman at his feet. "You held out much longer than most."

Inka's weeping eyes fixed on the gloves as they landed in front of her face. "I did not suffer as much as Christ did," she said. "Yet I failed Him."

"He will forgive you, won't he?" Sam said with a trace of sarcasm in his voice. "Isn't that what your faith is all about? Repenting and being forgiven?"

Inka looked up at him. "Yes," she said. "I will repent and ask for forgiveness. And He will forgive me." There was a long pause during which she took in a deep breath. "And I forgive you," she finished.

Sam chuckled, then reached into his vest pocket and pulled out the derringer on the end of the chain. "Thank you," he said with a laugh. "Now, you and your Jesus can talk it all over." He pressed the derringer against the woman's forehead, cocked the hammer and pulled the trigger.

The top barrel of the 2-shot weapon clicked as if on an empty chamber.

Sam frowned and raised the tiny pistol to his eyes. He had never had a misfire with this derringer before. Pointing it back down at the woman on the floor, he cocked it and pulled the trigger again.

Once more, the weapon failed to discharge.

Sam flipped the switch on the side of the weapon and broke open the barrels. Both were loaded, and he could see the dent in both primers at the end of the casings. Lifting the gun up, he dumped the two bullets and reached into his pocket, coming out with another pair of .32-caliber hollowpoint rounds. Reloading the weapon, he aimed it at Inka's head once more.

And experienced two more misfires.

A rare chill passed through Sam's body, causing his shoulders to shiver. Was it faulty ammunition? The derringer had never failed him before. He dumped the unfired cartridges again and reloaded for a second time. Twice more he tried to shoot Inka in the head, and twice more the derringer clicked empty. Yet again he checked the primers. Both were dented.

This time, instead of emptying the gun, Sam closed it again, locked the barrels back in place and pointed it at the wall. The small caliber roared inside the tiny dwelling as a hollowpoint round drilled into the wall. He aimed it down at the woman again.

Click.

Sam rarely lost his composure, but when he saw Inka smiling up at him through the blood dripping down over her eyes, he tried to shoot the expression off her face. Again the gun misfired

His anxiety turning to anger now, Sam aimed at the bare wall once more. The .32 exploded again, sounding like a high caliber rifle round within the confines of the small house.

Sam felt fear and anger sweep over him as he jammed the derringer back into his vest. There was something wrong with the tiny gun. It was something that caused it to misfire when pointed *down*, but allowed it to fire when aimed horizontally. That had to be it.

Reaching behind him, he drew the kris from the sheath in the small of his back. He looked down at the woman on the floor. There was fear in her eyes, but there was something else, too. Something he couldn't name. Something that made him more uneasy than ever. It was something that shouted out, "Go ahead and kill me if you must. I will be far better off than *you*."

Sam held the wavy blade of the kris in front of him. He started to kneel next to the woman in order to cut her throat, then stopped as a sudden wave of nausea swept over him. He remembered the flashing lights of the police cars and ambulances. It had to be some delayed reaction to those lights. He thought of the stream of blood that would shoot from the woman's throat after he sliced through it, and knew much of it would end up on his hand and arm. Some would soak through the suit he'd changed to in the back of the police car, and would wet his chest and stomach.

The thought not only sickened Sam further, it made him realize he didn't have a third suit with him, and he would catch the eye of everyone—friend and enemy alike—as he made his way back to his vehicle near the bombed-out chapel.

Some of the blood might even splash up to cover his face.

The flashing lights were dancing in Sam's head as he turned to the woman's side, bent over and regurgitated until his stomach was empty and he shivered in dry heaves. When he finally had control of himself again, he stood back up, leaned over the bucket of water and washed his face.

Then, standing over the woman once more, Sam said, "You are right. You are nothing but a poor old widow, and you are not worth killing." Then he sheathed his kris and hurried out of the house to find this church where Father Adisa was hiding the bishop.

MAKING SURE THAT their weapons were concealed, Bolan, Paul and Jabari had left the walkway and turned to walk past several police cars and a half-dozen officers. The men in uniform had each stared at them, then turned away, waiting for whoever was in command to give further orders.

As they continued walking, a blue van marked with giant letters announced to one and all that the SWAT team the Executioner had heard about had arrived.

Bolan, Paul and Jabari walked past the van as men in black BDUs poured out of the vehicle. They were a half block away, and feeling as if their departure without being detained was about to become a reality, when they heard a voice behind them.

"Halt! All three of you!"

Bolan and the other two men turned to see one of the men in black. In addition to the BDUs, he wore a matching drill instructor's cap and black combat boots. His badge was embroidered onto his BDU blouse rather than pinned there, and in his hands he held a sawed-off Remington pump-action shotgun.

The man aimed the weapon at the trio and swaggered forward. "You three," he said in an arrogant tone of voice. "I saw you come out of the walkway between the buildings."

Bolan knew his accent would give him away if he spoke. So he waited, hoping Paul or Jabari would do the talking, but neither man spoke. The soldier's leadership had been unofficially recognized, and the fact that his voice would stand out obviously hadn't crossed the others' minds.

So no one answered, and the situation became awkward.

Finally, the SWAT team member racked the slide on his shotgun and chambered a round. "Perhaps your silence is due to the fact that I did not phrase what I said as a question," he stated. "So let me try again." He moved in closer, the short barrel of the Remington almost touching Paul's abdomen. "What were you doing back there?"

Bolan realized that keeping quiet now was just making things worse. "I think you've mistaken us for three other men," he said, doing his best to sound as if he were born and raised in Nigeria.

It didn't work.

The swaggering SWAT cop immediately pulled the shotgun barrel away from Paul and jammed it into Bolan. "You are American?" he demanded.

"Through and through." The soldier had looked down in his peripheral vision and seen that the man's finger was not on the trigger. He held it outside the trigger guard.

Just as he'd been taught by some range instructor who'd never been in a real gunfight.

"What are you doing here?" the SWAT man went on.

Bolan took a deep breath and let it out. Behind the officer, he could see other men in black, as well as others in regular blue police uniforms, moving around the area. None of them seemed to be paying any attention to what was happening down the block.

"I came to teach you two things for future reference," Bolan said.

"Oh really?" the officer queried, cocking his head to the side. It was another show of arrogance, and it made Bolan feel better about what he was about to do.

"Yes, really," Bolan replied. "First, never get this close to a man when you have a weapon trained on him. Second, keep your finger inside the trigger guard. You don't have to have it *on* the trigger, if you're inexperienced and afraid you might shoot accidentally. But if it's outside the guard, this can happen." In a blur of speed, Bolan wrapped his left arm over the weapon. His forearm knocked the SWAT officer's hand to the side. Then, reaching across his body with his right hand, the Executioner grabbed the shotgun barrel secured in his armpit and pulled it down as his other arm jerked the stock up.

The shotgun flipped out of the officer's hands before he knew what was happening. Bolan pulled it away, then drove a right cross into his chin.

The SWAT man collapsed onto the sidewalk.

Bolan glanced back down the street. It still didn't look as if anyone had paid any attention to what was happening.

Reaching down, he dragged the unconscious man against the glass of the storefront next to them. When he looked up again, a taxi was creeping down the street, the driver's mouth open like some idiot as he stared at the police action down the block.

Paul didn't have to be told what to do. He flagged down the cab.

And a minute later, they were heading toward the Isaac Center.

CHAPTER ELEVEN

The reunion at the Isaac Center was not a happy one. A few police still remained, measuring distances and shot angles in front of the building where the first assault on Bolan and Layla Galab had taken place. They had left there only a few hours earlier. But to Bolan, it seemed as if years had gone by since then.

To avoid the cops and their questions, the Executioner directed the cabbie to drive past the front of the building and onto the street at the rear of the dorm rooms. He, Paul and Jabari got out. The soldier paid the fare, then led the others through the dorm building to the offices at the front. The door to Galab's office was closed. Bolan tried the knob. Locked. So he and his companions moved on to the reception area.

He was a little surprised to find Galab there, talking to her receptionist. Tara was the woman's name, if he remembered correctly.

The Isaac Center director turned to Bolan and flashed a smile.

"How did you get here?" Bolan asked.

"By cab," she replied. "The same as you."

The Executioner frowned. "How'd you know we caught a cab?" he asked.

"I saw you get into it right after you knocked out that policeman." She made a fist with her thumb sticking out on top and begging to be ripped off. Then she swung her arm through the air in a punch that wouldn't have hurt a newborn puppy. "As soon as I got the rest of the people to run out the back," she went on, "I ran, too. And when I was clear of the danger zone, I blended in with the crowds on the street and circled the block."

Bolan made sure a frown didn't show on his face. "The gunfire would have been heard on the block behind the Bokos in the alley," he said. "Are you telling me that people on the sidewalks just kept strolling along and going about their business as usual?"

Galab nodded. "People in this country are used to the spontaneous outbreak of gunfire." She stopped speaking, but the seductive smile stayed on her face. "I caught the next cab that came along."

Bolan nodded. He supposed it *could* be true. He glanced out through the glass front of the building. Several bullet holes were evident, and some had spiderwebbed to encompass a whole pane. The police were gathering up their equipment, and the carpenters were beginning to bring theirs out again.

"You came in the front door," Bolan said. "The cops didn't stop you and have any questions?"

Galab shook her head. "One of them recognized me as the director," she said. "And I denied any knowledge of the gunfire this morning. I felt it was far more important that I meet with you and continue our struggle against the terrorists."

Again, Bolan kept his poker face. This, too, could be true. But it sounded awfully thin.

The Executioner knew they had a leak somewhere. Boko Haram had known to attack him and Galab when they had left the Isaac Center for the bakery building. Then they had somehow learned about the bakery itself, and that it hid converted Christians. Paul had assured Bolan that none of the people in the congregation room had cell phones. The exception to that was Galab. After she'd arrived, she had admitted to calling to check on her mother, and calling her office in order to alert the police to what was going on during the long-running gun battle in the twists and turns of the bakery building.

Had she also called someone in Boko Haram? Was Layla Galab herself the leak? It was beginning to look more and more that way. Bolan didn't want to believe it, but he had to face the facts. He could take her cell phone and check the numbers she had called. But even if a number appeared that wasn't connected to the Isaac Center or her mother's house, she could just lie about it. And there would not be time for Bolan to double-check whatever story she came up with.

There was one other possibility, however, and he could check it out almost immediately.

Bolan was still running all these things through

his mind when the muscle twins—still Red and Blue to him—walked past the cops without any of the officers giving them a second look. They had both added cutoff sweatshirts to their sweatpants, and didn't draw as much attention as their bulging biceps did when they were bare-chested.

The fact that the police didn't pay them any attention gave a little more credence to what Layla had just said. Disinterested or downright lazy cops could be found among their more dedicated brothers and sisters the world over. The police outside the Isaac Center just might have ignored Layla and the twins in order to keep from getting tied up in more interviews and interrogations.

In any case, Red opened the door, and he and his brother entered the reception area to join them.

"Shall we go into my office?" Galab asked.

Bolan nodded.

As they passed the reception desk, Galab looked at the woman sitting behind it and said, "Tara, if any more people come in looking for me, send them back, please."

"Yes, Miss Layla." She had been typing on a keyboard and gazing at a computer screen. She continued that task as she spoke, never once looking up at her boss or any of the men.

Once inside her office, Galab took a seat in her chair behind the desk. She looked exhausted, both physically and emotionally.

There weren't enough chairs in the office to accommodate all the others, so Bolan and Paul stayed on their feet while Jabari, Red and Blue sat down. The soldier walked to the front of the desk, then turned his back to her, leaned against the edge and started to speak to the men. But he stopped when Paul suddenly convulsed into one of his violent coughing fits.

While he coughed into a handkerchief, Bolan turned to look at the phone on Galab's desk. It had multiple numbers and clear plastic buttons along the bottom of the instrument that could be punched to access a specific line. When one of the numbers was in use, a light appeared in the button.

It was an old-fashioned means of setting up multiple phone numbers. But for a developing country like Nigeria, it came as no surprise.

At present, none of the buttons was lit.

Bolan kept leaning against the desk, but shifted position in order to keep one eye on the phone. When Paul had quit coughing, he said, "What happened to the older white-haired man and his son?"

Red looked down at the floor. "They were both cut down during our escape," he said in a low voice. "I saw them—"

Bolan interrupted him in midsentence. "I'm sorry about that, and we'll all mourn for them. *Later.* Right now, we've got to strike while the iron is still hot, so to speak." He looked to Paul, who was still holding a handkerchief to his mouth. "We didn't get all of the Bokos inside the building," he said. "Not by a long shot. And there are dozens of others in the Ibadan area who are probably ready to go on to their next strike while the cops are still spread thin between the university chapel and the bakery. All of which means we've got to move and move fast."

He stopped speaking long enough for his words to sink in. While silence fell over the office, his mind drifted back to the man with the curling beard. He looked to Paul and Jabari.

"There was a man with the Bokos," Bolan said. "I narrowly missed him. He had a sparse goatee that curled out and up. And even though I only saw him for a fraction of a second, I sensed something evil about him. Do either of you know who I mean?"

Paul didn't hesitate. "I know the man of whom you speak," he said. "His name is Dhul Agbede. And you are correct that he is evil. The man is a monster."

Bolan continued to look at Paul. "We need to get moving," he said. "Pull out one of those papers that you got from the dead men."

From a pocket in his tunic, Paul drew out the sheet of paper that had come from a computer printer. He was about to read the address when Bolan saw one of the line buttons at the bottom the phone suddenly light up.

He held up a hand, palm out. "Wait," he said in a low voice. "And don't make any noise. Any of you." When he saw that the men understood, he gently depressed the button, then reached for the receiver and gingerly lifted it from its cradle.

Covering the mouthpiece at the bottom with his hand, the Executioner held the instrument to his ear.

"...and several of them are here *now*," Bolan heard the receptionist whisper into her own phone. "Including the big American you want so badly. Paul, as well. And the police sergeant who killed one of your men. I think he killed many more today at the bakery building."

A man's voice said, "Do you know where they are going next?"

"No," Tara replied. "But I will try to find out." She paused for a moment, and when she spoke again her voice was nervous and shaky, the voice of someone asking for something but afraid the request would anger the person. "I have done well, have I not?" she said.

"You have," the man answered.

"Then perhaps you could see your way to including a small bonus with my usual payment?"

"We will see. Get back to me when you learn more."

"I will. Thank you, Mr. Hayat," Tara said.

Bolan heard two clicks as both parties hung up.

He placed the receiver back on the cradle. Looking at Paul, he said, "Do you know a Mr. Hayat?"

"Fazel Hayat," Paul said. "He is the top dog of the Bokos here in Ibadan and the rest of south Nigeria."

Bolan turned to glance at Layla Galab. The good-looking Isaac Center director had already realized what was going on. She seemed completely defeated. "I am…*so sorry*," she said, staring down at her desk.

"It's not your fault," Bolan replied. "Your job is to help people. I'm the one who's supposed to figure these things out and eliminate the human scum who try to stop you."

He turned back to Paul. "Read off the address," he said.

"It's 11637 Yejide Street."

In his peripheral vision, Bolan saw Jabari's face turn an ashen gray. The Executioner switched his attention to the former police sergeant.

Paul obviously recognized the address, but couldn't quite place it. "It means something to you, Jabari?"

It took the man wearing the stripes on his shoulders a moment to find words. But when he did, he said, "Yes. It is a church. And one of the smaller safe houses here in Ibadan. Relatives maintain the place." He curled his right hand into a tight fist and held it with his left. "It is where I left my wife, my daughter and my son."

Bolan nodded. "Then we'd better get to that address, and do it *now*." He walked to the office door and opened it, to find Tara standing there. The receptionist held several sheets of paper in one hand.

"Oh," said the woman in the expensive clothes and diamond rings. "I was just about to knock. Miss Layla, these documents need your signature."

Galab came around her desk and Bolan stepped

aside. Tara was a good head taller than her boss. But when the Isaac Center director swung her fist at the other woman, it produced a good deal more power than Bolan would have guessed it would.

Tara went down for the count.

Bolan looked at the muscle twins. "Were you guys ever in the army?" he asked.

The heads atop the thick necks shook back and forth.

"Any experience with firearms at all?" the soldier went on.

Again, the bodybuilders shook their heads. "We can fight, though," Blue said. He held up his fists and the muscles in his forearms rippled like tsunamis.

"I'm sure you can," Bolan said. "But the kind of fighting we're about to engage in involves guns and blades, and strong as you are, it won't matter how much you can bench press or dead lift."

The twins appeared devastated, and Bolan could tell they really wanted to help. "Besides," he said, "I've got something else important for you to do." Reaching inside his robe to the vest, he found the pocket where he'd stuck several sets of plastic cuffs. He pulled out one set. Then, dropping to his knees next to the unconscious woman on the floor, he rolled her onto her stomach and twisted the strips around her wrists.

Looking up at Red and Blue, he said, "You two, and Layla, keep her in custody after she wakes up and until we're finished. If this Fazel guy or Dhul or anyone else calls, get her to find out all she can from *them*. And make sure she gives them plenty of misinformation. Got it?"

The twins grinned. They were back in the contest. Galab nodded.

Bolan, Paul and Jabari moved toward the door. Just before he exited, the Executioner looked back at Galab. "Don't ever again say you're not a fighter," he told her. "You punch like a heavyweight champ."

The woman smiled as they left.

SAM WASN'T USED to getting shaky, and he didn't like it. Not one bit. So, as he left Inka's cracker-box house and started through her backyard, he was already coming up with reasons why his derringer had misfired so many times.

There *had* to be some scientific explanation for the whole debacle that had taken place inside the house. Maybe it had seemed as if Allah was stepping in to save a woman from being killed. But that simply couldn't be.

She was an infidel Christian. He was a dedicated Muslim.

Allah simply didn't work that way.

By the time Sam had reached the next block, he had quit shaking. He stopped to straighten his tie in the reflection of a window of a house even smaller than the one he'd just left, then turned toward the church Inka had finally told him about.

As he started down the packed dirt street, it reminded him of a story a young Christian his al Qaeda brothers had once captured had told him. In spiritual desperation before he had given his life to Christ, the young man had tried to kill himself. He had driven out into the countryside and parked on a dirt road far from prying eyes. Then he had jammed his father's 12-gauge shotgun—loaded with double O buckshot—up under his chin and pulled the trigger with his thumb. When the shotgun misfired with a click, he had opened the door and gotten out of the car. Aiming down at the dirt road, he had pulled the trigger again and blasted a crater into the dirt. Back in the car, he'd shoved the barrel into his mouth and tried again. Once more, the weapon misfired. So he got out again, aimed at the ground, and once more the exploding shot dug a crater in the packed dirt.

The young man was convinced that his Jesus had saved him both times. Sam had been tempted to explain that sometimes a firearm could become broken in a way that allowed it to function when it was pointed down but not up. But the young Christian would die soon enough, and he'd decided to let him go on believing in this fantasy of his own creation.

Sam continued down the street. He had regained control of his unaccustomed uneasiness, but was still slightly confused. What had just happened back at the woman's house couldn't *quite* be explained away by his memory of the man with the shotgun. It had broken in a way that allowed it to shoot down but not up. Sam's derringer had performed exactly the opposite. It had not worked when he aimed it *down* at the woman, but it had fired when he raised it *up* and shot the wall. Sam was an expert at using weapons, but he was no gunsmith who understood the way they functioned. Could a derringer become damaged in the opposite way the shotgun had? Could some broken part inside the little pistol leave it in a state where it would shoot when the barrel was tilted up but not down?

He didn't know. But if that was the case, it still didn't explain why the derringer had misfired, and that bothered him.

He saw the church in the distance, on the left side of the dirt road. As he headed toward it, Sam reminded himself to take both the suit he now wore and the one covered in the cop's blood to the dry cleaners as soon as he had killed the bishop from New York.

The rest should be simple, Sam thought as he cut across the grass and walked to the front door of the church. He knew his suit acted as a type of camouflage in situations like this. The bishop hiding inside the church, and the Catholic priest who was hiding him, would not suspect Sam to be the assassin that he was until it was too late. And Sam guessed that there might be other Christians hiding inside.

It would be his duty as a dedicated member of al Qaeda to kill them all.

As he approached the front door, Sam drew the derringer with his right hand and the kris with his left. He climbed three concrete steps to the porch, took three more steps, then kicked the door with his right foot.

It swung open, and Sam found himself in a small foyer. Beyond the deserted area, he heard voices in what he knew would be the sanctuary. Pushing through to the pews he could see through windows in the several doors before him, he looked up to find a huge crucifix on the wall behind the pulpit at the other end of the room.

A battered and bloody Jesus hung on the crucifix, and his eyes seemed to be staring straight into Sam's soul.

Perhaps a half-dozen men and women were seated in the pews, facing the cross and the penetrating eyes of the crucified Christ. But there was no service going on, and standing in an aisle that led to the stage was a man wearing a cassock much like the one Sam had found back at Inka's house. This would be Father Adisa, the priest she had finally told him about. The cleric was talking to another man in work clothes—a khaki shirt and pants. Sam knew that these had to be the garments the woman had given Joshua Adewale from New York City.

Sam had finally found the bishop.

And he could kill him, the priest and all the other Christians hiding inside the church.

Sam walked forward as the two men in the aisle turned to look at him. Neither appeared frightened, and that irritated the man with the derringer and the wavy blade, because both weapons were in plain sight in front of him, and there could be no mistake as to his intentions in coming to this church.

The derringer held two shots. One for each man. He was close enough now that he could carefully place a round in each of their brains.

"Do you have any last words, infidels?" Sam asked.

The man he knew was the bishop had turned to squarely face him. Now, he looked at Sam, and still there was no fear in his eyes. "God spared me in the explosion," he said in a steady voice. "He has something He wants me to do."

A chill ran down Sam's back, but he refused to let his nervousness and confusion show. "And what great task is it that Allah has assigned to you, Bishop?" he said sarcastically.

"I do not yet know," Adewale replied.

"And you never will," Sam said. He lined up the derringer with the bishop's head and prepared to squeeze the trigger.

But Sam never got a chance to fire the derringer and see if it was working again.

It was just like the old adage said: he never heard the shot that killed him.

DHUL AGBEDE HAD taken only four men with him, because the Christian church invasion, he suspected, would be even easier than a home invasion. Many people, especially police officers, kept weapons in their homes for protection. But while there were exceptions, few carried them into churches.

The fools seemed to think that stained-glass windows and wooden figures hanging from a cross were all the protection they needed.

And Agbede was about to prove to them just how wrong they were.

Yet even he could not believe how easy it was to get into the church. The front door was wide open, as if they'd *invited* him. So, with his men following him, their rifles raised and ready, he walked up the steps and into the foyer.

And through the glass in the upper half of the doors leading into the sanctuary, Agbede saw that he had been awarded the rare opportunity of killing three birds with one stone, to put a small twist on the Westerners' expression about two birds and a stone.

Sam was standing in the middle of the aisle, facing two men who could only be the church's priest and the bishop from America. Of course, neither was the reason Agbede had come to the church. His mission was to kill the cop named Jabari and his family. But this situation was simply too good to pass up.

Agbede looked over his shoulder as the four men he'd brought with him stopped behind him. "Wait here," he said. "I will only be a second." Then, walking up to the glass in the door, he looked down the barrel of his AK-47 and lined up the front and rear sights. Without further hesitation, he pulled the trigger and watched the back of Sam's head explode in a mass of blood, skull, brain and flesh.

The two men behind Sam flinched involuntarily. But by then the 7.62 mm bullet had passed on through Sam's face and missed both of them.

Agbede turned and looked back at his men. "Alaba," he said, staring at a man dressed in surplus jungle camouflage fatigue pants and a plain black T-shirt. "Leave the door open, but watch it."

Alaba frowned so hard his forehead looked like three giant riverbeds.

Another of his men, Yakima, asked, "How do you know which one is the bishop?"

Agbede could barely refrain from striking him, but he controlled himself. "Unlike you illiterates," he said, "I study these things. The priests' garments are not the same as a bishop's. And the man wearing the khaki shirt and pants looks uncomfortable in them. They are not what he is used to wearing."

Alaba was still nervous. "But if the big American and Enitan happen to come here they will know—"

Agbede finally let loose and slapped the man across the face. "Do not question me!" he shouted. "If they come, I *want* them to know we are here. We will use the people inside as hostages, lure them in, then kill them. Now, do as you were told."

He turned to the other three men. "Come with me," he said. Then he turned back around and saw the round hole that the 7.62 mm bullet had pierced in the glass. Cracks led from it all the way to the edge of the wood, and the top of the door looked as if it might break into shards at any second. And it did as

Agbede swung the door open, with pieces of glass falling to the carpet covering the floor.

The people in the pews gasped as he entered the sanctuary, the broken glass crunching beneath his boots. His men didn't have to be told what to do. One of them walked down the aisle toward the priest and the bishop. The other two spread out, covering two more exits from the sanctuary.

Agbede watched as his man in the center aisle used his rifle barrel to prod the priest and bishop into taking a seat in one of the pews. He looked at the priest. He would, of course, kill that man in addition to the "three birds" he'd thought of earlier. That would make four birds: Sam, the priest, the bishop, and Jabari, if he could find him.

The man with the curling beard scanned the rest of the people in the pews. Somewhere in the crowd was Jabari's wife, son and daughter. That would make three more birds, and he would kill them first—in front of the Nigerian police sergeant. In actuality, he realized, he would eventually kill all the people in this church. But not until he'd had his fun with the women.

So Agbede changed the old adage once again. I'm killing a whole flock with one stone, he told himself, and the knowledge of what was to come made him smile.

He had to force himself not to strut as he made his way down the aisle to where his man stood, still guarding the priest and Bishop Adewale.

Agbede continued to scan the people in the pews. He had never seen Jabari in person, but Hayat had provided photographs, and he didn't see the man now. "Where is the man called Jabari?" he demanded.

No one answered.

"All right then," Agbede said. "If Jabari is not here, where are his wife, his daughter and his son?"

Again, he got no response.

But he would, he thought as he slung his AK-47 over his shoulder and pulled out the glistening, gold-inlaid machete from its scabbard. He would get a response. And he'd get it *soon*.

THE ISAAC CENTER'S Maxima had been riddled by gunfire when Bolan and Galab had first left to go to the bakery safe house, and it wouldn't run. But the center also had a fifteen-year-old Buick LeSabre with tinted windows that had been donated, and it was in this vehicle that Bolan, Paul and Jabari now approached the small church on the packed dirt road: 11637 Yejide Street.

The address was making sense now, and the other loosely related clues and leads were beginning to fall into place, as well.

The sun had set a half hour earlier and darkness shrouded the city. Bolan had a hard time believing that everything that had happened since his arrival had occurred in a matter of hours.

Even for the Executioner, it had been quite a day.

Paul was in the shotgun seat next to him. "I remember this place now," he said as they neared the church. "A Father *Something* who helps hide Christians who've been put on the Boko Haram radar." He shook his head in wonder. "We have so many places like this now that it's hard to keep track of them. But I should have known better."

Bolan slowed the Buick as they reached the church. In large numerals on the side of the building he saw *11637*. But what stood out even more was the man in the jungle cammies just inside the door. He was gripping one of the Bokos' favorite weapons—another in what seemed like an endless collection of AK-47s. "Looks like they beat us here," the Executioner said grimly.

"That man's name is Alaba," Paul said. "I know him well. And he knows Dhul Agbede well. If Alaba is here, then the Bokos are being led by Dhul."

Jabari was sitting behind Paul, and now he leaned across the vehicle toward Bolan. "They are looking for me," he said.

In the rearview mirror, Bolan could see the man's face. Sweat poured down from his hairline across his skin as if he was standing in the middle of a rainstorm. "Agbede will not just kill my family when he finds I'm not there," he said in a low, gravelly voice. "He will torture my son and daughter first." His voice rose slightly and took on a shrill sound. "And my wife—"

The Executioner didn't let him go on. "That's not going to happen," he said. "Any of it. We're not going to let it." They drove past the front of the church. Bolan noted that Alaba followed the car with his eyes, but the tinted windows kept him from seeing the men inside. And the Boko with the rifle didn't seem to be overly concerned about the vehicle.

Bolan turned left at the corner and guided the Buick around the block. Behind him, he could hear Jabari quietly praying for his family. The soldier waited until the man had stopped, then pulled the Buick over to the side of the road and threw it into Park.

"Okay," he said. "This situation isn't complex. We've got a group of people inside the building who we've got to believe are being held hostage by Boko Haram. They left the door open with their man out in the open to make sure we knew that. They're expecting us to negotiate with them. We're not going to do that. There won't be any negotiations. We're going to attack, hard and fast, and take out every Boko who puts up a fight."

Paul frowned. "But how can we get in fast enough to do that before the hostages are killed?" he asked.

Bolan had worn the Kel-Tec over his shoulder on a sling during the drive. But now he handed it to Jabari and reached inside his robe and vest and drew the sound-suppressed Beretta 93-R. "This Dhul character is expecting his man at the door to warn them if someone attacks," he said. "Or at least he expects to hear gunshots, which will give them a few seconds warning." Bolan pulled the Beretta's slide back slightly to make sure a round was chambered, and saw the brass case. "They aren't going to get that warning."

"Just tell us what to do," Paul said.

"Again, it's going to be simple," the Executioner replied. "As soon as we turn the corner in front of the church, I'm going to pull up on the grass. We'll drive like bats out of hell until we're right in. You two need to have your doors open. As soon as I stop, I'll fire on the door guard and take him out, then we'll all bail out."

"Then we all go through the front door?" Jabari asked.

"Correct," Bolan said. "If we do this right, we should all be inside the sanctuary before Dhul and the other Bokos even know we've arrived."

"Let's do it," Paul stated. "Let's do it *now*." He and Jabari both grasped the pistol grips on their AK-47s at the same time. "Like you said, it's simple. And I don't want to overthink it and start second-guessing everything."

Bolan nodded. In answer, he threw the transmission into Drive and took off down the street. At the corner, he twisted the steering wheel to the left and moved off the dirt into the yard of the church. As he floored the accelerator, the Buick's tires tore up the grass.

Bolan had already rolled down his window. Just before he came abreast of the church's front door he moved his foot from the pedal to the brake. More grass flew through the air as the rubber tires suddenly stopped rolling and skidded the last few feet.

The vehicle came to a rocking stop directly in front of the door.

The man Paul had ID'd as Alaba stood motionless for a split second, his mouth falling open in surprise. As he started to raise his rifle, Bolan aimed the Beretta at Alaba's head.

The near-silent 9 mm hollowpoint round from the 93-R flew an inch or so below the spot where the Executioner had intended it to go. Instead of drilling through the bridge of the guard's nose, it went in through his open mouth. But from there it angled up into his brain and the rear half of the top of his head blew off, splattering the wall behind him.

Bolan threw the vehicle into Park. He had heard the other two men exiting the Buick a split second before he pulled the trigger, and now he used his left hand to open his own door. He was the first to the church entrance, leaping over Alaba's body and landing inside a foyer that led into the sanctuary. He could see a bullet hole in the shattered glass in one door, and wondered briefly exactly what that meant. He didn't know, but it hardly made a difference at this point.

The Executioner shouldered his way into the sanctuary, transferring the Beretta to his left hand and drawing the Desert Eagle with his right. He could sense Paul's and Jabari's presence right behind him as he quickly scanned the pews. Two men with AKs were standing halfway down the middle row that led to the stage and the pulpit. A third man—Bolan had no idea who he might be—lay just in front of them on the floor, with blood soaking into his three-piece suit.

Two more terrorists covered the doors on the sides of the large room.

All four men raised their weapons as Bolan's pistols zeroed in on them.

With his left hand, the Executioner used the Beretta again, this time to down the man in front of the exit to that side. Behind him, he heard the explosions of rifle fire as Paul and Jabari joined him in eliminating that threat.

Bolan's right hand lifted the Desert Eagle and pointed it toward the man in front of the exit on that side of the sanctuary. The Beretta had been whisper quiet, but the mighty .44 Magnum pistol roared, drowning out the AK-47s behind him as the Executioner double-tapped a pair of death rounds into the Boko on that side.

By now the two men in the center of the aisle had reacted to the sudden shock. Bolan saw that one of them was the terrorist with the goatee that curled out and up. It was the man he had only caught glimpses of throughout the day, but who he recognized as one of the Boko leaders. It was the man Paul had told him was Dhul Agbede.

But the other man, wearing a full set of desert-camouflage BDUs, was slightly quicker than Agbede and already had his assault rifle up and pointed toward Bolan, Paul and Jabari. So the Executioner was forced to concentrate on him first, flipping the Beretta's selector switch to 3-round burst and letting the trio of rounds drill into the man's chest and explode his heart.

Bolan turned both pistols toward the final man, Agbede, the sadist he'd heard so much about.

Who already had his rifle aimed at the Executioner.

Even as he pulled back on the triggers of his pistols, Bolan knew he was too late. Perhaps only a hundredth of a second too late, but a gunfight wasn't like playing horseshoes. Close didn't count.

And there was no second place winner.

But just to the side of Agbede, a man wearing a khaki work shirt and matching pants had risen to his feet. During the fraction of a second that Bolan worked the triggers, the man swung what looked to be a book around and slammed the bound edge into Agbede's throat.

At the same time the terrorist instinctively recoiled from the attack on his throat, three rounds and another booming .44 Magnum bullet left the Executioner's weapons. The 9 mm rounds formed a near-perfect two-inch isosceles triangle in the center of Agbede's chest.

The .44 Magnum hollowpoint round disposed of the curly beard for all eternity.

Suddenly, the sanctuary fell silent. Then a woman

wearing a simple cotton dress, a teenage girl who looked very much like her and a younger boy who resembled Jabari rushed down the aisle past the Executioner.

Bolan turned to see all three members of Jabari's family trying to hug him at the same time. The former police sergeant looked up at the Executioner as tears ran from his eyes.

His lips silently formed the words, *Thank you*.

Bolan turned back to the man in the khaki work clothes, who still held the book that he'd used to strike Dhul Agbede in the throat.

The Executioner wasn't surprised to see it was a Bible.

EPILOGUE

Eliminating Fazel Hayat turned out to be the easiest part of the mission.

The Executioner drove the Buick and spoke into his cell phone as Paul directed him to the Boko Haram headquarters.

"Okay, Jack," Bolan told the pilot who was still waiting for him at the airport. "Tell Hal we'll lift off as soon as I've taken care of this final detail."

Bolan parked the Buick in the driveway, and he, Layla Galab and Bishop Joshua Adewale got out and walked to the front door. The Executioner thought of Paul. He had planned to bring the man along for this final phase of the mission. But Paul had known he wasn't really needed, and elected to begin checking the other safe houses to ensure that the people who had fled the bakery building had all arrived safely.

"Bishop, Layla," Bolan said as they stopped on the front porch. "This probably isn't a fit place for you to see. Why don't you wait here until I come back for you?"

Both of them nodded.

One front-thrust kick from the Executioner opened

the door, and he walked in. Bolan strode through the house, passing more naked and scantily clad women than he'd ever seen in one place at any time in his life.

When he reached the room with the swimming pool, the soldier drew the Desert Eagle. Fazel Hayat reclined with three women on a huge pillow at the end of the swimming pool. The Executioner gave him a moment to make a move, hoping he'd scramble away from the women. As Hayat lunged toward a nearby divan, Bolan put a single .44 Magnum round into the Boko Haram leader's brain.

The explosion rebounded off the walls as well as the water. But then, as it died down, it was replaced with what began as a hesitant clapping on the parts of a few of the women. The acclaim gradually grew as the victims of Boko Haram's white slavery and human trafficking trade began to realize they were free at last and would not be punished for their impromptu celebration. The cheering and applause grew until all the women were standing and clapping their hands in joy.

Bolan had seen several sets of eyes staring through the glass into the pool area, and guessed that they belonged to more Bokos, but when they saw their leader die, they immediately disappeared.

Another day, Bolan thought. As much as he might like to, he wasn't going to take on all of Boko Haram terrorists at the same time. Turning to a woman wearing a short diaphanous gown and red shoes, he said, "You and a couple of the ladies take the body into a back room somewhere. Then all of you find some clothes. You're about to have a couple of guests." Then he retraced his steps to the entry.

The front door was still open when he arrived there. As the bishop and Galab entered, Bolan realized he had been so preoccupied with the final gunfight at the church, and the elimination of Fazel Hayat, that he had neglected to ask Galab what had become of her traitorous receptionist, Tara.

"What did you do with your receptionist?" he asked, as she and Adewale followed him down the hallway.

"The police came and took her," Layla said.

"Police that you *trust*?" the Executioner asked.

"Police I *think* I can trust. But you must remember that it is impossible to know from one day to the next who is trustworthy."

"I guess that leaves an opening for the position of receptionist at the Isaac Center," Bolan said.

"I don't think it will be a problem," Galab replied. "The bishop has told me about a fine woman named Inka who helped him after the chapel exploded. I plan to offer her the job, and a dorm room to live in at the center, which should be much better than the house the bishop described."

Bolan nodded. "I know that orphans are your specialty," he said. "But there are a lot of women in here who may be grown, but are very much *like* orphans. Can you help them?"

"That is why I came with you," Galab said. "I will

find a way to get them back to their home countries or wherever else they want to go, now that they are free."

Bolan led them into the pool room. The women who made up the harem had found enough clothing to cover at least the essentials, and another round of applause broke out when they saw the Executioner again.

Galab threw a knowing smile at him. "It must be very difficult for you to say goodbye to so many women who seem to worship the very ground you walk on," she teased. "Especially when they are so elegantly dressed. Are you sure you don't want to just stay and take Hayat's place?"

Bolan grinned. Fazel Hayat's body had been removed from the room at his request. Only a few spots of blood remained where he had been before the women took his corpse away. "If you could see Hayat now, Layla," Bolan said. "You'd know that *nobody* would want to take his place."

"You are as solid as an oak, Matt," the woman stated. Her voice still held a trace of good-natured sarcasm. "I *so admire* the fact that such a massive display of female flesh has had no effect on you."

"I never said it had no effect on me. After all, I'm only human. I just said I didn't want to stay and take Fazel Hayat's place."

Bishop Adewale spoke up for the first time. "I do my best to be a man of God," he said. "But I am only human, too, and the flesh is weak, as the Bible says." He had spoken to both Galab and Bolan, but now he turned his full attention to the Executioner. "To paraphrase the Lord's Prayer," he said, "You have delivered us from much evil, Mr. Cooper. But now I think it is about time that you led us away from temptation."

Bolan and Layla both smiled. "Fair enough," said the Executioner. "Let's get you out of here and away from it all."

Galab suddenly turned and hugged Bolan. "Thank you for all you have done," she whispered into his ear. "But I was hoping we could have at least a little time together before you left. Just the two of us."

Bolan held her at arm's length. "I wish I could," he said. "But you remember the call I got on my cell?"

Galab nodded.

"It seems I'm needed elsewhere, and we barely have time for goodbyes." He let go of her, and he and the bishop retraced their steps back out to the front porch.

"You can open your eyes now," the Executioner told Adewale.

The bishop laughed. Then his face turned serious. "God spared my life during the explosion at the university chapel, where so many other bishops died," he said. "And He delivered me from death at the hands of that man wearing the suit, and others, a number of times." He took a deep breath, then said, "I know He had some reason for doing that, some task he wants me to perform. But I still don't know what it is."

The Executioner looked the man square in the eye. "I'm sure all will be revealed in due course. But for the time being, somebody's got to help reorganize the church here in Nigeria, rebuild the chapel at the seminary in Ibadan." Bolan turned and led the way to their vehicle. "That's a start."

* * * * *

COMING NEXT MONTH FROM

GOLD EAGLE®

Available April 7, 2015

THE EXECUTIONER® #437
ASSASSIN'S TRIPWIRE – *Don Pendleton*

American high-tech ordnance has gone missing en route to Syria. Determined to destroy the stolen weapons before they can be used, Mack Bolan discovers nothing is what it seems between the Syrian regime, the loyalists and the beautiful double agent working with him.

SUPERBOLAN™ #173
ARMED RESPONSE – *Don Pendleton*

A rogue general sets out to stage a coup in the drought-stricken Republic of Djibouti. Hunted by the police and the army and targeted by assassins, Mack Bolan won't stop until the general and his collaborators face their retribution.

STONY MAN® #136
DOUBLE BLINDSIDE – *Don Pendleton*

The killing of US operatives in Turkey threatens US–Turkish relations. While Able Team moves to neutralize the threat in the States, Phoenix Force heads overseas, where they discover the dead agents are just the beginning.

COMING SOON FROM

GOLD EAGLE®

Available May 5, 2015

THE EXECUTIONER® #438
THE CARTEL HIT – *Don Pendleton*
Facing off against a Mexican cartel,
the Executioner races to secure the lone
witness to a brutal double murder.

DEATHLANDS® #122
FORBIDDEN TRESPASS – *James Axler*
While Ryan and the companions take on a
horde of hungry cannibals, something far
more sinister—and ravenous—lurks beneath
their feet…

OUTLANDERS® #73
HELL'S MAW – *James Axler*
The Cerberus warriors must confront an alien
goddess who can control men's minds. But are
they strong enough to eliminate this evil interloper
bent on global domination?

ROGUE ANGEL™ #54
DAY OF ATONEMENT – *Alex Archer*
A vengeful fanatic named Cauchon plans to
single-handedly resurrect the violence of the
Inquisition to put Annja and Roux on trial…
and a guilty verdict could mean death.

A crack rent the air.

The unexpected noise came from behind the Executioner. He turned his head quickly to witness the black canopy opening, then checked the altimeter on his right wrist.

The parachute was deploying too early.

An invisible hand grabbed Bolan by his neck and jerked him into an upright position, his head snapping backward. His hands flew automatically to the risers that would enable him to gain some semblance of control in his descent. They weren't there, and his terminal velocity hadn't significantly decreased.

Bolan looked up and cursed. The black parachute, all three hundred and seventy square feet of it, had collapsed and become entangled in itself. Bolan plummeted toward the ground completely out of control.

He had only seconds to react. The gear bag had slipped from between his knees and was now hanging by its quick-release cord. The weight of the equipment in the bag was causing him to gyroscope, spinning him to the left in ever-quickening circles. Soon it would be impossible to maneuver. He forced his right hand slowly down to his belt, fighting the gravitational force. He fumbled for several seconds, unable to locate the emergency-release cord.

Suddenly it was in his hand and he tugged hard. Immediately the gear bag dropped away, disappearing into the darkness. With the loss of ballast, Bolan began to spin slightly slower. His fingers were throbbing, his head felt as if it were about to pop from the blood being forced into his extremities. Gritting his teeth, he found the emergency release for the parachute with his left hand and depressed it.

There was a snap as the faulty parachute let loose.

Bolan was once again in free fall.

Instinct told him that his time was almost up. He curled into a ball, rolled over and threw his limbs out in a star formation. He pushed aggressively down with his right arm and leg, and the spin was quickly brought to a halt. Reaching down, he tugged on the cord for the reserve chute.

Don't miss
ARMED RESPONSE by Don Pendleton,
available April 2015 wherever
Gold Eagle® books and ebooks are sold.

THE EXECUTIONER
DON PENDLETON'S

*The mission's simple: get in, get out—with the hijacked
ordnance and without starting a war...*

*Read on for a sneak preview of
ASSASSIN'S TRIPWIRE
by Don Pendleton.*

Bolan froze. His nostrils flared.

The smell was unmistakable. It was human body odor,
and if he was smelling that, it could mean only one thing.

There were enemy soldiers right here, right now.

He ripped his knife free and slammed the blade into the
dirt next to his knee. A horrifying scream welled up and
blood darkened the arid soil. Bolan left his knife where it
was lodged and threw himself into a forward roll.

The ground erupted around him. Half a dozen soldiers,
concealed in shallow grave-like depressions, popped up
all around him. The soldiers pushed themselves to their
feet, their weapons and web gear trailing plumes of dirt.
Weapon-mounted lights cast hazy beams in the dusty air.

Bolan's suppressed Beretta pistol was already in his
fist. He pivoted on one knee, tracking the weapon lights.

The Beretta coughed out 3-round bursts as the
Executioner tapped out a Morse code of death on the
trigger. He fired, rolled and fired again, changing
position with each shot. The metallic clatter of
Kalashnikov rifles rolled over him; the enemy weapons
ripped the earth around his body.

The Beretta's 20-round box magazine cycled dry. Rather than dump it and attempt a reload, Bolan shifted the weapon to his left hand. He drew the Desert Eagle with his right, still avoiding enemy gunfire. The Israeli hand-cannon belched flame each time he pulled the trigger. He was careful not to look directly at it, doing his best to salvage his night vision.

Bolan heard the shots before he saw the new shooter. He threw himself backward in the dirt before he could fix the new threat's location. The chopped AK, a Krinkov with a folding stock, cut down the last two soldiers in the circle of resistance. Bolan had swung his Desert Eagle in the direction of the approaching form but stopped himself before pulling the trigger.

The figure that came to stand over him pulled a desert scarf from mouth and nose. Bolan saw, against the night sky, long hair falling free of the square of cloth. The distinctive sound of a classic fuel-oil lighter snapping open was followed by a flare of light. In the flame, a beautiful woman with dark hair and darker eyes looked back at him.

Don't miss
ASSASSIN'S TRIPWIRE by Don Pendleton,
available April 2015 wherever
Gold Eagle® books and ebooks are sold.